Blind Truth

For Carole
Best Wishes
Margaret Sheldon

Also by Margaret Sherlock

Fiction
AGAINST ALL ODDS

Non-Fiction
SEVEN SISTERS DOWN UNDER

Margaret can be contacted through her
website at
www.margaretsherlock.net

Margaret Sherlock

Blind Truth

Shorelines  Publishing

First Published in 2012
by
Shorelines Publishing
3 St. Mark's Drive, Torquay, Devon.TQ1 2EJ

Copyright © 2012 Margaret Sherlock
ISBN:978-0-9559710-3-7

Cover artwork tracey.turner@blueyonder.co.uk
Typesetter elainesharples@btinternet.com
Printed by Short Run Press Limited, Exeter

Dedicated to Lil

My sister and best friend

Hell, is the truth learned too late.

Chapter 1

The rhythmic rocking of the windscreen wipers, beating perfect time to music that filled the air space of James's car, began to grate. Lyn knew the CD was being played in an effort to lessen the palpable tension, but the necessity for keeping vision clear whilst driving in torrential rain, caused it to fail miserably. A snatched sideways glance, revealed that James too was unaffected by a melody than was renowned for its ability to soothe; his jaw was set tight and the rigid muscles twitched under the strain. He very rarely swore; but twice in the last fifteen minutes, and without apology to Lyn, he'd blasted his horn and verbally abused two women drivers for travelling too slowly. They were half an hour into their journey to Heathrow airport and Lyn's departure, to Sydney- Australia, wasn't until 10-00pm. There was no need to rush. She could have taken a train—an easy run from the local Torbay station—but James wouldn't hear of it. She should have insisted. Resigned, she closed her eyes on the heavily laden sky, mirrored in the rain-slicked tarmac that disappeared beneath the wheels at seventy miles per hour.

She'd known James for almost a year. This trip to Australia had been planned together and was meant to be a shared experience—a celebration to mark the first anniversary of their meeting. He had boyishly hinted at presenting her with a special gift during the three-week holiday. But suddenly everything changed! Ten days ago, without the slightest hint of regret or apology, he'd revealed that he couldn't afford to take the time off. Lyn had taken this revelation literally and had offered to pay for them both. James's acrimonious response left Lyn in no doubt that his feelings toward her had changed. Her first reaction, had been to cancel the trip altogether, a convenient excuse in the long line of many, thrown up through fear of the unknown; but apart from not wanting to give him the satisfaction of causing even more disruption to her plans, she knew in her heart that meeting Jennifer Beck—her supposedly, long dead mother, needed to be faced.

James gave an audible sigh of relief as he turned left onto the A380, leaving behind most of the choking traffic that had hindered their progress so far. Wearing a sheepish half-smile he glanced over to Lyn, relieved that her eyes were closed and he could return to his own thoughts without giving an apology that wasn't truly meant. He *had* been looking forward to spending three weeks of glorious sunshine with the woman he loved. And apart from meeting up with Lyn's mother (a reunion which was bound to be strained and emotional under the circumstances) he would have had her all to himself. No long spells of loneliness as she worked on floral arrangements that needed to be transported to London. No visits from Jill, her partner, to discuss venues and then staying the week to catch up on old times, leaving James excluded and at a loss. And most of all, no contact with Candy Laverne and, (if James's suspicions were correct, Carl) two unsavoury characters who, at this point in time, seemed to be dominating his every waking thought.

Their relationship had been developing favourably. Lyn had met his family on several occasions and she was liked and admired by both Helen, his sister, and Mother. Flushed with confidence and pride James had, with the help of Helen, discovered Lyn's finger-size and bought her a surprise present of a diamond ring, to mark the first anniversary of their meeting! This special celebration, conveniently aligned with a long-overdue reunion of Mother and Daughter, alas, was not to be.

Ten days ago, two separate incidents which were obviously linked, caused James, not only to re-consider his planned trip, but to wonder if there was any future in a relationship filled with secrecy and deception. The unscrupulous Victor Carlson had reappeared! And this time, there was no doubt in James's mind that Lyn was involved. Why else would Carl be sniffing around the only property for sale on The Terrace, and why else would he be well known to Lyn's new colleague, Candy Laverne? Once and for all, James intended to get to the bottom of these unsavoury liaisons; but this could only be done whilst Lyn was out of the way.

Clicking noises in the area of the dashboard told Lyn that James was fiddling with the CD player. The music had stopped a minute or two earlier leaving the dominant sound of wipers ruling the airwaves. Hoping and praying that it wasn't about to be replayed, Lyn stole a glance. Her eyes opened at the precise moment that her mobile phone, placed on the central console between them, indicated an incoming text message; and James's hand reaching to retrieve it!

"Sorry! I thought you were sleeping. I was just about to turn it off."

"No need, it's only a text message."

"Well, aren't you going to read it?"

"Why is it so important to you?" As expected, no answer was forthcoming, leaving Lyn to wonder for the umpteenth time why so much had changed between them in the last week or so.

The only other time she remembered him being this way was very early in their relationship. After months without gainful employment and mounting debt, due to the corrupt shenanigans of Vinny Conway, she had, by a fortunate twist of fate acquired a substantial windfall. For a while, James had been obsessively curious about this sudden influx of money, especially as Lyn had been using a large chunk of it to purchase part of his next door property. Although she had never revealed the truth behind the good fortune, he'd accepted her word that it was come by honestly. She might have thought twice about buying his property, had she known that Vinny had already moved into the basement flat below her, a fact that James had kept shamefully to himself; so *his* lack of disclosure about Vinny and *her* lack of information about her windfall, sort of evened things up, laying down an unspoken respect for each others little idiosyncrasies.

Two weeks spent apart over Christmas and New Year, whilst Lyn visited her daughter Sarah in Ireland, confirmed the strength of their feelings for each other and as 2009 progressed, so had their relationship. In fact, the summer months were particularly fulfilling and their togetherness seemed complete when James found a buyer for Lyn's Victorian house, enabling her to purchase the upper floors of her business premises for accommodation. Even the daunting prospect of meeting Jennifer, the famous artist of Australia, didn't seem quite so intimidating with the strong arm of James for support. However, their togetherness took a distinct downward turn after Lyn had agreed to use her office and workspace for one of Candy Laverne's exclusive underwear parties.

Candy Laverne, a larger than life character from Blackpool, had worked the Northern Clubs as a dancer in the early sixties. Her greatest gift, apart from being a thoroughly decent person with a heart of gold, was her knowledge of underwear design. From individual designers to the creators that filled the fashion houses of the world, before it filtered down to the high street stores, Candy recognised, evaluated and used their products to greatest effect. Her clients, drawn from an exclusive list of extremely rich businessmen, paid dearly for the pleasure of seeing beautiful young women modelling the crème de la crème of silk lingerie—obviously with the option to buy.

Jill had met Candy first; as with all the London venues, *she* secured the work and Lyn designed and made up the floral arrangements. Two such events were carried off with great success and far more profit than the usual wedding reception.

Being an astute businesswoman, Candy had been toying with the idea for some time that venues held outside London would both lower her outgoings and increase her scope for a wider client base. In spite of the recession,costs had been escalating; but this was a rich man's pastime and those in the know increased their charges to make up for cutbacks elsewhere. Lyn had also been anxious to maximise profits and minimise travelling time to London, so after a lengthy discussion, it was agreed that the 20th of October venue would be held in Torbay, as a test for its suitability in the future.

She had spent almost a week sourcing and making up the distinctive floral arrangements that Candy specifically preferred—sensual arrangements for a sensual event—was a mantra used regularly between them. When Candy first mentioned her preferred blooms, which were costly and not always easy to source, Lyn and Jill, felt justified in thinking it was just another of her many jokes; but after Candy enlightened them to the hidden meanings (used extensively in Victorian times) and how closely certain flowers resemble human form, their respect for Candy's knowledge deepened and her wishes were followed to the letter.

On the morning of the event, Tuesday 20th October, James returned from a trip to his bank looking distant and disturbed. Lyn had asked him if everything was alright. Instead of a response, he locked his office door and disappeared into his apartment. Putting this strange behaviour down to preoccupation with a business matter, Lyn returned to the preparations for the evening ahead.

The event was a great success. Nine businessmen, although Lyn had been sure Candy had only invited eight, and six of Candy's favourite models, created the perfect balance of friendliness and intimacy. Broad smiles and several cheeky winks, told Lyn that Candy was raking in plenty of orders for the exquisite lingerie. The majority of the men were well on into middle age, which begged the question, who were they buying this underwear for? Lyn's role, apart from providing the venue and floral arrangements, was to serve refreshments and merge into the background. Only after the last guest had left, was she allowed, along with the models, to sample the champagne and caviar.

Whilst helping to pack away the samples, Lyn drooled over a particularly lovely, French corset and matching knickers. She'd watched spellbound as Elena, a beautiful Bulgarian model, had moved with complete ease amongst the guests, each one unable to resist touching the garment. Suddenly, Candy was beside Lyn urging her to try it on. The second glass of champagne, coupled with a sense of camaraderie with the models, soon found Lyn stripping down behind one of the portable screens. All were in agreement that it was perfect for her; but suddenly aware of how rash she was being in view of the expensive trip to Australia, Lyn shook her head. Leaning in close, Candy whispered that she would like her to have it as a present. "Take it with you on your trip. You told me that James is giving you a special gift for your first anniversary; this can be *yours* to him; but don't let him catch sight of it before the special day and believe me when I say that every anniversary from then on will carry the memories of the first. A wise woman will make that night as special as possible."

Filled with emotion at such generosity and sound advice, Lyn had grabbed a tissue from a nearby shelf. "I'll just dash upstairs to look in my full length mirror," she'd remembered saying, anxious to do just that but mainly to quell the threat of blubbering in front of half a dozen beauties. As she ran up the stairs to her apartment, bare-footed and dressed only in the corset and knickers, she came face to face with James who was just about to descend! She couldn't remember anything that was said; but the look of astonishment on his face sent her panic-stricken and giggling into her room—locking the door behind her to preserve at least some remnant of the surprise.

The sound of a second text message to Lyn's phone cut melodiously through the monotony of droning engine, swishing wiper-blades and driving rain. James had barely spoken a word since apologising for his unbridled urge to read the first; but the strain to remain silent was now too much. "Aren't you concerned that the messages might be important?"

"Do you mean important to me, or revealing to you?" Asked Lyn as she reached for the phone and brought up the message. "Both are from Jill", she said banefully. "The first says, *Bon Voyage sweetheart, u r not alone, I will be thinking of u all the way.*" A hard swallow and few seconds of silence followed as Lyn brought up the second message. "*Don't forget the aspirin! Luv u Jill!* Satisfied now?" The phone was then turned off and casually replaced on the central console.

"It seems strange to me that two women should use such terms of endearment."

"Lots of commonplace things seem strange to you James; could we stop at the next motorway services so that I can take the aspirin that Jill was referring to."

"How could she possibly know that you need an aspirin?" James was trying to make light conversation, but everything he said was tinged with the negative edge of disordered reasoning.

"The aspirin is to help prevent deep vein thrombosis, a condition which can develop after taking a long-haul flight." Lyn's tone was that of a school mistress imparting news to a class of seven year olds. After assuring her that he'd stop as soon as possible, whilst at the same time thinking that she could just as easily swallow the damn tablet whilst sitting in the car, James returned to his disturbed thoughts.

There was no doubting the fondness between Lyn and Jill. A year ago Vincent Conway had been convinced that they were lesbians after catching sight of them locked in a long embrace. The pair hadn't been in touch for twenty–five years so this show of affection was proof enough of their strong bond of friendship. But proof of Lyn's sexual preference for men over women had been delightfully confirmed in their love-making that had grown more satisfying over the months. The sweetness of these happy memories suddenly turned sour when, unbidden, an image of Lyn dressed like a common prostitute filled James's head. The look of horror on her face because he'd almost caught her red-handed! Broken pieces slotting neatly into place as James recalled witnessing only hours earlier, a clandestine meeting between Candy Laverne and Victor Carlson.

This was a subject that James didn't want to think about; not now while he was hurting so badly. Not now when he needed all his focussing power for the road ahead which was crammed with heavy goods vehicles, irresponsibly manoeuvring from one lane to the next and spewing cascades of water from beneath their huge tyres. A sign showing, SERVICES 10 MILES AHEAD, was momentarily visible before disappearing behind a tall removal van on the inside lane. James groaned inwardly with the thought that at least twenty minutes would unnecessarily be added to this frustrating journey.

Chapter 2

4.10pm

Peter Radcliffe was behaving like a teenager preparing for his first date, instead of a mature gentleman of means about to spend the evening with a beautiful woman who was soon to become his wife. The place had been scrupulously cleaned, there was champagne on ice and a table booked at an out of town, exclusive restaurant; so why was he feeling so nervous? A sly peek at the ornate box on his bedside cabinet offered a certain amount of reassurance.

Two weeks ago his world had been falling apart! News from his doctor, that he had no more than three to four years left, before dying from a condition that had only recently come to light, had sent him into a downward spiral of depression. His only investment, his property on The Terrace, was also starting to fall apart. Lack of maintenance over the years had taken its toll. Loose slates that wouldn't have cost too much to remedy (if only the miserly old dentist below him had agreed to cough up part of the cost) had subsequently been ripped off in storms that seemed to be more and more frequent. This had caused leaking and creeping dampness on the upper floors, where Peter now resided. The ground floor, which happened to be the most valuable section of the building, had been for sale for nearly a year; but several prospective buyers had been put off by the fear of high costs in putting right the years of neglect. Refurbishment was needed but due to the recession, Peter no longer had the means.

Then suddenly, and as if by magic, salvation arrived in the form of a handsome, blue-eyed Scandinavian named Carl; showing him a way to make his remaining years free from financial restraint and to fill those years with the intelligent companionship of a beautiful young woman, whose loyalty and devotion would be guaranteed.

Carl sat on the covered balcony of his hotel suite, sipping tea from a bone china cup as huge waves crashed over the sea-wall below. Like the ocean, he was roused. The young Bulgarian woman, Elena Petrov/a, would be here soon. Arrangements and paperwork would be finalised, giving *her* the financial security she sought, and Carl the opportunity for owning a property on The Terrace.

Elena had been the most beautiful of the six models and he hadn't been surprised that Radcliffe had chosen *her*. She carried more weight than the others; but her curvaceous body and exquisite bone structure belied this fact. Carl had never been a womaniser; his mother, the greatest beauty in his life, had never been equalled. He carried a photo of her everywhere; not an image showing her decline into old-age; but as a twenty one year old, crowned-beauty-queen. Clutching the photograph to his breast, he closed his eyes and thought of Elena. There *were* similarities; her hair wasn't as fair as his mother's and the eyes were darker, but her skin was aglow with youthful promise just like his mother's had been.

Gentle knocking on the hotel's heavy, wooden door brought an abrupt end to Carl's reminiscing. He reverently placed the photograph back inside his wallet and walked slowly to the door. "You are ten minutes late Elena and I am a very busy man!" Carl led her to the balcony and offered to remove the leather jacket that was spotted with rain.

"Why do you choose to sit in the open when you have such luxury at your disposal?" asked Elena feeling the sharp contrast in temperature between inside and out.

"It reminds me of home and the daily grind that my brothers have to endure. Come and sit with me awhile, the paperwork is completed except for signatures." As he spoke, Carl slid the jacket from her. Elena said nothing as he placed his arm around her shoulders, teasing up the sleeve of her cashmere jumper to expose bare flesh. A gasp escaped her tightened lips as he manoeuvred the same cold hand beneath the cushioning of soft wool, in search of more exposure.

Before she realised what was happening, the garment was abruptly removed and abandoned, without care, out of her reach. She crossed her arms protectively across her chest, then thought better of it and dropped them to her sides before asking "What's this all about, Carl? I'm soon to be married. Remember?"

"I'm just examining the goods. As far as I'm aware, your body could be covered in needle marks or other signs of a depraved life." As he spoke, he gripped both shoulders and twisted her around, enabling him to remove her bra. He expected a reaction. Non was forthcoming. "You have beautiful skin, Elena, such a waste! such a waste!" His fingers, even colder now, lightly traced her neckline, shoulders and upper body. He was lost in a reverie of thought.

It was still raining as Elena strode back to the tiny bed-sit that she'd rented for the week; but her jacket remained open to the elements. The feel of cleansing, cold driving rain was considerably more pleasurable than the hot breath of the man she knew only as Carl. Straightening her back she marched on more purposefully; soon she would be married to a gentleman. Soon, the financial burden of the last three years would be eradicated; freeing her from unwanted licentious looks and demands. And most important of all, her two younger brothers would be given the chance of further education; freeing *them* from falling into the corrupt hands of the Bulgarian Mafia.

She had met with her husband-to-be once only and this was in the presence of Carl; but tonight they would be alone, giving each of them the final opportunity to decide whether to commit or not. Elena had no doubts at all. Carl had told her that Peter was terminally ill; not the sort of illness that required a daily nurse; when that became necessary in approximately two to three years time, arrangements had already been made. In the meantime, Peter wanted nothing more than intelligent companionship and help with day to day domesticity. As recompense for sharing his last few years, Elena would inherit everything on his death. Peter's wife had died years before and the couple were childless. The only living relative was a nephew in South Africa who hadn't been in touch since moving there in 1990, so there was no one to challenge this arrangement.

Cold, wet hands struggled to connect door key to door lock. Eventually the door opened and a smell of dampness filled the air. She flicked on the small heater and prepared to run a hot bath knowing that the steam would only add to the humidity that pervaded everything in the four metre by four metre space. She'd wanted to spend more time at Carl's plush hotel, reading carefully through all the fine print of the documentation; but after his weird behaviour, she was happy to just sign and leave, accepting his word that she would be given copies of everything after the marriage.

She had almost two hours before the rendezvous with Peter, and as she slid beneath the warm scented water, Elena thought about what she knew of the man who was soon to become her husband. At the age of sixty-four and mainly due to his illness, Peter was no longer sexually active, but he did crave affection and assurance that he was still attractive to the opposite sex. He was retired from his profession as an accountant—living now on the generous pension that had accrued over the years. All this information, given in the strictest confidence, was supplied by Carl. Elena had only seen the lovely property, that Peter owned, from the outside—part of it was rented and this would continue whilst Peter was alive—but once it became wholly hers, she intended to bring her family from Bulgaria and share her good fortune with her brothers.

Stefan, who would be twenty-two in three days time had been trying to reach her, it broke her heart ignoring his messages. Elena knew he would disapprove of what she was about to do; but her mind was made up. Very soon, a family celebration would be arranged for Stefan and Dimitar to meet their new brother-in law; then all would be well.

With dry martini and tonic water in hand, Candy paced the length of her sumptuous sitting room. She had made it a rule never to work weekends and this included making or taking telephone calls relating to work. In the whole of her working career she had resented working at the weekend; but for the first twenty years or so she hadn't had any choice. Things were different now. She'd created a niche that suited both her and her models; and all respected the sanctity of the weekend.

Three times in the last hour this sanctity had been violated by phone calls from Stefan, Elena's younger brother, demanding a whole cartload of information; but mainly, where she was. Candy couldn't help him because in truth, she didn't have a clue where she was. Four days ago she'd received a message from Elena, saying simply that she'd decided to get married and she could no longer work for the agency; but thank you for all your help. Candy had been a little hurt but mainly worried by this brief message. She knew for sure that Elena didn't have a regular boyfriend; and, the generous wages that Candy paid—a large chunk of which was being sent to her family in Bulgaria—should have kept her free of marauding parasites. Elena had worked with her for over three years and was regarded almost as family; and Candy's belief in supporting family was unshakeable.

Candy Laverne had never taken her situation in life for granted. Her mother had died of internal bleeding two days after giving birth to her. Both parents had been warned against further pregnancies; but their desire for another child, took precedence over the doctors' warnings. Alice, the older daughter, was thirteen at this tragic time and the void of sudden loss helped her to slip easily into the role of surrogate mother. Working as a team, Father continued to bring in the money and Alice snatched whatever time she could and continued her school-work from home. Mindful of the sacrifices that her family had made on her behalf, Candy had always felt that the most appropriate recompense would be to live her life to the full, and in due course, take care of the ones that had taken care of her.

Alice, who was now eighty-two, resided in an upmarket apartment overlooking the sea at Lytham-St-Anne's. Candy took care of her every financial need and drove the three hundred miles, at least once a month, to spend twenty-four hours of quality time with her sister. Her overnight bag was already packed but Candy knew in her heart that she wouldn't be able to go. Not this weekend!

Chapter 3

6.45pm

Feeling lonely and vulnerable, Lyn stood in line, at the appropriate 'check-in' counter

"Why are you so glum; you're heading off to the land of sunshine and happiness?"

She turned in the direction of the voice and came face to face with a young man who looked as though he'd just returned from the land of sunshine and happiness. His sun-bleached hair and bronzed complexion belied any notion that he'd spent the last few months on British shores.

"Sorry, I was miles away, answered Lyn cutting off the sadness that she'd felt at James's hurried goodbye."

"Didn't mean to pry; but I've just had this horrible thought, you're not going to a funeral are you? Mum's always ticking me off for putting my foot in it. My name's Andy by the way." Andy shifted his back-pack and made available a sun-kissed hand for her to shake.

Lyn, touched by his warmth and friendliness, smiled, introduced herself and laid to rest his fears of an imminent funeral. There was still fifteen minutes before the check-in desk was due to open; but already a long line of sun seekers was forming. For Lyn, this was the first big milestone of the long trip to the other side of the world. She'd heard and read about all kinds of horror stories connected to airport security and especially about check-in procedure; so she was particularly grateful to have a companion in the queue who was a regular traveller. Andy, she quickly learned, had spent the last eight months in Australia and had only returned to England for two weeks to celebrate his mum's fortieth birthday. Confusion must have been apparent on her face as she mentally calculated how young this guy must be if his mother was only forty.

"I know what you're thinking, and no, she wasn't a child bride, she's my gorgeous step-mother."

A two-way conversation flowed easily as Lyn gave a brief account of what part of Australia she was visiting. She learned that Andy was the same age as Sarah—her daughter—but the similarities ended there. She could never remember talking in this affable way with Sarah; and after the sudden death of her husband, Martin, when Sarah was fifteen, for several years they barely talked at all. There was less strain between them now that Sarah was married and living in Ireland. And with the arrival of their first child in the summer, a tentative bond was beginning to form. Even so, Lyn would have preferred to have seen Sarah experiencing a little more of the wider world before settling down with a much older man.

Security proved to be much trickier than check-in. Lyn's suitcase, although large, was well within the permitted weight and Andy's only item for the hold, a guitar nestling within a strong, hard case, weighed even less. Andy had suggested that they sit together for the duration of the flight and there'd been no problem accommodating this request; however, Lyn was beginning to wonder if she'd been a little rash when Andy was carted off for a thorough search after his rucksack revealed something on the x-ray machine. Ten minutes later he found her in the departure lounge and they laughed and joked about the dildo he'd bought as a present for his landlady—a recently divorced woman who was missing the night time company of a man. Andy, feeling that he was being targeted as substitute husband, had obviously made this common knowledge to his family. The dildo had been his step-mother's idea and she had bought it. Andy couldn't wait to phone her and tell her the trouble she'd caused. As Lyn studied his happy, animated face, she felt envious at the obvious closeness between them. With plenty of time to kill before boarding, it wasn't long before Lyn was revealing parts of her life that she normally kept to herself. Andy was a good listener, appearing to be genuinely interested in the ups and downs that Lyn had overcome. Suddenly her phone rang, bringing an abrupt end to the revelations.

Stuck once again in a long line of traffic, James had decided to phone Lyn. Part of him—the cowardly part—had hoped that her phone would be switched off; leaving a message would be much easier than sensing the hurt and disappointment every time they spoke. He'd hated the way he'd behaved; but he couldn't allow this woman to make a fool of him. His wife had done that all those years ago; he'd trusted *her* and she'd betrayed that trust in the worst possible way. But there might not be another chance to convey how he felt before learning the truth, and if the truth turned out to be as he suspected, he would never speak to this woman again, no matter how strong his feelings.

He'd punched in the easily remembered number and after the second ring they were connected. "I'm glad your phone's still on, I...I just wanted to wish you a pleasant flight and hope that all goes well with...You know... Meeting your mother."

Amongst the hesitancy of the words, Lyn sensed a shift in attitude and instinctively moved to a quieter space. "Couldn't you have spared a few minutes at the airport to say this James?"

"I know it's a pathetically lame excuse Lyn, but I need to get back to the office as soon as possible; but, as it happens, I'm caught up in a long traffic jam."

"Well don't expect me to feel sorry for you, I'm stuck in a crowded departure lounge, all alone, I'm about to take my very first flight, all alone and spend three weeks on the other side of the world, all alone, thanks to the man who I thought loved me." She turned her head from the phone to disguise the sound of a sniffle and her eyes caught sight of Andy, who seemed to been watching her every move. Her attention moved back to James and his silence.

He found it impossible to utter any words of love; the recurring image of Lyn disappearing into her apartment, dressed only in a fancy corset and knickers, mocked his feeble attempt to speak at all. Before ending the call he heaved a sigh and said "Take care Lyn, what I'm doing needs to be done; for both our sakes!" James inched forward two car lengths then punched in Vincent Conway's number. Again a connection was quickly made. "Vincent, any sign of Carl?"

"Radcliffe and his young tart left ten minutes ago, all dressed up, probably going for a bite to eat before getting down to the real business, but no, there's no sign of the slippery bastard, what do you want me to do?"

"Watch and Report; nothing more! I'm stuck in a long tailback on the M5! Don't take your eyes off Radcliffe's place, phone me the minute the situation changes." James cut the connection and tossed the phone on the front passenger seat, relieved that Vincent was on the ball and curbing his aggressive instincts.

James and Vincent were diametrically opposite in every way; but each had experienced, first hand, the calculating deception of a man who had almost succeeded in robbing them of hundreds of thousands of pounds. This happened almost a year ago before Carl, having spent a three month period in Torbay, returned to London and disappeared in the elusive world of high-finance. But he was back! Threatening Vincent with financial reprisals and threatening James's future relationship. This time, both men were determined to bring him down!

Vinny walked slowly back to his car, satisfied that Radcliffe's place was left as he'd found it. There were two other methods where he could have entered illegally— without any noise or chance of being seen—but as he was now in possession of his own his own back door key, he'd chosen the easiest. Jimmy had stressed several times that everything was to be kept within the law, and Jimmy was the boss. Well, at least he thought he was. In reality, Vinny was now his own boss and never again did he intend to be at the mercy of anyone else.

Unbeknown to the solicitor, Peter Radcliffe had approached Vinny several weeks previous, wanting him to run over his place and point out any weaknesses in its security after a couple of yobs had attempted to break in. Vinny had obliged, making sure that whilst weak locks were replaced with strong five lever ones, an extra key had been cut and kept for any future eventualities. Vinny had taken to doing this on a regular basis with his clients. Disguised within an ordinary cardboard box on the top shelf of his office cupboard, lay a biscuit tin containing several similarly acquired door keys, all carefully tagged with names and addresses. Jimmy would be horrified if he knew the half of it. Watch and Report only, was what Vinny had been hired for.

Watch and Report could be quite rewarding; especially when hired by a middle-aged wife who was well past her sell-by-date and the trendy hubby sought younger flesh. Armed with no more than a camera and notebook, and paid handsomely for several months, Vinny would take great pleasure in recording the clandestine antics of the husband (especially the sexual ones.) He'd also picked up work from several insurance companies who needed his services on Watch and Report. These in the main, were toerags that had had a slight bump in their car, and were claiming they could no longer walk or carry on working. It gave Vinny a great thrill and the Insurance Company a sigh of relief when he proved without a shadow of a doubt that the claimants were also lying, cheating bastards.

This assignment was quite different. Carl, the guy they were trying to nail, was as slippery as an eel. Jimmy was determined to bring him down using the full force of the law; and being a solicitor Vinny could understand where he was coming from. But it wasn't going to happen. Not in a million years! He'd experienced first hand how Carl worked. All his dealings, although corrupt, were kept a fag-papers-width on the legal side. A mixture of animal-cunning and brute force was the only way to deal with Carl and eventually Jimmy would see it.

The last year had been pretty good for Vinny; mainly due to the small basement flat he'd bought from the solicitor. The posh address, giving credibility to his newly chosen career, had secured him plenty of work. Two days after Christmas, when Charlene had disappeared without a word, he'd already picked up enough, about the workings of his computer, to manage on his own; and saving the cost of keeping her and paying her wages, more than made up for sleeping alone. Even Lyn Porter had started being civil to him. Vinny put this down to the release of sexual tension. She'd got under Jimmy's skin pretty bad and it made Vinny squirm sometimes to see the two of them behaving like teenagers discovering their first taste of a good shag.

But something happened recently that upset the whole damn caboodle and altered Jimmy's plans. Several times

Vinny had broached the subject only to be given the cold shoulder; then out of sheer frustration, blurting out, "What the fuck's happened between you two," caused a flicker of reaction. He'd remembered Jimmy asking.

"Vincent have you ever wondered how Lyn managed to buy the most expensive section of Number 4 when only a week previously, she was out of work and deeply in debt?"

Vinny had thought about this, convinced that it was a trick question. He'd then answered in the most obvious way, saying that he hadn't given it any thought at all, he'd just assumed three things. One: The forty grand that Vinny had tried to swindle her out of, was used as the deposit. Two, *you* gave her a very favourable price because you wanted to get inside her knickers and three, it has to be said, she is a bloody hard worker and this has enabled her to keep up the hefty mortgage payments.

In typical legal jargon, the solicitor had responded. "You are wrong on all counts!" And then had gone maddeningly quiet and turned to walk away leaving Vinny in a stew of wonderings and confusion. "Hold on!" He'd shouted after him "What do you mean, wrong on all counts?" After a heavy sigh, Jimmy had then revealed how Lyn had bought the place cash *and* paid for several alterations without having to borrow a single penny from the bank. A long, piercing whistle had escaped Vinny's lips which seemed to have the effect of encouragement as Jimmy added, with a weird, distant look on his face. "Lyn has always refused to reveal where this large sum of money came from."

"Giving a woman a good slapping usually does the trick." Vinny had said, mainly in jest, but Jimmy hadn't laughed. He'd retreated back into some unknown place in his head leaving Vinny stumped for words.

Later on that same day, Jimmy had come down to Vinny's flat and in his usual over-polite manner had asked if he might have a word. Vinny had responded by opening his door in a wide arc, something which wasn't done often, not in his line of business. The solicitor had entered seeming agitated and hesitant, so Vinny had made it easier for him. "Come on man, spit it out, I haven't got all fucking day!"

"Vincent, are you and Victor Carlson working together again?"

The question took Vinny by surprise and thinking back he realised how gormless he must have looked, but gradually the penny dropped. "Are you 'aving a laugh? He tried to con me out of every fucking penny I had!"

Jimmy had then turned to leave but Vinny had kicked the door shut as he'd shouted "You can't ask a question like that and just walk away without explaining yourself!"

"I'm sorry if I've offended you Vincent, but I've seen Victor Conway on two separate occasions today and naturally I'm curious."

Vinny had plonked a lukewarm cup of coffee in front him and demanded to be told the details.

Carl checked his watch. It showed fifteen seconds short of nine thirty. Radcliffe's appointment was at ten, allowing him time to drop Elena off, but not enough time to try out the wonder pills that Carl had secured for him—with strict instructions that they weren't to be sampled until after the marriage ceremony. On setting up this proposal, Carl had emphasised that Elena Petrov/a, was a devout Christian, and any attempt to sully her, would cause the whole arrangement to be cancelled.

Radcliffe was a tight-fisted, old fool, who had played right into a trap set barely a week ago. Normally Carl would need at least a month for this type of stratagem; but the previous two weeks had been particularly auspicious, allowing him the opportunity to uncover the whereabouts of Vincent Conway; which in turn led to the discovery of Radcliffe's property on The Terrace. Carl allowed a smile to crease his normally passive features as he thought of the ironic twists and turns of life.

Catching sight of Charlene Dais at one of his favourite haunts, The Prospect of Whitby, on the Thames foreshore, had resulted in forming the catalyst for the plan. With a little coercion, she had not only revealed Vincent Conway's whereabouts and how the scoundrel was earning a living; but after further threats and pressing, she had revealed that Lyn Porter was now the proud owner of the spacious, commercial, ground floor. A twitch, barely perceptible, beat erratically from the corner of Carl's left eye as he remembered how he'd felt after hearing this news. The two people, who had thwarted his plans a year ago, were now both occupying the very building that he had set his heart on acquiring for himself.

During the month of August, when London teemed with tourists desperate to find shelter from the never ending rain, Carl had attended one of Candy Laverne's little 'private functions'. He'd attended several others in the past; not because he was interested in purchasing underwear at a grossly inflated price; but because it served his purpose in a much more lucrative trade.

A new acquaintance of his, whose life had become incredibly lonely since losing his wife to another man, had taken up Carl's offer of providing a solution which would benefit all parties involved; with the exception of Candy, who would no doubt lose one of her best models. This particular function had turned out to be enjoyable as well as profitable. The new acquaintance made his choice, choosing also to purchase every item of lingerie that the young Eastern European woman had modelled, which should have alerted Candy's suspicions, but her attention had been elsewhere that evening. Lyn Porter, looking as though she'd undergone a complete makeover since the time he'd last seen her, was apparently sharing the role as hostess and both were caught up in each other's conversations.

Not wanting to be recognised by Porter he had kept a low profile; and when the opportunity presented itself, he'd found out all he needed to know from a colleague of hers named Jill. The evening had ended well. The new acquaintance, an elderly industrialist from Amsterdam who owned a superb apartment in Westminster, had secured a prospective, young wife. The young wife had secured a prospective, lavish lifestyle and Carl, as well as securing a fat fee for this arrangement, had secured the prospect of the superb apartment passing to him on the death of the elderly industrialist.

A nervous cough broke the silence of the hotel lobby and interrupted Carl's satisfying thoughts. An upbeat tattoo of knocking, on Carl's hotel door, followed by Radcliffe's scratchy voice caused him to stiffen with irritation. "I'm a little early Carl… Are you decent?"

Carl didn't respond. There was almost ten minutes before their appointment and he had no intention of spending a single minute longer in the company of someone that he loathed. This man carried with him the scent of death. He'd noticed it the moment he'd been compelled to shake the man's hand. His property had reeked of it and no amount of camouflage could hide it. Air fresheners, fabric softeners, even expensive perfumes, were in a short space of time pervaded by the scent of a body polluted by disease.

An image of Carl's mother snapped into his head! It would be her birthday in ten days time, and by then the next course of Chemotherapy would be over. He should be with her now. Every year at this time, he would return home for three weeks of celebrations; but he couldn't bear the pain of seeing her like that. His current business venture would be completed in good time. Then, as usual, he would, bring her an armful of Orchids—the flower that represents beauty—and he would fill her heart with pride as he discussed his latest acquired property.

Chapter 4

10.00pm

Driving to Heathrow from Chelsea wasn't Candy's idea of a good night out! But it was much better than staying home alone worrying about people she loved. Stefan had phoned again. This call, made less than ten minutes after the third, caused Candy to worry even more. In a cold, determined voice he had demanded the full address of Elena's last venue. He'd been about to board a flight from Sofia to Heathrow, then continue on to the address that Candy had repeated to him several times—innocent of the fact that Torbay was at least a three hour drive away from Heathrow, even when travelling in a fast car—and Stefan didn't even have a driving licence, let alone the money to hire a car.

For the umpteenth time, Candy reminded herself that she was sixty-nine! Too old to be chauffeuring angry young men in the dead of night! Too old to even be out of bed; knowing how her face would wither in protest the next day. But in all honesty, the impetus of doing something positive, instead of just worrying, had sent her blood pulsing around her veins and stoked a determination to equal that of Stefan's.

The plane was due to touch down at 10-30 and as Stefan had no luggage to wait for, Candy's timing should be just about right. The rain, after petering out to a light drizzle had stopped completely, allowing her to push her Jaguar just that little bit more. All things being equal, they should arrive at the pre-booked Torbay hotel by 2-00am, not bad going, thought Candy smugly, considering the impromptu situation.

Marching purposefully into the 'arrivals' area, Candy was struck by the lack of noise. Lots of people filled the space but like *her* they were here to welcome and collect and judging from their lack-lustre, sombre expressions, they'd been here for some time.

"Damn it!" she exclaimed, checking the airports bulletin board and comparing her watch against the airports clock. The flight from Sofia had just landed; but its arrival was fifty minutes later than scheduled. Earlier that evening Candy had altered her watch in line with the ending of 'British Summer Time' (a habit she'd adopted years ago after forgetting to adjust the time early on a Sunday morning at the end of March and the consequences had cost her dearly.) Fortunately the forgetting of this evening's earlier adjustment would mean just another hours less sleep.

Frustration mounted as she scanned face after face of the young, Eastern Europeans that suddenly started pouring into 'arrivals', all of them looking tired and weary from their journey. But Stefan wasn't amongst them! Almost at the point of giving in and returning to a bed that was comfortingly familiar—reasoning that Stefan had taken her earlier advice to leave things a few more days—she was suddenly jerked from behind and wrapped in a strong embrace.

"Candy, is so good to find you!" Stefan said haltingly. "I thought you would have grown tired of waiting."

Offering the six foot two inch, young man a reassuring smile and guiding him over to the only kiosk serving hot drinks, she soon learned how Stefan had been singled out for a thorough search because he wasn't carrying luggage— not even hand luggage. Security had found nothing untoward but had refused to let him use his mobile phone until he'd reached the outer confines of the airport. All this was relayed to Candy in broken English, as he gulped on a large black coffee. Lines from tiredness and worry, which had no place on one so young, tore at Candy's heart; but practicalities took precedence over emotions as she realised that they would have to visit a twenty-four hour store before heading down to Devon.

It was ten twenty-five when Peter Radcliffe returned home, alone. After making sure that the front door was locked securely, he mounted the stairs to his upper rooms. He flicked on the light in his front sitting room and moved over to the window. He opened the window wide and leaned out taking several gulps of air. He didn't notice the black four-wheel-drive parked below and slightly to the left. And even if he had, it didn't matter. The car belonged to his neighbour four doors away, whose presence was hidden behind the dark tinted glass.

After several long deep breaths of the bracing sea air, Peter gathered up his coat, shrugged off on entering the room, and made his way to the back utility area. With spectacles carefully positioned he opened the front panel on the newly installed boiler and adjusted the settings. He'd wanted the place warm and inviting, just in case Elena had accepted his offer of a nightcap. Just as well she hadn't, the heat was overbearing. Moving into the bedroom, Peter proceeded to empty the pockets of his coat before hanging it in the rosewood wardrobe. Cheque book and receipts were filed neatly in the top drawer of the matching tallboy and his car keys were placed in the drawer of his bedside cabinet.

Tucked at the back of this drawer was a silver-framed photograph of four people. Peter pondered over the faces of these people before kissing each in turn, which left four damp areas of condensation marring the glass. Before returning it to its hidden place, the glass was polished by a clean, folded handkerchief. His eyes moved to the ornate box—a gift brought back from India by a client who had made a fortune back in the days of Margaret Thatcher, when fortunes were easily made. The box, correctly categorised as a 'bidri' cigarette box, was an attractive mix of gold and silver wire, intricately inlaid on a blackened, zinc-alloy base. It hadn't held cigarettes for years. Now it contained the promise of pleasure far greater than tobacco! Before dragging his eyes from the box, Peter tapped four bony fingers gently on its gold and silver surface. "Patience old man, won't be long now," he announced to the empty room, then turned off the light and returned to the fresher atmosphere of the sitting room.

Leaving the window open, he poured himself a scotch and soda and lit a small cigar, a habit now confined, to special occasions only. He turned on the radio and sang along with Matt Monroe. "Strangers in the night, exchanging glances..." wafted through the damp night air, laced with the scent of cigar smoke.

Whilst sipping on his nightcap, Peter's thoughts ran over the meeting with Carl. Everything was in place for the 6th of November; and all parties were in complete agreement over the arrangements, although Peter still couldn't quite understand why everything should remain secret and he and Elena should be denied contact until that day. But he had agreed to Carl's terms when the arrangements were first hatched so he couldn't very well complain now. Even so, the man didn't have to be so damned discourteous about inconsequentialities. And, it was the height of rudeness to ignore a proffered hand, especially on sealing a deal. Obviously, business protocol is different in Scandinavia.

Feeling the chill of the damp air starting to creep into his bones, Peter crossed to the open window. The driver of a vehicle, having just pulled into the kerb several doors away, sent two flashes of headlights, brightening up the road and attracting Peter's attention. After grabbing his spectacles, Peter recognised the car and was grateful that James Fairbank had taken the trouble to signal a greeting, albeit an unorthodox one. He returned a goodnight wave before closing the window and retiring to his bed. He was starting to feel the effects of the wining and dining on food far too rich for his digestive system; not to worry, soon he would be married to this beautiful woman and the rest of his days would be blissful domesticity.

Making absolutely sure that Radcliffe had gone through to the back of his premises; Vinny climbed out from the rear seat of his car and locked the door with the minimum of noise. He walked on soft-soled-trainers to where Jimmy stood waiting in the porch of his property.

"What the fuck was that all about?" Vinny whispered through clenched teeth.

"I'm not sure what you mean Vincent." James was preoccupied trying to get the right key to unlock the porch door.

"Well I'll spell it out for you! When I'm on surveillance, I don't expect an associate, even if that associate is the one paying the bill, to turn up with lights flashing and signalling to the whole fucking neighbourhood that someone is being watched."

Having succeeded in opening the door, James said in a reasonable voice. "Vincent, the only thing that Peter saw, was a neighbour arriving home and sending him a goodnight gesture; and you will have noticed, if your attention had been on him and not me, that he returned that gesture with a wave."

"Oh very neat; I'll have to remember that when *I'm* caught flashing!"

"Vincent I'm tired and in need of a drink, come upstairs and you can bring me up to date."

Vinny followed knowing that the solicitor wouldn't be pleased that there'd been no sign of Carl. If he'd been allowed to do things *his* way and follow every move that Radcliffe had made, the result might have been different. As it stood, a tart arrived at 7-30pm, they both left in Radcliffe's car at 7-51pm and Radcliffe returned alone at 10-25pm, feeling satisfied enough to make him break into song, the lucky bastard. But it was in Vincent's own interest to prolong the telling of the evenings events. He wanted to make sure that Jimmy consumed enough of the bottle of wine that had just been opened. He wanted to make sure that Jimmy slept soundly through the early hours of Sunday morning.

Mindful that eating a decent meal and catching up on much needed sleep was what his body needed, James had headed straight for the mahogany wine rack that sat neatly at the end of the granite counter. His appetite seemed non-existent lately and he could only sleep after several glasses of wine. He pulled the cork expertly, releasing a pleasing 'pop' to the silent kitchen. Removing two balloon glasses from the cupboard, he held them up to the light to check that they were blemish-free; stealing the opportunity to read Vincent's features. Their eyes met and the silent game of manoeuvring was over. Vincent had very little to report; why else would he be sitting relaxed in the leather armchair.

"No wine for me Jimmy, I'll just have a small beer."

"It's an Australian Shiraz Reserve."

"Doesn't matter how fancy the name, red wine gives me the shits! And I can't afford for that to happen in my line of work."

James handed him a bottle of chilled lager and a glass

tumbler. Vincent accepted the bottle only and drew two deep gulps before opening his notepad and reading aloud what had transpired whilst on watch at the property, four doors away.

"Vincent, what makes you so convinced that the woman who Peter was with is a prostitute? Maybe she's Carl's secretary or girlfriend."

"Carl always works alone and he's not interested in skirt."

"Is he homosexual?"

"No he's not queer, he's just not interested in sex; he gets his rocks off making money."

James refilled his wine glass then walked over to the window. The rain had stopped and a stiff breeze was creating erratic movement amongst the boats in the harbour. "It might have been Peter's daughter, she lives in South Africa but she could be over on a visit."

"How old is the daughter?"

After a few seconds of contemplation James answered, knowing that this train of thought was a complete waste of time. "She must be in her late thirties by now."

"Jimmy, this tart was young and beautiful, big tits, lovely arse; every normal guys dream, so why else would she be wasting her time on an old codger like Radcliffe, unless he was paying her? You've got your knickers in a twist over Carl's involvement with Radcliffe, if you had let me do things my way, you might have had more to go on. And why the hell are you so convinced that Carl is involved here? It seems obvious to me that Radcliffe's found a buyer at long last and the old bastard's having a bit of a fling!"

"I agree; the, For Sale, board has gone and he's spending money as though there is a never-ending supply; restoration on these period properties are extremely expensive so how come he can afford the work before the sale is completed?"

"Simple man, he decided to take out a loan!"

"Well, Victor Carlson and Peter Radcliffe were certainly deciding on something when I caught sight of them together in a private room at the bank." James noticed that he had shocked Vincent with this revelation. He had been hoping to find out for himself, through speaking to his bank manager, why a man who had caused so much heart-ache and who had supposedly left the employ of this particular financial institution, was here at all? But he was informed by the assistant manager that his boss was on leave and wouldn't be returning for another week.

"There's nothing more I can do Jimmy. If Carl *is* involved with Radcliffe as you say, then you're only chance is to get Radcliffe to talk."

"And how do you suggest I do that? Hold a gun to his head?"

"He's your fucking long-standing neighbour; talks in the same, public school, pompous way. Have a few glasses of that fancy wine together; I've already told you he likes to sing! He's in bed now, you'll have to arrange something with him tomorrow; but take my advice and have a lay-in first, you look knackered." Vincent scribbled out an invoice and handed it to James before disappearing out of his kitchen.

Lyn was barely two hours into the twenty-three hour flight and already the advice given by several well-meaning, well-travelled people had been cast aside. Andy was young, carefree and very persuasive. They'd eaten a hearty supper of lightly-spiced lamb served with rice and stir-fried vegetables; proceeded by an interesting mix of raw salad and nuts and followed by a red-berry-mousse. They'd enjoyed a glass of champagne with the starter, had another to compliment the mousse; and the two glasses of red wine in between went perfectly with the lamb. When Lyn had started to protest at the amount of alcohol being consumed, Andy had reminded her of his promise.

"I want to make your first experience of flying, as memorable as possible. You need to get a period of quality sleep and in my experience, a few glasses of alcohol is the very best way to guarantee it."

Before settling into this period of quality sleep, Andy asked Lyn to make sure her valuables were out of sight. After tapping her nose and attempting to look coy, she patted the slight bulge, reassuringly felt strapped around the right side of her waist and almost invisible beneath her loose fitting jumper. Armed with a boyish grin, he then recommended that while visiting the bathroom, she remove anything from the close fitting pouch that would be needed during the flight such as passport and tickets etc and place them elsewhere but easily accessible, like her handbag, or even better, a secure pocket in her jeans. "The last thing you want is someone eyeing you up whilst you fiddle with your underwear to remove your passport." He gave another grin and a cheeky wink before continuing.

"I've stashed cash in the most ingenious places, but if a thief is on the prowl, he is watching you at the most vulnerable times; times when you need to get to your passport for instance. Thankful for this sound advice, Lyn weaved her way unsteadily down the narrow aisle clutching her toilet bag.

On her return she found both their seats reclined with a nest of blankets and pillows waiting to be arranged. Andy was sitting in *her* seat by the window.

"Hope you don't mind me changing seats Lyn, I know all about women and their frequent visits to the loo after binge drinking. I don't want to be woken by your legs rubbing against me."

"I thought the drinking was supposed to help me have some 'quality' sleep." Lyn wiggled both her fore fingers in the air whilst making a loud hiccup.

Chapter 5

Sunday—3.30am

Candy pulled into the twenty-four-hour garage and made a dash for the toilets. Coffee had never been one of her favourite drinks, but she had happily downed three mugs of the stuff since setting out. The expectation of non-stop conversation from Stefan, to stimulate and prevent drowsiness, hadn't materialised; and after several attempts, the monosyllabic responses, led her to believe that he was just too exhausted to bother.

Feeling buoyant from relief and knowing that within the hour she would be tucked up in a comfortable bed, Candy whistled a tune as she slid back into the driver's seat; then realising that Stefan was still sleeping, put a stop to her birdlike rendition of 'twenty-four hours from Tulsa'. Stefan was producing his own noises—soft, puffing snores, muffled because his head was cushioned against the window by a plump carrier bag. The carrier bag contained three sets of socks, underpants and sweat shirts, and all nine items were black. He'd refused Candy's offer of new jeans, the ones he wore (which were also black) were his best, and he didn't like the style of the supermarket brand.

Stefan had matured a lot since the time Elena had turned up with him at one of the modelling sessions. Clutching her younger brother's hand, she had begged Candy to allow him to stay in the background until the session was over. He'd come to London to find work and lodgings of his own; but in the meantime he'd be sleeping on the floor of Elena's bedsit. Candy was soon to learn of the desperation behind Elena's plea! Their father, after raising the large amount of money to send his beautiful daughter to England as a trainee model, had instead been duped into buying her a life of prostitution. This same father had been brutally murdered trying to bring to justice the gang of people traffickers; and Stefan would be next if the so-called Bulgarian Mafia had their way.

Most of Candy's models were Eastern European and most had been rescued (at considerable expense) from the hands of such low-life. All had thought they were heading for a chance to make lots of money in one of the world's fashion capitols; but instead of the catwalk they had become street-walkers; desperately trying to earn enough to keep their Bulgarian pimps happy. For the hard-working majority of Bulgarians, the situation had improved since entering the European Union; but the opening up of borders, had made it even easier for the determined trafficker to prey on the vulnerable.

Elena, now free of the financial chains that bound her to a life of prostitution, was doing well. The money she had been sending home each month had been used wisely to improve the lifestyle of her mother, disabled by multiple sclerosis, and her youngest brother, in need of further education. But the recession was worldwide and money difficulties back home brought even more pressures to bear here in England.

Candy smiled as her memory fixed on that first encounter with Stefan; this young, intelligent-looking young man, built like a tank but holding on to his sister as if his life depended on it. And in a way it did, because his command of the English language was virtually nonexistent. Eventually Candy managed to secure him work through a builder she'd known for years—words weren't that necessary for mixing cement, carrying bricks and demolishing walls—but within a year, as the recession began to bite and banks were loathed to lend money, the builder, reluctantly had to let him go. God knows how he's earning a living now, thought Candy as she drove into the grounds of her favourite hotel.

Stefan felt the motion of the car change as it turned into a wide left arc and then slowly come to a standstill. His eyes opened on a large crescent-shaped building. Concealed lighting from ground level, fanning over the cream-coloured paintwork, highlighted the splendour of its elegant architecture. Candy was moving to the rear of the car; and suddenly aware and mindful of manners, he jumped out and removed her two bags from the trunk. She told him to go ahead while she parked the car elsewhere, indicating with her finger the way to reception. Stefan could see the way to reception; he wasn't the ignorant baboon he used to be. Even so, it was an unexpected bit of good fortune that he should find himself alone in the entrance leading to reception. Positioned on his left, was a rack holding dozens of pamphlets showing places of interest; but Stefan's eyes soon located what he needed—a street map of the area. It was folded and secured in his jeans pocket before Candy returned.

"There won't be any time for sight-seeing Stefan, lets get some shut eye love, then we'll decide how to proceed after breakfast. It's deathly quiet in here; I hope there's someone to show us to our rooms."

Stefan had no intention of taking more sleep. In spite of Candy's persistent chatter, he had managed to grab sufficient rest on the journey here. The English always wanted to talk. Stefan was tired of talk. He was ready for action!

Lyn awoke from a dream that was both tantalising and disturbing. She stood naked against the trunk of a giant tree fern. Unlike the normal tree fern, this dreamland species had a smooth trunk and as she pressed her body against it, the trunk moved and moulded to her shape. All around her were exotic plants; their form and colours mesmerising as they swayed in the warm perfumed breeze. In the dream, she'd wanted to move away from the giant fern, eager to touch and explore this paradise of a garden; but she found she couldn't. The fronds of the giant fern, which had originally teased and brushed lightly against her flesh, wrapped grippingly around her waist the second she tried to move away. Three attempts were made before the dream dissipated into reality.

The cabin was dark and almost silent. The soft hum of the plane's engines defied the capability of keeping such a large craft travelling at such speed and height. Lyn was in awe of so much; but in particular, she was amazed at how you could travel in such comfort and in so little space. She had Andy to thank for this. The two seats he had managed to wangle, flashing that boyish grin which seemed to melt every female's heart, were a Godsend because of the extra leg room. With the same charming smile he had managed to secure a double ration of blankets and pillows; which were used more for padding than for warmth. Due to his acclaimed expertise as a frequent traveller, Lyn had allowed him to organise their sleeping positions for maximum rest, and she had drifted off contentedly amongst the hubbub of other peoples light conversations and the flickering of several, silent computer screens.

Feeling thirsty and stale in the mouth from the earlier over-indulgence, she reached forward for her bottle of water, anchored in the pocket of the seat in front. But her body came to a sharp halt! Confusion faded when she realised her seat belt was fastened across the blanket; but on remembering that this wasn't so before she fell asleep, the confusion returned. She also noticed that the arm that separated the two seats had been lifted to the upright position, allowing Andy's arm to wrap around her waist. Torn between needing a drink of water, and not wanting to disturb Andy's sleep, Lyn did nothing. Eventually, nature galvanised her into action—she needed to pee! Unlike the dream, her escape was quite straight forward; Andy's arm was gently lifted and the seatbelt released, permitting an easy glide to freedom.

As Lyn squeezed out of the toilet cubical she came face to face with one of the female cabin crew.

"Is there anything I can get for you madam?" The hostess asked in a whisper.

"I'd love a glass of water please." Lyn followed the woman to the back of the plane, enjoying the chance to stretch her legs. She drank the water in one long gulp and asked if she might have another? The hostess smilingly obliged.

"Tell me," Lyn asked hesitantly, "did you fasten my safety belt, after I fell asleep?"

"We always recommend wearing your seat belt madam, especially whilst sleeping; it saves us disturbing you if we enter any turbulent conditions."

"Thank you very much." Lyn made her way back, carefully balancing the glass of water and amused that the obliging woman hadn't quite answered her question.

Unable to drift back into sleep but reluctant to reach over and open the window-blind Lyn checked her watch, remembering simultaneously that Andy had advised her to remove it. He had spent a good deal of time and energy promoting his views on the best way to travel long-haul. Lyn had listened, not because she was that interested in the time differences and its effect on the body, she'd listened because it had seemed ages since someone had actually bothered to talk to her. Even Jill, her oldest friend, seemed so wrapped up in her family that there was barely time for any talk other than business matters.

Candy arriving in her life was like a breath of fresh air. She'd reminded Lyn of Beryl—her old boss from years ago. Not because they were alike in looks; Beryl was grossly overweight, had brown frizzy hair, which she'd insisted on dyeing too dark a shade for her age, and, Beryl didn't give two hoots about fashionable clothes. But the merriment and the love that had exuded from the heart of her, had bound a relationship that spanned over twenty-five years. Lyn realised just how much she missed her new friend from London. She also wondered, and not for the first time, if she would ever see Candy again. James couldn't stand her! Like most things, he would never discuss the reasons why with Lyn; but the dislike was apparent on his face every time Candy Laverne's name was mentioned.

"You look miles away and very sad" Andy's sleepy but cheerful voice cut through Lyn's meandering thoughts and his arm took possession of her waist once again.

"Sorry Andy, I didn't mean to wake you, do you know what time it is?"

"Haven't got a clue and couldn't care less, here let me fasten your belt and make sure it's visible, before the cabin dragon descends."

"I wondered who it was that bound me to the seat.

"Well actually it was me; I told the Gestapo Lady that we were lovers so it was quite natural that I would make sure you were safe and comfortable."

"Andy, I feel so embarrassed now! I'm old enough to be your mother."

"So what, I prefer older women, besides it was great to see her squirm with jealousy." As he spoke, his arm tightened and he snuggled his head down onto her shoulder.

"You know that I have a boyfriend in England and…"

Andy interrupted by pressing a finger to her lips and said "My simple philosophy on life is this: if you need something and an opportunity comes along to satisfy that need, well, need I say more." Again that broad smile and the cheeky wink! "Shouldn't be long before the breakfast trolley will be rattling down the gangway and all the lights will be blazing. If you need more sleep, now is the best chance you're going to get."

Chapter 6

The alarm from the digital clock, kicked in at precisely 5am, competing with the sound of running water. Vinny, anxious to stop it before it reached its crescendo, dashed from the shower to his bedside, leaving a trail of wet footprints on route. He knew the chances of it being heard this early were slim but he felt irritated that he'd forgotten to turn it off before getting up. Since finding his perfect niche in life, he had become more orderly and focussed—a necessity in his line of work—but for the last week, something had started nibbling at his guts and causing havoc with his peace of mind and ordered routine.

The bits and pieces of info that he'd squeezed out of Jimmy weren't much help but they were a start. Personally, he couldn't give a flying fart that Carl was corrupt; he worked in banking so it was to be expected. But he cared very much when that corruption reached out to him with the prospect of undoing all the hard work of the last year. Several official-looking letters had arrived over the last few weeks, threatening action relating to False Declarations of

Bankruptcy and Outstanding Payments of Capital Gains Tax. Vinny knew who was behind it, Carl's methods of intimidation were well known to him and they were just that, methods of intimidation. But Vinny had his own professional standing now and the last thing he wanted was to be blacklisted. The thought of Carl actually living and working from a premises just four doors away from his own, made him break out into a cold sweat.

But first things first he thought, as he skated the used bath-towel over the wet patches on the laminate flooring whilst drinking the last two inches of coffee from his mug. He needed to find out how Lyn Porter had come by such a large sum of money. Jimmy was convinced that she was involved with Carl. But Vinny just couldn't see it.

For a second time, Stefan walked along the length of the row of premises known as The Terrace. It had been easy to find. The street map was very clear about the whereabouts of the harbour and Candy's tit bits of information had provided the rest. There had been plenty of street-lighting as he'd walked along the water's edge, the rising tide chortling as it lapped against the small anchored boats; but up here it was dark and deathly quiet. He stood in the gap opposite the premises of number 4, and with his back to the harbour he imprinted on his memory everything about the place: its four-story-height, its strong front door—elevated from ground level by a short run of concrete steps—and the antique sash windows that were commonplace in properties of this period. Before returning to the hotel, he would walk along the rear of The Terrace, carefully counting out the individual doors, just to make sure. Not all back entrances showed a number, but all gave an indication of how easy they could be accessed. He glanced one more time at the ground-floor room where Elena had last modelled for Candy Laverne. Before she had disappeared! Suddenly, something caught Stefan's attention! A small moving light, within that room flickered on and off. He crossed the road in just a few strides, and craning his neck over the waist-high-iron-railings to the porch, he could just about see into the window. A small torch-beam revealed a heavy-built man, crouching with his back to the window as he rifled through paperwork. After watching for a while, the body-language of the crouching man suddenly changed; he had found what he was looking for and the torch was switched off.

Afraid of losing the opportunity, Stefan knocked on the door, gently at first, but after realising that he couldn't be heard or was being ignored, the knocking grew louder. Still no response. Filled with an energy born out of stifled frustration, Stefan beat on the heavy wooden door with both his fists and with all of his might. Suddenly, the door was yanked open and he was seized around the neck by a large, fat-fingered hand.

James had groaned with irritation as he'd fumbled for the switch on his bedside lamp. The knocking had dragged him from sleep that had begun troubled and fitful; but due to the amount of wine he'd consumed, had gradually settled into a comatose restfulness. Glancing at the clock provoked more groaning. Even allowing for the extra hour, which marked the end of British Summer Time, it was far too early for any sensible person to be up and about. When the knocking had become more urgent and angry voices could be clearly heard in the area of his front porch, he'd leapt out of bed, muttering about how the neighbourhood was being taken over by all manner of unsavoury characters.

Halfway down the central stairway he halted. The profiles of two men, animated by an aggressive struggle, were visible through the pane of the half-glazed inner door. His porch door, which he clearly remembered locking, stood wide open! Tightening the belt of his dressing gown, he flicked on the lights and strode purposefully down the rest of the stairs.

"The police are on their way, what's going...?" James's angry outburst fell short as he recognised one of the hoodlums! "Vincent, what's happening here?"

"This... This foreign piss head was attempting to break-in," he shouted, spittle flying in all directions, whilst making a show of the fact that he managed to twist the man's arm halfway up his back. "We don't need the cops involved; I'll sort him out."

This other man, clearly shaken at the mention of police involvement, said nothing in defence of Vincent's accusation. He was clean-shaven and dressed simply in skin-hugging black jeans, tight-fitting black sweatshirt and black shoes. The only item missing which would complete the perfect ensemble of a night burglar would be a hooded jacket; but he wore nothing more to keep out the chill of the dark, early morning.

"Why were you knocking on my porch door? Mr...

Whoever you are. And I don't believe for one moment that my neighbour's assumptions are correct."

"Jesus H Christ Jimmy, I caught the fucker red-handed! Go back to bed, like I said, *I'll* sort it." Vincent's last three words were emphasised with a further push on his captive's arm, releasing from him a sharp intake of breath; but apart from this, the stranger remained silent.

"Right, the police it is then!" James turned to re-enter his hallway, but before he'd opened the door, another scuffle broke out! The captive had freed himself and landed a heavy punch directly in the middle of Vincent's face. Vincent's body creased in pain and he rocked back and forth as his hands tried to stem the blood that oozed from his nose. The assailant, eager to make a dash for freedom whilst he had the chance; but blocked by Vincent's bulk, turned his appealing eyes on James.

"Please, I no criminal; I just look to find Elena."

In spite of the obvious discomfort, Vincent dragged himself up leaving a smear line of blood on the pristine magnolia-painted wall. "I've already told you, you fucking foreign idiot, this is not a brothel, so piss off to wherever you belong!"

"Vincent, go and get cleaned up, I'll deal with this."

"I'm not leaving you alone with this thug, he's probably armed!"

"I think it's pretty clear from what he's wearing that he's not carrying any weapons, please go and attend to your bleeding nose."

"Candy Laverne give this address to me; this is last place Elena work."

James bristled at the mention of that name!

Vincent's voice, sounding nasal from the swelling, cut in. "You're in the wrong fucking neighbourhood mate, there are no tarts plying their trade around here."

Quick as a flash, Vincent was seized by the throat! And the man, dressed solely in black and standing at least four inches taller, pinned him against the wall.

"I know meaning of word, tart, and if you call my sister by this name again, I will break all teeth from your dirty mouth! You understand?"

A silent, communicated affirmative must have shown on Vincent's face. The stranger's hands released their hold and Vincent disappeared out of the confines of the porch.

The smell of coffee and warming croissants created an atmosphere of calm and pleasant normality; but Stefan wasn't fooled. Both men needed information and this show of goodwill and hospitality from one, was the first step in a complicated dance. From his seat at the table, Stefan studied James Fairbank as he busied about in his smart, expensive kitchen, the quality of this man's quiet strength, worn like the designer-label dressing gown he had recently discarded, his every question and every statement made would have been carefully thought out. Usually, Stefan preferred this; talking just for the sake of it was a waste of energy for the talker and a headache for the listener. But right now, a headache would be good.

James Fairbank placed the silver pot of steaming coffee on the table and took the seat directly opposite. He raised his fine-bone-china cup in the fashion of a 'toast'. "Here's to finding your sister, Elena!"

Stefan's cup remained on the table. "I will not leave this area till I have, Mr Fairbank."

"Stefan, please call me James, I'm your friend and I want to help you. It is Sunday and I am not in my role as a solicitor." The solicitor's hands made the open gesture to study the way he was dressed. And it was true, the faded jeans and the cable-knit jumper created the image of a regular guy, a handsome, regular guy, the sort that are always chosen for Hollywood movies. But the eyes told a different story. The eyes never stopped searching for…For what? Their greenness drew you in, a swirling pool of crystal water, inviting you to remove your outer covering and dive into the depths where burdens could be released. Stefan turned from the greenness to drink his coffee and lay jam in the croissant. Talking ceased as both men satisfied their hunger.

With all the croissants gone and the coffee cups refilled, talking began again. The obvious things were covered; Elena's age, how long she had worked in England and what she looked like. Stefan had produced a recent photograph as an answer to this last question. James Fairbank had studied it closely and placed it beside him on the table. The talking had moved on to boyfriends of Elena; and on this, Stefan had been adamant. "Elena does not have, what you call 'boyfriend'. I am her brother, I would know if she had met someone and fallen in love. In Bulgaria, marriage is a sacred ceremony and all family are invited to celebrate it. Elena has given up good job which she has enjoyed for three years and she doesn't answer phone or my messages. Something is not right! And it starts here, in this building!"

"Tell me about Candy Laverne."

Stefan sensed the dislike as the solicitor spoke her name. "She is good friend to me and Elena. She is honourable lady who cares much for people who work with her, and she also, worry where Elena is."

Stefan felt a vibration in his Jeans pocket. He removed his mobile to check the caller. The hint of a smile softened his serious features as he thought of the English saying 'Talk of the Devil'. It was Candy; but he wasn't going to speak here.

"I have to go, Mr Fairbank, thank you for hospitality."

"Well at least give me your phone number and tell me where you are staying, it's in my own interest to find out what's happening here. I feel sure that you will find Elena very soon." A pen and notepad were pressed into Stefan's hand. Looking into the greenness was resisted as he wrote down his phone number and nothing more.

The solicitor followed him down the stairs, and after shaking Stefan's hand watched as he fled towards the town. When it was safe to do so, Stefan turned and walked in the opposite direction.

Chapter 7

Sunday—9.00am

Elena loved the ocean. Whilst growing up in Breznik—a small town forty kilometres west of Sofia—there were only three occasions when she'd been fortunate enough to visit the sea-shore and the memory of each was deeply etched. She stood overlooking the small beach that was situated directly in front of Carl's hotel. He had phoned an hour ago and told her to pack all of her belongings and meet him here at nine o'clock. Naturally she had complied. For five more days she would bow to his every whim, and then she would be free. How wonderful, she thought, to have all this within a short walk. How fortunate to be able to open your sitting room window and allow the salt-laden breeze to fill your home. And how especially satisfying to be able, eventually, to share that home with your sick mother and two younger brothers. The stiff breeze whipped at her long coat and pulled her hair from the elasticated ribbon; it was chilly and it was overcast but her surroundings were still achingly beautiful.

Her phone rang and she hesitated. Carl had warned her against taking calls from friends and family, they would want to talk her out of the decision she had made, which was only natural; but a call from Candy earlier that morning had caught her off-guard and had been very disturbing. Stefan was in England, looking for reassurance that his sister was alright. Elena rummaged in her bag to retrieve the singing phone. Suddenly, a steely grip clamped her arm.

"Leave it!"

"Oh! I thought that might be you ringing to say you'd be late.

"As you know Elena, I am never late." The phone stopped abruptly in the middle of a melodious bar and Carl allowed her to see who had been trying to reach her. It was Stefan. She explained to Carl how her brother and her boss were good friends and they were just anxious to know she was alright.

"Ex-boss, Elena. You are now your own boss and you will soon be in a very enviable position; let me demonstrate a simple way of keeping these irritating interruptions out of your way" Without waiting for her answer, Carl plucked the phone from her hand and removed the phone's sim-card from its housing. She watched in astonishment, as he dropped the little square of plastic to the floor and ground it into pieces using the heel of his polished, leather shoe. The lifeless phone was then slipped into his own pocket.

"Now, back to more important matters; we need to move you to a more secure place until the day of your marriage."

"Why? I can't think of anyone who wishes me harm."

"Peter Radcliffe knows where you are staying and he is an extremely lonely man. I'm sure that you wouldn't want him pestering you before the appropriate time."

"He seems like a perfect gentleman, I feel sure…"

Carl cut her off by impatiently raising his hand. He knew how much she wanted this and she knew that she would have to go along with whatever he'd arranged to achieve it. Doing her best to sound light-hearted she asked where they were heading and if she would be allowed to go shopping. "I only brought the minimum of clothing to Devon and none of it is suitable for getting married in."

"Leave everything to me Elena, all your needs will be met. We are moving a little further down the coast, that is all."

Candy sat in front of the dressing-table mirror. She was half-heartedly applying make-up to a face that was puffy from lack of sleep and fiddling with hair that refused to lay flat. Her usual pre-bedtime routine of cleansing and plastering on the moisturiser, then stretching a net over a hairdo that had cost a small fortune, had been cast aside in favour of ten minutes extra sleep. But the sacrifice had been for nothing. It had taken ages to slip over the edge into unconsciousness and what little sleep she did get, was of poor quality; her head had constantly tossed and turned into her pillow. A few facial exercises would bring a bit of colour to her cheeks, she thought, but this meant pulling your face into several grotesque expressions and she wasn't alone. A quick glance over toward the window showed her that it hardly mattered that Stefan was in the same room, his back was toward her and he was lost in his own troubled thoughts.

She'd woken early; far too early considering the time she'd gone to bed, and on a whim had decided to ring Elena. To her great surprise and utter relief Elena had answered! Candy had then babbled on about anything and everything except the most important thing—where on earth are you? The only snippet of information gained from the call, was that the marriage would take place on the following Friday; and the only bit of information given, before Elena suddenly announced that she had to go, was that Stefan was in England.

Without a second thought, Candy had then run along the corridor to Stefan's room and knocked on his door. There'd been no response. Knocking louder and calling his name produced no more than an angry outburst from the adjoining guest, which had sent her back to her own room feeling more than a little frustrated. Undeterred, she had rung reception and asked to be connected by phone to Stefan's room, only to be informed that he'd left the hotel in the early hours and hadn't yet returned. By now, frustration had developed into exasperation and determined to give him a piece of her mind she'd phoned him on his mobile; but the young rascal had refused to answer. By the time they had finally spoken—each blaming the other for an opportunity missed—Elena could no longer be reached.

Candy pushed away the closed vanity case and took another sip of the strong coffee which Stefan had produced (as a sort of peace-offering.) Coffee was the last thing she'd wanted, apart from causing another row, so she had smiled and accepted it graciously. Now all she had to do was drink the stuff by slow and moderate degrees, then start the conversation flowing again.

"Stefan, I know you must be sick with worry over Elena's decision to marry; but I can't see what either of us can do about it; perhaps coming here was a bad idea, love."

"No Candy, is good thing to come here. I have been to place where Elena was last working; a man was there in the dark, searching through papers. Something bad is happening; I feel it here." Stefan thumped the middle of his chest with a clenched fist. "My sister is marrying for wrong reasons, and I cannot allow this to happen. I will show her picture to everyone in this town if necessary... Govno!"

Candy recognised the Bulgarian swear-word and knew that Stefan only used such language, in her presence, if the situation was dire. She watched as he feverishly emptied his wallet, then the pockets of his jeans. "What is it love? What have you lost?"

"The photograph of Elena, I leave it at the solicitor's place!"

The printer was playing up again. James had been threatening to replace it for over a year; but it had become so conveniently easy and so satisfyingly pleasant, to just pop across the corridor to Lyn's office and make use of her up-to-the-minute model, that he hadn't bothered. He was hurriedly attempting to copy the photograph of Elena, knowing that time was of the essence (Stefan would be back as soon as he realised he'd left without it) but three attempts proved the fact that a recognisable image was not going to be produced. Disheartened, he turned off the deficient equipment and grabbed his jacket.

Vincent looked sheepish as he opened the door to the basement flat and relaxed a little when he saw that James was alone.

"They carted him off then?"

"We both know that Stefan wasn't here to break-in and steal from anyone, Vincent. Only you could have opened that door and only you could have disengaged the burglar-alarm. What were you doing in Lyn's office?"

"That's it! Take the word of a fucking foreigner; you afraid of race-relations coming down on you; you joined up to all this political correctness crap or what?"

The last thing James needed right now, was to get embroiled in one of Vincent's pointless tirades. He needed a favour; he would have to leave his other concerns for later.

"Vincent do you mind me using your photocopier; mine needs new cartridges and there's no chance of buying them on a Sunday."

The sudden change of tack left Vincent stumped for words; but only for a few seconds.

"It's about time you upgraded your office, get rid of all that depressing, heavy wood and leather, give it a make-over, you can't beat these modern materials. There's no poncing about with furniture polish, just a quick flick with a duster."

James had been hoping to keep the acquired image of

Elena to himself; but the thought of Stefan returning any second to claim it back, forced his hand. He stopped Vincent in mid-stream as he launched into the merits of acrylic-corded-carpet, versus old-fashioned rugs on original wooden floor boards.

"It's a photograph of Stefan's missing sister, so a slightly enlarged image on good quality paper, would be very much appreciated." James blurted out, as he fanned the photograph under Vincent's nose.

Halfway across his, power hub, Vincent's description of the three-by-four-metre space where his computer and the necessary accompaniments to his profession were arranged, he suddenly stopped.

"That's her! That's the tart I saw with Radcliffe. Sister my arse, foreigners are all fucking liars and you can tell that to the fucking race relations board, I've been proved right, she's on the fucking game!"

Peter Radcliffe dropped the phone back into its cradle as a broad smile creased his worn, leathery features. He had expected today to be just like any other Sunday—boring. The long-handled broom, which he had been using to clear an accumulation of damp, slippery leaves from the back door steps, was again taken up. With the broom head uppermost and a tea towel draped fetchingly over the damp bristles, Peter proceeded to waltz with it around the kitchen floor. As per usual, the tempo was set from the radio.

When the crooner and his accompanying music ceased, Peter laid aside the broom and considered the afternoon ahead. A home-cooked Sunday roast in the stimulating company of a fellow businessman, who conveniently, happened to be a neighbour. He had no doubts at all that James Fairbank was also feeling the pangs of loneliness. If his memory served well, Lyn Porter should be well on her way to the other side of the world. Such was the way of the heart when once again it had been stirred by the opposite sex. Why on earth he had changed his mind about flying out to Australia with her was anybodies guess; but it would be interesting to discover. He would give his neighbour the benefit of his extra years and fuller knowledge of the workings of a woman's mind. He would also like to find out when he intended to make Lyn Porter his own. Life was too short to dither. Life was far too precious not to reach out and take advantage of an opportunity.

Peter checked the time once again and decided on a cup of tea; the usual time of eleven o'clock was still half an hour away. He hated the altering of clocks, his body rhythm was already under strain with the amount of medication he was on, but he wouldn't fuss over that today. Today there would be no main meal to deal with and today was another day closer to his hearts desire.

After five minutes of brewing, the Darjeeling tea was poured into a porcelain cup and carried into the sitting room. A brass band was booming from the radio and Peter reached over and lowered its volume. He needed to think; he needed to work out what pills he could safely take before the afternoon visit and which could be safely left until his return. He had no intention of advertising the fact that he was ill. A couple of glasses of full-bodied red wine would be fine with the roast; but he must resist the port that would be offered later. Doctor's warnings to hold alcohol levels down to a minimum and Carl's warnings to keep the marriage secret grumbled around his head as he began to realise how restrained the shared dinner would be. He would just have to rely on James to set the tone of conversation.

The phone rang again as Peter carried his empty cup to the kitchen for a refill. "Oh my, I'm a popular guy", he sang as he soft-shoe-shuffled to the phone table.

"Anna, what a lovely surprise, how is life in sunny South Africa?"

"I take it that Gerald and the boys are well, good, it's nice to hear it."

"No, no I can't possibly do that, not this Christmas, I've already made plans. Maybe during the spring would be better."

"Well of course I want to see you all sweetheart; but my life's a little hectic right now…I'll phone soon and we'll arrange something. I promise. Goodbye dear, give my love to the family.

It had been at least ten months since Peter had last heard from his daughter—a Christmas card holding a snapshot of his twin grandsons on their fourteenth birthday—but it had been over nine years since he'd had the pleasure of their company.

Oblivious to the biting chill of the on-shore wind, James stood on the top step that led down to Vincent flat; fingers turning blue as they gripped the photograph and copy of Elena. He was in a quandary. Under pressure from Vincent, he had just invited his neighbour for a 'traditional Sunday roast'. Trouble was, his fridge and his freezer, were devoid of the necessary ingredients. His own plans for today had been to drive over to Exeter and pay his sister a surprise visit. Ever since Helen's discovery that he wouldn't be travelling to Sydney with Lyn, she had pestered him to have dinner with her. Today he'd planned on satisfying her curiosity while he satisfied his need for a nourishing home cooked meal.

He had to agree, it did make sense to arrange an informal get-together with Peter Radcliffe, and endeavour to extract as much information as possible, but James had wanted to do this at one of the many local restaurants. This suggestion, had sent Vincent into hoots of laughter and derision as he played out in his usual colourful manner how, everyone within earshot of their table, would be privy to the saucy antics of Radcliffe and his tart, or worse, Radcliffe would quite rightly clam up and the opportunity would be lost. James had had to agree he had a point, and in the final analysis, had agreed to drive out to the nearest supermarket for the necessities. This wasn't the only thing that kept James rooted to the spot in a troubled dilemma. Whilst Peter Radcliffe was safely out of the way, Vincent would be entering his premises and, giving it a thorough going over.

The sound of a hand-break being engaged and the sight of a well-polished Jaguar stopping directly in front of him, dissipated all thoughts and concerns of unlawful entry. A woman, whose face he instantly recognised, climbed out of the driver's seat.

"James, it is you! I thought Stefan was having me on. Why aren't you on your way to Oz. Is Lyn around?"

The friendly tone of Candy Laverne's voice was obviously as false as her name, and although James's first reaction was to ignore her, enter his own premises and slam the door, he realised grudgingly that this would be counter-productive.

"Lyn's flight was yesterday, unfortunately something came up and I couldn't manage the time off."

"Couldn't manage the time off! Do you realise how important this trip was to Lyn? How she'd been looking forward to sharing that time with you?"

James flinched at the audacity of this woman's words; but again held back from speaking his mind. Candy Laverne came even closer, so close that he could smell her perfume and define the slap-dash way she had applied her make-up.

"Ah, I see you have made good use of the time since Stefan accidentally left this behind."

Candy Laverne's red-nailed talons snatched the photo easily from James's chilled fingers. She handed it to Stefan, who by now, was standing beside her. A single red-nailed talon pointed to the copy.

"This implies that you know more than we do about Elena. Shall we go into the warm to continue our little chat?"

Chapter 8

Changi Airport-Singapore

For the second time, everyone filed dutifully off the plane, and although most would be returning to the same plane and the same seats within the hour, they had been told to take all their personal belongings with them. This announcement had caused a wave of discontent; nothing that could be defined as an outright verbal complaint, just a rippling of negative murmurs and the slamming of overhead lockers. A scheduled, three-hour stop for refuelling had already been made at Abu Dhabi airport, and like everyone else, Lyn had been grateful for the chance to stretch and walk around the airport's exotic surroundings; but having settled down once again for what should have been the last, uninterrupted leg of the long journey, no one was especially pleased to be again ousted from their temporary comfort zone.

"You didn't say anything about more stops." Lyn was sifting through her bag looking for the boarding card which Andy had given the impression wouldn't be needed again.

"I've never flown with this airline before; like everyone else, I assumed there was just the one stop." As he spoke, Andy pulled and guided Lyn in front of him before a large-built woman and her even larger-built husband choked up the gangway with their extra wide bodies and their several pieces of hand-luggage.

Eventually the mass spilled out into a quiet corner of Changi International Airport. They were welcomed by a loud speaker announcement, broadcast in several languages, it stated that Singapore had a zero tolerance to drug smuggling and anyone found guilty risked the death penalty. Lyn's mood brightened on seeing a sign indicating Toilets and Showers; but on approach was dismayed to see the long, winding queue.

Andy placed a comforting arm around her shoulder. "Believe me, we don't have the time. You'll appreciate that long soak in the bath all the more when we arrive in Sydney, let's take this opportunity to stretch our legs again, there's still a lot of cramped hours to go."

After walking at least a hundred metres along a wide corridor devoid of any stimulus, apart from the odd advertising bill-board, they emerged into a completely different type of zone. Kiosks and open-fronted shops, selling all manner of goods from snacks to clothes, titillated the senses and brightened the mood of all that had taken the trouble to follow their lead. The refreshment areas were given a wide birth by Lyn and Andy; food and drink were plentiful on the flight and neither were money wasters; but an item caught Lyn's eye and after careful consideration, she decided that she wanted to buy it.

Taking her out of earshot of the eager assistant, Andy did his best to dissuade her from buying it. The Pashmina, woven in a blend of cashmere and silk and hand-finished in a mixture of mauves and soft silver grey, was the perfect gift for Candy. Lyn took on board everything that Andy was saying about the wealth of shops that Australia had; but in her heart, she knew she wouldn't find a more perfect item for her friend, and the cost, considering the quality of the shawl, was so incredibly reasonable. Without mentioning that the item was for someone else, Lyn persisted. "I appreciate all that your saying Andy, but I really want to buy it."

"Ok… I agree, it is beautiful and it's perfect for your colouring; but you can only have it if you let me buy it for you."

Andy bartered his way to a ten percent discount and paid the smiling assistant the money whilst waving away Lyn's protests. He then kissed her on the cheek, took her by the hand and led her away from the glam and glitter of the other stalls. "Better get back to the boarding gate, this lot wouldn't have any qualms about leaving late passengers behind."

"That was very generous of you, especially after what you've told me about your lack of funds; but I can't in all conscience let you buy this for me."

"I'll find a way for you to pay me back." This was accompanied by a broad grin and a cheeky wink.

Torbay
Two leather chairs were positioned in front of James Fairbank's large mahogany desk. Candy and Stefan were

told to sit! No please or would you like to, just one tiny little word that sounded like the hiss from a poisonous snake. The solicitor's office was cold from the weekend's lack of heating and Candy made a point of wrapping her woollen shawl more tightly round her shoulders. Stefan had told her everything that had gone on earlier; including the hospitality received in an apartment that was comfortable and warm. Candy needed warmth. She also needed to understand why this man, whom she had only met once, very briefly, resented her.

The solicitor positioned himself on the business side of the desk, seemingly unaffected by the room's frigid atmosphere.

"Pardon my boldness James, but if we're to remain in here do you mind switching on the heating."

For several seconds, Candy was treated to his undivided attention. His eyes, unwavering, bore into hers and because the rest of his face remained impassive, she was left uncertain as to how he would respond. Eventually, the twin pools of green lowered.

"I'll make us some coffee." James stated, placing his manicured hands on the desk and rising to his full height.

"I don't want any coffee, I'm sick to death of coffee, so if a hot drink is all you're prepared to offer, I'll have a nice cup of tea, no sugar and not too strong, and before you go, I'd like to know why you're behaving in such a hostile way? As far as I'm aware, James Fairbank, I've done nothing to deserve it." Again, Candy was subjected to his deep penetrating gaze before he spoke.

"A woman of you're age, speaking in a Lancashire dialect, was never given the birth name of Candy Laverne. I have an aversion to falseness, especially when it involves something as important as ones name. So I'll make you your 'nice cup of tea', Candy Laverne, but when you have drunk it, unless you are prepared to deal in complete honesty, which includes sharing the name you were given via your parents, then I'm afraid you will learn nothing of Elena from either myself or my colleague."

The solicitor left the room; and although it was done in a quiet, dignified manner, Candy sensed his inner turmoil.

"The toffee-nosed, pompous son-of-a…" Stefan suddenly rose to his feet.

"I go outside for smoke, give me loud shout if you need me, yes."

"I thought you'd packed up smoking Stefan,"

"I be just outside, yes?" She smiled and nodded. Her heart went out to him, he looked lost and he looked beat.

Closing her eyes and concentrating on deep breathing Candy tried to relax. Without encouraging it her mind drifted into a childhood memory that transported her back to when she was four years old. She was on her way to school for the very first time. Alice, who was seventeen at the time, had taken the morning off from her teacher-training, to share in what *she* regarded as a very important occasion. There was no such person as Candy Laverne, back then in the innocent, uncomplicated world of a pretty fair-haired, four-year-old child. She skipped merrily along beside her older sister, who was doing her best to impart some words of wisdom to her young charge. Doreen Crapper was the child's name back then—Doreen, which was her mother's name and who had died giving her life and Crapper, from her father, who had instilled in both of his daughters the proud historical origins of the family name—which simply put, meant cropper or reaper of crops.

Alice was earnestly warning little Doreen how to deal with the childish cruelty that had blighted *her* early years in school, due to the misfortunes of fate. Every morning, when register was called, the class fell silent; and in alphabetical rote, the crystal-clear voice of Miss Sharples rang out—"J. Brown, P. Collins, A. Crapper…!" Naturally the teacher put an end to the outright laughing and blatant sniggering with a mixture of punishments; but the bullies found silent ways of poking fun and showing their distaste of the name.

Intrigued, but not particularly disturbed by Alice's concern, little Doreen had asked what she should do if she was teased in the same way.

"Just take no notice of em, it just shows their ignorance."

Doreen remembered the advice well enough; although for the life of her she never did understand the reasoning behind it. She had found a more immediate and satisfying way to stop the teasing—a smart punch on the nose with a tightly closed fist! The delivery of several of these within the first week of school led to two things. The other kids in her class never laughed at her name again, at least not in her presence, and the teachers, including the head, thought that although little Doreen had the face of an angel, she possessed a capricious bent on account of not having had the benefit of a mother's love. Father was visited by a big wig on the Education Board, who no doubt expected to find a home devoid of discipline and decency; but was instead, treated to a lecture on the medieval origins of the 'Crapper' name and how it had been bastardised in recent times by the American servicemen. Things settled down in Doreen's close-knit community and her surname, with its various connotations, was never an issue again; until seventeen years later!

Alice Crapper had known from a very early age where her future lay; she wanted to teach at primary-school-level. Although she had no desire to marry and have children of her own (she'd already experienced that role with her mother's untimely death) she felt that she had a lot to impart to children who were in their formative years. But Doreen took after her mother—a born extrovert who liked to show-off. To the dismay of her father and in spite of doing well in all subjects at school, Doreen's greatest desire was to become a dancer. After several years of part-time working to fund places at various dancing schools, Doreen was given her first big break. She was signed up by The Max Fuller Entertainment Agency, the most prestigious agency in the North West.

During the initial interview, which was quite informal, Max told her that although she looked and danced like a star, she would never make it in the entertainment business with the name Doreen Crapper. At twenty-one, Doreen had long since outgrown the urge to punch anyone on the nose who ridiculed her name. Besides, Max was giving sound advice, and if she chose not to act on that advice, he told her she was free to 'sling her hook'. Suddenly, concerned that her big chance might be pulled from under her, Doreen had blurted out the first thing that had come into her head.

"Oh I do have a stage name; I just thought you'd need my proper name for your records and that," she'd said, feverishly wondering if she dare mention the name of her first dancing instructor whom she'd once had a teenage crush on. "It's Cristiana Laverne, shall I spell it for you?"

"No don't bother", Max had said, obviously unimpressed. He liked the 'Laverne' part but said Cristiana was too dramatic, said we needed to, Americanise the first name. Concern about what her father would think was soon suppressed beneath the joy of a signed contract for three years of stage engagements under her new name of Candy Laverne.

Forty-seven years on, there was only one person alive, who would know Candy by her original name. And Alice always used it.

Several voices, including the distinct clipped words of Stefan entered the chilled office as the door was held open for James. He pushed through carrying a large tray. Stefan and a stockily-built man with a shorn head followed.

"It's fucking freezing in here Jimmy! Has your heating packed up? Hollered the shorn-headed man before dropping his eyes on Candy. "Sorry love I didn't see you there."

All eyes turned on James Fairbank. "Naturally, it's set to cut out at the weekend and I didn't particularly want to alter my settings."

"Fuck the settings; you can see the old biddy's half frozen!"

The solicitor placed the laden tray on his desk before responding. He stretched his arm toward Candy, "Vincent may I introduce…"

Candy stood, turned to the shorn-headed man named Vincent and interrupted Fairbank's annoyingly, formal introduction.

"Doreen Crapper, pleased to meet you." Candy took hold of the large, fat-fingered hand and gave a squeeze.

"Good God woman with a name like that you'd need to be able to land a hard punch!"

"Oh believe me I can!"

With four people in it, Vinny's power hub seemed almost claustrophobic; but at least it was warm. In spite of the complaints, Jimmy wasn't going to budge on his decision to leave the central heating system on the pre-set mode. Nor did he seem keen to invite the four of them up to his rooms; so Vinny, pissed off with his weird mood, had picked up the tray saying. "Follow me everybody!" And they'd all traipsed down the steps to his flat.

He had moved the most comfortable chair, his black-leather swivel, close to the radiator and had insisted that the old girl sit in it. He'd also brought in two stools from his breakfast bar but so far, no one had taken advantage of their availability. Stefan, who had earlier asked for, and been given, two cigarettes from a box that Vinny had had kicking around for five months and three days, stood in the far corner with his back to the light of the window. Jimmy, half-standing and half-sitting against the work top, was positioned diametrically opposite; perfect, as usual, for gauging the reactions of others. Starting to feel like a mother-hen whose chicks had proved to be capable of fending for themselves, Vinny perched on one of the imported bar stools and for the first time in five months and three days felt the strong need of a smoke. Fighting the urge to disappear through the back door and satisfy the need, he reached for a pen and note pad and tried his best to appear professional.

The old girl had drunk her first cup of tea in one long swig and was nursing her second in both hands. Jimmy hadn't said a word; but on draining his cup and replacing it carefully on the tray, he turned to Stefan.

"I can understand your concern for your sister, Stefan, the only thing we know, is that she was seen, last evening, in the presence of a much older man who happens to live a few doors away." Jimmy held up his hands as Stefan suddenly became activated. "Believe me; she is not in his house now."

"Why are *you* so interested in this older man?" asked the old girl, rising to stand between Stefan and Jimmy.

The solicitor's answer was aimed only at Stefan. "There is an obvious connection between my neighbour, Elena and Victor Carlson."

"And who the hell is Victor Carlson, when he's at home?" Interrupted the old girl, turning pink from frustration at this peculiar way of communicating.

Vinny sensed the rising tension and swept his eyes around for any loose objects that might be easily thrown. This feisty old bird reminded him of his aunt Beryl and she thought nothing of flinging the odd ornament, especially at him, when she got frustrated.

"Ms Crapper…" That did it, Vinny, already on tenterhooks and desperate to relieve the tension, started to snigger; and the sniggering turned into hearty laughing that couldn't be controlled.

"Right let's get one thing straight, here and now!" Candy slammed her almost empty cup down hard on the nearest surface; splashing its contents and commanding everyone's attention. "For forty-seven years I've been known as Candy Laverne. It's the only name I use; it's on my passport and every legal document I possess. And contrary to what some might think," at this point she turned her eyes on Jimmy and riveted them, without wavering, on his own. "I like my name and I want to be addressed by it."

"Very well, Ms Laverne, but I would just like to point out, before moving on to the subject of Victor Carlson that 'Crapper' is an early medieval name that has nothing to do with lavatories…"

"Spare me the lecture; we are here on the serious matter of finding Elena. Who is Victor Carlson and what is his involvement with Elena?"

"I was rather hoping that you might enlighten us here; I saw you covertly handing the man an envelope, on the day Elena was working here."

Vinny hated it when Jimmy played the role of solicitor. He had a sneaky respect for the old bird and couldn't understand why Jimmy was giving her such a hard time. He needed to ease the sticky situation and the uncomfortable atmosphere that filled his work-space. "Victor Carlson is usually known only as, Carl! I keep telling Jimmy it's pointless using his full name, which is probably only one of many, when no one knows it."

Relief and recognition dawned on Candy's furrowed brow. "Thank you Vinny; I take it that's what you prefer to be called, and, as to the covert envelope you're referring to, Carl had phoned me and asked for a favour on behalf of a friend of his who lived in Torbay. My fashion shows are attended on an-invitation-only basis and I didn't see the harm in supplying him with one. He sometimes introduces clients to my London venues. Having said that, on several occasions, models have suddenly decided to leave my agency after Carl has been on the scene; but these are grown women and I can't see what we can do. I've spoken a couple of times to Elena by phone and she says she wants to get married. The most worrying thing for her family and friends is the fact that no one knows who the prospective husband is!"

Making sure that he didn't use any objectionable words in the presence of Stefan, especially after suffering the earlier consequences, Vinny felt it was time to stop pussy-footing around and get down to business. "Well it looks pretty obvious to me that the lovely Elena has agreed to marry Peter Radcliffe. He is old and decrepit but no doubt worth a few bob. It happens all the time and there's no law against it. Thing is, if Carl *is* involved, there's more to it, and this is what we need to be sorting. We've all got something to gain from learning the truth, so I suggest we cut the crap on personality differences and get down to the nitty-gritty of what's going on!"

Chapter 9

Sunday Afternoon

Floor to ceiling glass sliding doors, that moved easily with the push of one finger, were the only barrier between Elena and the rugged coastline that lay two kilometres outside the coastal town of Lyme Regis. During the short drive here, Carl had emphasised, again, their need to keep out of sight and out of reach. His emphasising had been unnecessary. Elena no longer had any means of communicating, even this lavish house, with every other possible convenience, perversely had no sign of a landline phone, and, there were no immediate neighbours. Besides, she had no intention of jeopardising an arrangement that was so much to her advantage. These thoughts played at the back of her mind as she sought contentment from watching the rolling waves.

Carl had obviously been here before. On arrival, he'd retrieved a bunch of keys that had been hidden behind a cluster of stones that lay halfway along the broad winding drive to the double-sized garage. On pressing the top of one of the keys, the large garage door had rolled, almost-silently skyward, allowing Carl's black saloon to be swallowed in the cavernous space. A door, set in the back corner of garage, led to a short staircase and from there to the back of the house. A comfortable ambient temperature had welcomed them into a utility area that was scrupulously clean and tidy. Carl had walked over to a large chest freezer and lifted its lid. Apparently satisfied, he'd then moved to the adjoining kitchen and opened the two tall doors of the American style refrigerator. The right side was stocked with a variety of fresh-food; the left chilled space was taken up completely with bottles of champagne. He'd turned to Elena and spoke for the first time since arriving at the sumptuous property.

"We have everything we need right here Elena; just relax and enjoy your last few days of freedom."

"I'd like to unpack my case, which way is my room, Carl?"

"We have plenty of time for that;" Carl had said, as he'd checked his watch and removed a mobile phone from the inside pocket of his jacket. "It's time to phone Mother. Make us some coffee; I'll be back in ten minutes."

In spite of the unfamiliarity of the kitchen, Elena had a pot of filter coffee and all the necessary accompaniments set on a tray within five minutes. She placed it on a low table between two armchairs, which afforded a magnificent view across the Jurassic coastline.

As the tenth minute ebbed away, Elena heard Carl's footsteps returning down the ornate, spiral staircase. She filled her lungs one more time with the bracing sea air before closing the door on the free outdoors.

"Is your mother well, Carl?" It was an innocuous question that held no intention of prying into Carl's private life; but Elena sensed immediately that she'd touched on a raw nerve.

"This will be the only time that I haven't been with Mother on her birthday, which happens to be today, and naturally it is very disappointing for us both."

"But couldn't you have paid her a quick week-end visit?"

"No…!" Carl's hands closed into tight fists which relaxed again moments later. "After one more week, I intend to spend a whole month with Mother; we will then make up for this disappointment. Please, pour the coffee Elena and tell me about your family.

A light knock on the hotel door sent Candy rummaging through her handbag. Snatching her purse from the plethora of keys, makeup and other non essentials that always seemed to be carted around in her bag, she flicked out a ten-pound note.

"Thank you so much Millie, I promise to return it tomorrow morning." Candy pressed the ten-pound note into Millie's hand and relieved her of the bright-red water-bottle, brushing aside all attempts at refusing the tip. The young receptionist had been more than helpful; scouring the basement cupboards in order to satisfy the whim of an elderly guest who was only booked in for two nights.

During the last twenty-four hours, Candy had barely had any restful sleep—the gallons of consumed coffee had made sure of that—and on top of this, and due to the inconsideration of James Fairbank, she'd then been chilled to the bone. Past experiences told her, that if she didn't remedy the imbalance of her body very soon, she would be in for a nasty bout of flu or bronchitis. Draining the remains of the hot lemon drink and curling her body into a foetal position around the towel-wrapped source of heat, Candy nestled down into the heart of the bed and tried to make sense of what she was putting herself through.

Elena was far from stupid. Maybe she *had* decided to marry to improve her lot; Vinny had been right, it happens all the time, but both men seemed convinced that if Carl was involved, then nothing would be as straightforward as it seemed. Fairbank had been hoping for more information on Carl and had done everything, but accuse outright that Candy was lying, when she'd said that she had no way of contacting him. In truth, she'd never needed or wanted to contact Carl; he was a shifty so-and-so who just suddenly appeared when he wanted one of her invitations; something she wouldn't be doing in future. All of a sudden, the subterfuge and back-biting had got to her! A thumping headache at one end and frozen feet at the other had persuaded Candy to return to her hotel for a bit of peace and quiet. Stefan had refused to return with her, saying that he would stick with Vincent and find out what he could (Vinny hadn't minded him using the posh version of his name, after Stefan said it sounded more noble.) She had then left them to it, insisting that they meet later in the evening; she wasn't going to miss the chance of finding out what, if anything could be learned from Peter Radcliffe.

As warmth spread pleasantly from the rubber vessel, relaxing tense muscles and easing stiff joints, Candy felt herself drifting slowly towards a silken repose. An involuntary groan left her exhausted body as it teetered on the edge of sleep. Without warning, a thought shot through the shutting-down mechanism of her brain! Candy sat bolt upright and grabbed her handbag. After only a few seconds of rummaging she found her mobile and flicked through the message inbox.

"Yes, yes, yes!" she exclaimed to the empty room as she realised she still had the brief text message that Carl had sent on the day James Fairbank had seen her handing him the invitation. She read it aloud *"I'm outside now, bring it to me."* Those few commanding words, which had interrupted the organising of her show, had sent her hurrying outside. His earlier message, asking for the invitation, had been deleted straight away after answering it—her usual practice to keep her phone uncluttered. But here, and for her eyes only, was his number and therefore the means of finding out what was going on. Candy switched off the phone and curled back into her warm nest. She needed several hours of sleep before taking the next step.

Keeping two steps behind the man who was leading the operation, Stefan walked purposefully towards the back entrance of the property owned by the old man. The old man promised to his beautiful sister. He would not allow this to happen. Whatever it took, he would stop it! Elena had sacrificed enough for the family; it was time to put her needs first. He had remained silent during the meeting in Vincent's office; but everything spoken, and all that remained unspoken, but shown in the language of the body, remained in his head.

After Candy's departure, James Fairbank had made a list of items to be bought at a nearby supermarket and suggested that a coin be tossed to decide the shopper. Desperate to be useful,Stefan had volunteered for the job, without the aid of a coin. Vincent had then insisted on joining him, emphasising that it wasn't a matter of trust, it was to prevent any of the local yobs from ganging up on a foreigner and kicking the shit out of him. Stefan had remained silent; but one day he would explain to Vincent, how he dealt with such people. His security work, in the night clubs of Bulgaria, brought him into all kinds of dangerous situations. Far more dangerous than these people can imagine!

On reaching the back of the property, a recently installed, two-metre-high boarded fence with matching gate, barred their way. Stefan linked his hands and bending slightly at the knees offered them to Vincent as a means of scaling it. With a knowing smile and a one-finger tap on the side of his nose Vincent pulled a small bunch of keys from his jeans pocket and after checking that no one was around, selected the largest key and opened up the gate. It soon became obvious to Stefan that Vincent held a full set to the property.

Although the house was known to be empty—both men had watched from Vincent's window as Fairbank greeted Radcliffe on the steps of his porch—nothing was taken for granted, and Vincent went ahead, returning only when he was satisfied that the house was theirs to search without interruption. Without saying a word, Vincent indicated that Stefan should search the upper floor, whilst he covered the larger area of the main living quarters and Radcliffe's office. Both knew what they were searching for, any documents that could be linked to Victor Carlson and, more importantly for Stefan, any information that would lead them to the whereabouts of Elena.

Stefan stood in the doorway to the old man's bedroom and pulled on the latex gloves which Vincent had pressed silently into his hand before entering the gate. His eyes swept slowly and carefully over every detail. They stopped on a decorative box at the side of the neatly made bed. He took one step into the room, quietly closed the door behind him then moved swiftly to the far side of the bed. He gently lifted the lid of the box and studied its contents. A card of tablets, twelve in number and blister-packed, were taking up one third of the space. Alongside the tablets, which were coated in a bright-orange coloured shell with no indication of their use or ingredients, were several items of jewellery. Stefan emptied the contents onto the bed, closed the lid and gently shook the box. Something rattled in the lower section. It didn't take long to find and press the release mechanism of a small disguised drawer which held one thing only—a key. The hint of a smile crossed Stefan's serious features on recognising it as the type of safe-key that was commonly used in most holiday apartments across Europe. Before returning the box to its resting place, Stefan selected the scissors from his multi-tooled pen knife and cut two of the tablets from the strip. Pushing the tablets deep into his jacket pocket but holding the safe-key in his hand, he silently left the room to find his accomplice.

A neat pile of bank-statements lay to the right of Vincent. He was sitting at an old writing bureau in Radcliffe's office, engrossed in combing through the man's financial situation. A light cough from behind almost sent him flying from the spindly, straight-backed chair.

"Fuck it, Stefan!" He hissed through gritted teeth. "I thought Radcliffe had caught me red-handed!"

"Sorry Vincent, have you found something?"

"Well, there's definitely been a massive increase in the old boy's spending power recently; but no sign of where the money's come from, how about you?"

"We need to find the safe; it will be about this size." Stefan made two positions of his hands, indicating an area of about forty centimetres square.

"I know all about this old guy's security Stefan; take it from me, there is no fucking safe."

"Please trust me Vincent, there *is* a safe and time is passing quickly so we should put our efforts together and find it."

Vinny had started to like the guy, he'd been impressed by his ability to keep quiet over what was going on in Lyn Porter's place. He'd also made some useful suggestions about alternatives to a roasting-joint, which couldn't be bought at any price at that time on a Sunday; but he wasn't prepared to let a fucking foreigner dictate how he should do his job.

"If you're so fucking convinced, *you* find the safe, and don't fucking sneak up on me again!" Vinny straightened the paperwork that had been sent sprawling across the desk and replaced it exactly how he had found it. There was nothing more to be gained from the bureau. The small, decorative brass key was used to lock the rolling panel; and it was dropped back into its hiding place—a small vase on the nearby windowsill.

Two, floor-to-ceiling, white-painted doors to the right of the fireplace caught Stefan's attention; and as he walked toward the built-in-cupboard Vinny interrupted this attention.

"Don't waste your time I've looked in there; it holds the paperwork of his old clients, nothing else."

Disregarding the advice, Stefan opened the two doors and stood with his arms outstretched as he surveyed the shelves of box-files which were arranged in alphabetical order. At ground level, the rhythm of the arrangement changed; and Vinny watched as Stefan dropped to his knees and began removing everything from left to centre at that level.

"Come see, Vincent!"

Vinny moved closer. And sure enough, fixed in place at the back of the left corner, was a neat, metal safe about thirty centimetres high. It had been cleverly disguised behind shorter box-files to the front and an assortment of document-files on top.

"Right, all we need now is to crack the fucking code."

Stefan's smile broadened as he tapped the side of his nose with one, latex-covered finger and then splayed out the rest to reveal the key. Lost for words, Vinny watched as the key was slipped into the lock and after an easy half-turn, the metal door was pulled open. Stefan jumped to his feet and stood back to allow Vincent full access.

Sitting cross-legged amongst the scattering of files, with the entire contents of the safe balanced on his lap, Vinny carefully sifted through the pile. Beside him on the floor lay his notepad and pen which were used to give a scant description of each item.

Cash—£650.

Building Society Saving Book—Balance-£89-60.

Passport—1year left to run.

Copy of Will—Peter. R. Radcliffe.

Contract for loan of £100.00 via V.C. Enterprises.

Vinny's eyes fixed on the familiar headed page and his heart skipped a beat.

"Got you! You slimy bastard!" Vinny waved the document towards Stefan and at that same moment a vibration coming from his jacket pocket locked his satisfied grin into a look of stupefied wonder. Laying aside his prize, Vinny reached inside his pocket and flicked open his phone to read the text message from Jimmy.

LEAVE NOW! RADCLIFFE RETURNS!

"Shit, shit and more fucking shit, get all this back in the cupboard, as you found it, the old git's on his way back and if I'm caught, my career comes to a full, fucking stop. Oh God, I need to check the other rooms first! Stefan you'll have to do this."

"Go Vincent, I do this, then wait at back door for you."

Vinny forced himself to concentrate; leaving the cursing and name-calling of Fairbank, for not giving enough warning, and Radcliffe for…well for just being old and useless!

He started at the front of the property and checked each room he'd entered, making sure that doors that had been opened were now closed and furniture that had been lifted was back in the dimples of the carpet. All this was done in lightening speed; and as both men left by the back exit, Peter Radcliffe pushed his front door key into the brass, five-lever-lock.

The two men slipped back inside the basement flat, each uttering words from their respective languages that helped to relieve their pent-up tension.

"We did good, yes?" asked Stefan plonking himself down in one of the two chairs.

"We would have done much better with more fucking time; I needed to read that contract."

"Then read it my friend!" Stefan pulled the rolled up document from his inside jacket pocket and handed it to Vinny.

"Fuck me, Stefan, what if Radcliffe wants to take this out?"

"He will find it very difficult without this." Stefan held up the safe-key.

In spite of his concern, Vinny let out a bellow of laughter as he slapped Stefan on the back. Calming down, he switched on his printer and ran off three copies. Stefan rolled the original and placed it back in his inside jacket pocket.

"Tonight as the old man sleeps, I return this and the key; no need to worry Vincent, I be as quiet as little mouse."

While Vinny and Stefan were relieving their tension in laughter; Peter Radcliffe was kneeling in front of his downstairs lavatory, relieving his body of food that was disagreeable, and indeed forbidden, in his state of health. Stomach-cramps convulsed through his fragile frame as wave after wave of partially digested food hit the lavatory pan. Sweat poured from his furrowed brow and tears rolled down his hollowed cheeks.

All had been going well. Congenial chit-chat, helped along with a small dry-sherry, held the promise of a very pleasant afternoon. James had been particularly interested in how Peter was coping with retirement, and whether he might be considering moving to smaller premises, in order to keep running costs to a minimum. Peter had more than hinted that very soon he would have all the help that he needed in running the home that he'd loved and lived in for over a quarter of a century. James had remained tight-lipped on why he hadn't gone to Australia with Lyn, although he was more than happy to squeeze as much detail as possible on Peter's personal life; but Peter hadn't really minded, the whole neighbourhood would know soon enough.

Congeniality continued as luncheon was served; and it wasn't until the main course had been virtually consumed that Peter had learned what he'd actually been eating. Pig! You can dress it up however you like, and calling it Medallions' of Pork in Red-Berry Jus, didn't alter the fact that it was pig! And pig was the only animal protein that his doctor had advised against. Peter had automatically assumed that the tasty cutlets were lamb or veal, after all it is Sunday, and although a roasted joint had been expected and preferred, it wasn't unusual these days, to be presented with more exotic versions of the same thing. He blamed television. Too much air time was given over to cooking programs where celebrity chefs, earning a small fortune, were playing havoc with old-fashioned, English cuisine.

If only James hadn't asked outright. "Did you enjoy the pork?" Peter was convinced he would have been fine. But once the maggot of doubt had been allowed to burrow around in his mind; sending all manner of negative signals to his stomach, a downward spiral of unease and discomfort had developed. Suddenly and embarrassingly Peter had had to excuse himself. And not wanting to add to the embarrassment by vomiting in his neighbour's bathroom, he had fled the scene completely and returned home.

Chapter 10

Sunday Evening

The combination of two cups of tea, followed by a vigorous shower, helped to bring Candy back into the land of the living. She'd woken from a solid six-hour sleep, which had left her feeling groggy; but mindful of the all-important meeting that was to take place within the hour, she'd dragged her disorientated body out of bed and forced it to respond to her commands.

A light tap on the door indicated that her meal had arrived. Fortunately, the kitchen had still been open and the quick-to-prepare meal of omelette and salad, ordered before doing anything else, synchronised perfectly. She was ravenous, and as the welcome food was devoured, Candy wondered again where Stefan could be. She'd phoned him twice since waking and each time it had produced nothing, except an inane voice inviting her to leave a message. She'd also tried reception and his room, thinking that like her, he was catching up on sleep; but apparently he hadn't been in the hotel all day.

Putting aside her concerns for Stefan, Candy reached for her phone once again, hoping desperately that this time, her efforts would be rewarded.

"Hello Carl, Candy Laverne. I'm sorry to disturb you on a Sunday; but I'm trying to locate one of my models, Elena Petrov/a." Candy shifted the phone an inch or two away from her ear as Carl's response, although loud and clear, held no information on Elena: although the nature of his response, spoke volumes. At least now, she could arrive at the meeting, armed with a bargaining chip.

Every available seat was occupied in the main bar of Vinny's local. A football match between two popular national teams, flickered and blared from three television screens; but none were visible from where Vinny and Stefan sat. They had chosen a quiet, two-seater table, in the far corner of the billiard room. It was vacant because it's position was alongside the toilets. Neither were interested in football today; they'd come to the pub in search of food. Jimmy had offered them a meal, provided they arrive before the set meeting; but after being given a brief run down by phone, on how Radcliffe had turned a peculiar colour in the midst of his dinner—hence the sudden dash home—Vinny hadn't wanted to risk the same fate.

Neither had spoken a word since the plate of sausage, mash and onion-gravy had been placed before them; but as Vinny ran the last chunk of sausage through the thick, tasty sauce, Stefan, having all but licked his plate clean, broke the silence.

"Is good, no?"

"Good! No, it's fucking delicious! I've never been so hungry. Go get two more beers while I look at this again and try to make sense of it." He handed Stefan a fiver, knowing that the guy was skint and also aware that he was very embarrassed about that fact. He pushed his plate to one side and spread out the copy headed V.C. Enterprises, before Stefan could argue the point. He recognised the documents format and it was sloppy of Carl not to have changed it; but this indicated that this scam was prepared in a hurry, a definite plus in their favour. He also recognised Carl's signature, which was completely unreadable and because there was no printed form of his name, he would remain anonymous. It was a totally illegal contract, and unless Radcliffe was well on the way to senility, he should know this. The gist of the paper told of a hundred grand loan to Radcliffe, to be paid back on his death; but the rest of the information was laced with so much gobbledygook—an art form that Carl loved to indulge—that Vinny's eyes began to glaze over.

A collective roar and stamping of feet exploded throughout the pub. A goal had obviously been scored. Vinny looked up just as Stefan arrived gripping two straight glasses of frothing beer. Suddenly a football yob, eager to get to the toilet at this opportune time, knocked into Stefan who accidentally spilt a good dollop of the beer onto the table and onto the contract.

"Hey, watch how you go, please." Stefan placed the beers out of harms way and raised a conciliating hand, toward Vincent whose face flamed with anger.

The football-shirted yob retaliated "Free-loading-foreigner, piss off back where you belong."

Vinny jumped to his feet and grabbed the youngster, pulling him close by a handful of football shirt. "Watch your fucking mouth, sonny, or I'll make sure you get it stitched up!"

"Sorry mate", he mumbled and slunk into the washroom.

"No big deal Vincent, just high spirits."

Vinny wiped the document down with an unused paper napkin and then waved it around in an effort to dry it more. "I think it was a waste of fucking paper making a copy for each of us Stefan, Jimmy's the only one who is gonna be able to understand this shit!"

The young, football yob emerged; and once he was out of reach, gave Vinny a sly, sideways glance and stuck a finger in the air; but both men continued to sip on their beers, lost in their own thoughts.

Eventually a harassed-looking waitress approached with a tray. "Drinks, desserts?" She asked as she piled crockery on the tray and swiped the table with her cloth. She looked relieved when both men shook their heads. The match had just finished and she was anxious to get back to the bar.

"Let's go, before the fucking football songs kick-off." Vinny laughed at his own pun, wary about trying to explain it to Stefan; but Stefan slapped him on the shoulder in appreciation. "Good joke, no?"

Before leaving, Vinny decided to relieve his bladder of some of the chilled beer before half the pub decided on doing the same. Stefan waited patiently by the back exit, watching the people come and go. He noticed the young man who had knocked into him, accompanied by three others. One remained outside the toilet door and the others disappeared inside. Suspecting what was about to happen, He pushed past the restraining arm and was just in time to see two men grab at Vincent arms whilst in full-flow of relieving himself. They swung him round and golden liquid followed in an arcing fountain! The young football yob danced out of the way of the piss then closed in to land a clenched fist into Vinny's face. Stefan caught the fist; twisting it behind and up the youth's back before tossing him into a vacant cubicle. The other two men looked warily at the six-footer who was built like a tank.

"You want to fight?" asked Stefan, holding up his fists like a prize-fighter. Both men answered by darting out of the door.

"You should have bashed their fucking brains in!" shouted Vinny as he wiped his shoes and jeans with a wad of toilet tissue.

The walk back to Vincent's flat was uphill; and the weight of food and beer in their stomachs went partway to keeping unnecessary conversation at bay. But, there were several questions eating-away at Stefan's insides that needed answering. And they needed answering before the reins of this whole situation were handed over to the solicitor. James Fairbank was interested in one thing only, bringing the law down on Victor Carlson. In Bulgaria, nothing was this simple. Innocent people were always caught up in bringing people to justice. Stefan had already lost his father to this similar black and white idealism of justice, and he wasn't prepared to lose his sister in the same way.

"This man Carl, is he dangerous?" Stefan held Vincent's arm to stop his stride; this was a serious question and it was important that his friend understood him.

Vincent's mouth opened with an answer that contained no thought behind it; but as he turned to Stefan, his eyes registering the earnest look, he took a deep sigh and leaned against a nearby wall before answering. "Carl's mainly interested in scamming people out of money and classy properties. I thought we were pretty close friends once until I realised he was using me. I nearly lost every penny from the sale of my previous business and Fairbank nearly lost his magnificent building. When we were buddies, Carl told me that he always got what he went after; so in answer to your question Stefan, I don't know how dangerous he is when things don't go his way."

"Does he carry a gun or knife?"

"This is fucking England man!" Vinny realised too late what a stupid statement that was; everyday the papers held stories of gang warfare on city streets involving shootings and stabbings "I know you must be worried sick about your sister, but if it's of any help, Carl has no associates, and no friends to do his dirty-work. He's a sly bastard but I don't think he's stupid enough to go as far as murder!"

"Candy returns to London tomorrow and she is expecting me to go also; because I have nowhere else to stay." Stefan's admission hung in the air. A family of four, the father pushing a pram, walked slowly by, thanking both men for stepping off the kerb to allow them free passage. Vinny mounted the kerb and took his previous place by the wall.

"Here's the deal Stefan, *I'll* take you on for a week. I've got a bailiff-related job tomorrow and you have proved to be very handy in certain situations. You'll have a roof over your head and food in your belly: but I can only afford to pay you a hundred quid for the week."

"Thank you my friend. I promise you find me very useful."

James checked again that the drinks and refreshments were fully prepared. He was determined to keep the atmosphere amicable; but as this was his last chance to find the link between Lyn and Carl, and he was still convinced that Candy Laverne held the key to that link, he didn't want to waste precious time fussing about in the kitchen. He also didn't want to waste time locked in innuendos. Straight talking was called for and it was to that end that he had arranged for Candy Laverne to arrive thirty minutes earlier than the others.

His apartment bell rang at precisely seven-thirty. Candy was guided up the broad staircase and offered an armchair in his sitting room, where the ambient temperature was seventy degrees. He reeled off a list of drinks for her to choose from, adding, a nice cup of tea, when it seemed obvious that the woman wasn't showing interest in any of the others.

Candy's response was unexpected. "Where's Stefan and Vinny? I thought this was a meeting for laying *all* cards on the table."

Encouraged, James ignored the ingrained compulsion to offer hospitality the minute someone entered his home and instead took the nearby armchair and leaned casually forward. From this short distance, he marvelled at the positive change that a few hours sleep could make. The woman looked ten years younger. Her hair and make-up were immaculate and her upright posture and general demeanour indicated a strength that wasn't apparent that morning. Feeling a little diminished but still fired with determination, he pressed forward.

"Vincent and Stefan will be here shortly. Forgive me for asking; but I'm curious about an incident that happened during the evening of your…Your underwear party."

Candy smiled, but said nothing, allowing James to continue. He swallowed hard before doing so.

"Later during that same evening, I collided with Lyn as she ran up to her room. She wore nothing more than a skimpy piece of theatrical underwear and seemed very upset. Naturally I was shocked, but when I followed to find out what was going on, she'd locked her door."

Again Candy smiled; but it was brief and tinged with sadness. "Did it enter your head to ask Lyn what she was up to? Instead of jumping to your own conclusions."

"Of course I asked; but she wouldn't say." The strain of having kept a lid on his emotions for so long was etched deeply on his lined face and reflected in the haunted look in his eyes. He lowered them and watched as his fingers turned white from unconscious clenching. "Candy, I beg of you, what happened that evening? I too, would like to enjoy a decent night's sleep."

He listened, without any interrupting, to her explanation and gradually a weight was lifted from deep within his chest. But something still niggled. He tentatively mentioned Lyn's sudden wealth and how he suspected that Victor Carlson was involved in providing that money.

Instead of more information, Candy almost exploded with exasperation.

"For heaven's sake! You're asking the wrong person. It's obvious the two of you are in love! Why don't you just talk it through? And keep talking it through until you have all the answers you need."

He wanted to go on talking now. A fissure had cracked open in the dam and it was such a relief to allow the corrosive build up of doubt and suspicion to spill out; but before he could say another word, a knock on the door announced the arrival of Vincent and Stefan. The ingrained compulsion returned as he seated his guests and offered refreshments.

Vincent's voice resonated across the room. "I heard that Radcliffe's reported you to the health and safety mob; so don't try and palm his half-eaten dinner onto us. Hello Candy, you're looking very smart and attractive this evening; take my advice and don't eat anything." He then went on to give her a very colourful run down on the disappointing outcome of the luncheon with Radcliffe.

"It wasn't a complete failure." James cut in, trying to keep control of the situation. Peter all but admitted that he was getting married very soon and that his bride-to-be is much younger than he is." James looked over to Stefan offering a silent apology.

"We know this already; what did you boys find out?" Candy's forthright question put paid to the humour and focused their attention back to the serious matter at hand.

Stefan handed the copy of the agreement to James. "We take this from the old man's safe; please to read it very carefully it might hold valuable clues, yes?"

James took several seconds to absorb what was said. "Vincent, please reassure me that the police won't be arriving at Peter's any time now."

"Stop flapping! The original document will be returned later tonight, providing the old geezer can sleep after being poisoned like that." Stefan had remained mainly silent and sombre throughout the bantering. His sudden intervention altered the atmosphere in the room and focussed everyone's thoughts.

"In five days time, my beautiful sister who is only twenty-five, will be sold like slave. Elena does not marry for love; she wants only to help her family. I am her family and I will not let it happen. Mr Fairbank, will you try for making sense of the document; and I will speak with old man."

James gathered his coffee and the one-page contract and moved to a quiet corner of the dining room, leaving the others to argue over what more could be done.

He returned a while later to raised voices; and Stefan's voice was the loudest and most insistent. "You have spoken to him and he brush you aside, let me phone this time."

"Who do you want to phone Stefan?" asked James, aware of the young man's growing agitation.

Candy released a heavy sigh; then brought James up to date, as she had just done with Stefan and Vincent, on how she had remembered the last text message from Carl was still on her phone. She relayed again, Carl's few unhelpful words; and her own strong instinct that he knew where Elena was. Before Stefan could continue his badgering, she asked James what was enclosed in the contract."

"Put in simple layman's terms it's a contract laying down the terms of a £100,000 loan. Peter has already received the loan and as Vincent and I will bear witness, has probably spent over half of it improving his premises. The most unusual clause, in the terms and conditions set down, is section 3c of the small print."

"Get to it Jimmy! We haven't got all fucking night! Pardon my French, Candy."

James glared at Vincent and continued. "In brief, Peter doesn't have to start repaying the loan for six months; but if he should die within that time, the property, not the money borrowed against it, is passed into the hands of V.C. Enterprises."

"And what happens for Elena!" The anguish in Stefan's voice pierced and shattered what appeared to be four people rapt in genial discussion. James and Candy, eager to reassure him, pointed out the chances of Peter dying within that time were very slim. Stefan was not consoled. He delved into his jeans pocket and pulled out two bright-orange capsules and placed them on the coffee table for all to see.

"I see this drug many times in Bulgaria I work as security in night club and this," Stefan held up one of the capsules. "Is like Viagra but many times more powerful! Is used by Eastern European Mafia when they want to be rid of older man. Older man go to prostitute for good time and he take this for good time to last longer; usually he dies of heart-attack and no one ask questions. The old man Elena is to marry in five days time, has ten more of these in special box by his bed!"

Chapter 11

Sunday—9.30pm

The delicious meal, soft background music and pools of dimmed lighting, should have been enough to make Elena feel relaxed; but it had taken several glasses of champagne to ease away the tension that had developed since entering this house. Tiny lights glimmered in the distance like stars fallen to earth; but there would be no opportunity to discover and enjoy the sights of this popular seaside town, named Lyme Regis. She was a prisoner, held captive by a gaoler whose key was nothing more than a promise of a better life for herself and her family. The preceding tension began to form when she'd realised the implications of having lost all communications with family and friends. A phone call made earlier from Candy, had sent Carl into a rage, and a further call, made only a half hour ago, had induced him to remove his sim card and replace it with a brand new one.

They'd been discussing families and the heart aches suffered in the name of loyalties. The first call had interrupted Carl's unburdening of his life as a youth; he'd apparently been ill-treated by a father who was jealous of his youngest son's intelligence. Prior to the interruption of the second call, he had refused to reveal who this caller was, his mood had mellowed and he'd spoken reverently of his beloved mother. Elena had learned how she had sacrificed her prospects of becoming an international model, by producing five sons in quick succession for her selfish husband. She'd also learned, as Carl had continued to top up their Champagne-flutes, that his beloved mother had been cursed with the development of breast cancer; but was thankfully recovering after the latest invasive treatment.

The second unwanted phone call, had shattered Carl's softened persona and cut short the enlightening one-way conversation, leaving Elena wondering how she was going to make it through the next five days.

Candy pulled her woollen shawl around her shoulders and walked the short distance to Peter Radcliffe's home. After James had insisted on making the phone call to Carl, only to be disconnected the moment he got through, they were left with no alternative but to gather what information they could from Radcliffe. *She* had volunteered to be the gatherer of that information. James had had his chance and botched it, and although it wasn't really his fault, and everyone knew this, no one actually voiced it. Instead, Candy had announced, forcefully, that it was the least she could do bearing in mind that she was leaving first thing in the morning to drive back to London. Vinny had insisted on giving the outside of Radcliffe's place, the once over, making sure the old boy hadn't gone to bed and paving the way for Stefan to return the document to the safe.

She climbed the steps leading to the porch and looked up to the lighted room on the first floor. A window was slightly open and a net curtain lifted and danced; sending cigar smoke and words from a Frank Sinatra song into the breeze of the chill night. She waited for the final line of the song to fade out before ringing the doorbell. Overhead noises caused her to step back and look up. Peter Radcliffe's slender upper body hung over the sill of the fully opened window; a wool dressing gown draped around his striped pyjamas. Candy's resolve remained intact.

"Hello Peter, it's Candy Laverne; we met just over a week ago at Lyn porter's place. I'm sorry to bother you at this late hour; but I've got something very important to ask you and I'm afraid it can't wait. I promise I won't keep you long."

"Yes…Yes of course. I'll be down in a jiffy."

A minute or two later Candy was shown into the lighted room. The music had been turned off and a puff of air-freshener was struggling to banish the cigar smoke. Peter Radcliffe had hurriedly slipped into a pair of beige slacks and a brown cardigan, hoping that the blue and white striped pyjama top would suffice as a shirt. Candy gripped the cool, papery-skinned, proffered hand and accepted his offer of a drink from the corner cabinet. Vinny had drilled into her, to keep him from going to the back of his premises, so the cup of tea she would have preferred, was out of the question. They sat in opposite chairs, gripping their sherry glasses. Candy sensed his discomfort as her eyes looked down to his feet. He was wearing odd socks, and no amount of shuffling of the leather moccasin slippers in an attempt to hide this fact, was going to succeed. She took a sip of the golden, syrupy liquid and forced a swallow.

"Frank Sinatra is one of my favourites; I don't mind if you want to continue."

"No! No I wouldn't dream of…What was it you wanted to ask me? I haven't been feeling too well today and I was about to retire to my bed."

"Oh I'm sorry to hear that Peter; especially in view of you getting married soon, naturally you'll want to get as much rest as possible. I'll get straight to the point then. I'm here to ask for an invitation to the wedding. Elena is like a daughter to me and as you know she has no other relatives in England."

The next sip of Candy's sherry went down much more smoothly than Peter's. After recovering from the coughing fit, he asked how she'd heard about the forthcoming event when both he and Elena had taken such great pains to keep it confidential, and, both had agreed to a very private ceremony with no guests, on either side, attending.

"As I said, she's like a daughter to me and naturally she'd told me why she was leaving the agency. I don't want you to think that I'm here to pass judgment, Peter, Elena's a grown woman and both of you are entitled to a private ceremony if that's what you want; but I would like to give her a wedding present. I've driven all the way down here from London. I'm staying at a nearby hotel overnight and returning tomorrow, can you give me the address where she is staying?"

"Couldn't you have phoned and asked her yourself?" In the interim between question and answer, a creak in an overhead floorboard filled the silence, causing two pairs of eyes to glance at the ceiling. Candy grabbed for his attention.

"I haven't been able to reach her by phone, and to be honest, I was on the verge of contacting the police, stupid old woman that I am, then I thought of you and just knew that you'd be able to put my mind at rest."

"My dear woman, I can assure you that Elena is well and happy with the arrangement; but as to where she is at the moment, I can't help you, nor can I shed any light on why you can't reach her by phone. I don't even know where the ceremony is taking place. It's been planned and organised by Carl, you know the chap, and he'll be contacting me the day before the wedding with all the details. "If you leave me your number, I'll be happy to pass them on to you then: maybe sending a bouquet of flowers on the day will help to make you feel better." Peter stood and reached for her sherry glass, which was still over half full. Candy brought the glass to her lips and took another sip, foiling his attempt to be rid of her just yet.

"This is delicious Peter, I must make a note of the brand, my memory isn't what it used to be. I should have retired years ago; but I fear the loneliness of retirement. Tell me, these 'arranged marriages' that Carl organises, does he offer a similar service for old ladies and if so maybe I should give it some serious thought. Have you got his card?"

"No, I don't have a card and I don't have a telephone number for him either. He insists on contacting me.

Sounds odd I know; but the older I get the more I realise the world is mainly peopled by oddballs. Having said that, I can't complain, he offered me a good deal to turn my life around."

"And what will Elena gain from this wonderful deal?"

Peter stretched out both his arms and did a half turn, grabbing at his trousers when suddenly there seemed a serious risk that they may fall to his ankles. "Sorry about that, I've lost a little weight of late. What was the question, Oh yes, what benefits would Elena gain? Naturally, she would share all this with me; and after I'm gone, she'd be free to share it with her family."

"Sounds fair enough; and what does Carl gain from this match-making?"

"Money! A handsome lump of the stuff, believe me! That reminds me I must run over the details of the contract he gave me." Peter plucked the glass from Candy's fingers. "Well dear lady I must bid you a good night and safe journey back to the big city, I'm sorry that I couldn't be of more help."

Peter closed and bolted the front door on Candy Laverne then shuffled through the full depth of his property to check that the back door was securely locked. Damn the woman, he thought, as he went around checking that all windows were secure against any further unwanted intruders. She'd spooked him, no doubt about it. He gripped his lower abdomen as a sharp pain convulsed and sent him running for the lavatory; only to find that it was a build up of trapped wind. He had been enjoying his evening, and God knows he deserved it after the awful afternoon he'd suffered. "Damn and blast her thrice over!" He announced to the empty room as he turned off the lights and headed for the bedroom.

Should he read for a while, he wondered, knowing that sleep wouldn't come easily with all the old doubts circulating around his brain. Or should he do the sensible thing and buckle down and scrutinise every detail of that confounding contract? He'd tried once and ended up with a headache that lasted for hours! Maybe the best thing would be to allow James Fairbank to sweep his eyes over it. He couldn't charge much for that, might even throw it in as a freebie. He's probably still feeling a little sheepish over the luncheon disaster so I'll approach him first thing tomorrow. Feeling much better from having made such a sensible decision, Peter pulled the covers around his scrawny neck and was fast asleep in no time at all.

Carl was agitated, it didn't happen often, he'd prided himself of the fact that life could only run like clockwork if there was total control, and total control was what he demanded of himself. Everything he had strived for, since leaving college, was to please Mother. On the annual visits back home, he would spend many happy hours describing the places where he worked and the wonderful properties he had acquired. Her face would light up with joy and pride at having such a successful son. She particularly loved his description of Torbay in the South-West of England and was mortified when her precious youngest son was denied the property he had worked so hard to obtain. Carl's greatest desire was to overturn that mortification and prove to Mother, whilst he still had the chance, that her favourite son was all-powerful. The cause of the agitation had come from rushed and sloppy planning; and more specifically, two stray phone calls. He fully understood where Candy Laverne had got his number; but James Fairbank being able to ring him could only mean one thing—they were joining forces against him. No matter, they would soon find out that *he* was a much stronger force to be reckoned with.

Installing a new, unregistered sim card in his mobile meant that no one could reach him, not even Mother, but she sounded well after her recent ordeal and he would be with her in just over a week. His agitation calmed as he thought of her beauty as a young woman. The softness and glow of her skin reignited the wonderful memory of when she whispered in his ear and declared that he was now, a man. He drank the remainder of his champagne, rinsed and dried the glass, and walked slowly up the spiral staircase to Elena's room

The clock on James's bedside cabinet showed eleven-thirty. He was desperately tired; but a force far stronger kept him from slipping into oblivion. He'd been expecting a call from Lyn—just to say that she'd arrived safely. The plane had been due to land in Sydney almost two hours ago and although it's true that delays can happen, on long-haul flights it's quite rare. Since leaving her at Heathrow, he'd deliberately tried to keep his mind from thinking about anything connected to her; but since Candy Laverne's revelations of that ominous evening, he'd thought of nothing else.

Candy had returned from Peter Radcliffe's house, still bursting with energy and information that had been gained, but once it became obvious that Carl had become elusive once again, he had lost interest, feigning a stomach-ache and wanting his bed. No one questioned this in view of what had happened earlier to Peter Radcliffe. Before bidding him goodnight and a speedy recovery, Candy had apologised yet again for having to leave for London early in the morning but promised to keep in touch by phone. Stefan, having successfully returned Peter's property, had eagerly departed with Vincent; leaving James to wonder what they might have planned for the rest of the evening. But in all honesty, he didn't care. All he cared about right now was speaking to the woman he loved.

Chapter 12

The glare from the morning sun was almost blinding when Lyn and Andy left the confines of the airport to locate a taxi. After slipping on his sunglasses, conveniently stashed in the front pocket of his rucksack, Andy led the way to where a short queue was rapidly growing longer. A sudden spurt landed him fifth in line, beckoning Lyn to hurry before the next deluge of arrivals jostled her to one side. *Her* sunglasses remained at the bottom of the locked suitcase that she dragged like a tonne weight over the tarmac whilst keeping her eyes averted from the searing ball above.

"Much more economical if we share a cab. You look knackered!" Andy accompanied this with a playful nudge and one of his beaming smiles when Lyn finally joined him in the queue.

More than anything, Lyn felt disorientated and grubby. Since boarding at Changi Airport, she hadn't managed any more sleep. Out of boredom, the remainder of the flight had been spent watching films and eating everything that was offered. Overindulgence and lack of exercise had taken its toll, her lower abdomen felt bloated and the inside of her mouth tasted disgusting, in spite of the rigorous teeth-brushing carried out in the airport's washroom. Conversation had gradually dwindled into the odd flurry of words, spoken as and when necessary, both now eager just to reach their own individual destinations.

Viewed from the back seat of the taxi, as it sped toward Darling Harbour, Lyn thought that the heart of Sydney didn't seem much different to the centre of London, apart from the vivid blue of the cloudless sky, and not for the first time in the last twenty-four hours, she wondered if the cost and the effort of this trip, would be worth it. Several times her eyes closed involuntarily on the congested traffic and the colourful bill boards advertising familiar items and services.

Without realising that she'd slipped into a twilight state, the sudden halting of the taxi brought her back to reality. They had arrived at her hotel and Andy was already at the rear of the car removing her case. Feeling even more disoriented she groped around in her bag for money, dragging a twenty pound note from her purse as she scrambled from the car's cool interior.

Andy was beside her in seconds. "My stops further on, don't worry I'll grab the fair, besides if you pay in English bucks you'll be way out of pocket."

"Come on Andy, I can't let you keep paying." Lyn turned her back on the two men and began groping around her waist to locate the pouch holding her Australian dollars. Andy's voice stilled her hand.

"Lyn, I was hoping… I mean I don't want to presume anything but we do rub along quite well in spite of the age difference. Can I meet up with you tonight and show you the sights of Darling Harbour? I know you're here on business, but it would be sad to spend your first evening alone."

Lyn smiled and her weariness seemed less of a burden. "Thank you Andy, you're very sweet, but I insist on paying my way."

"Tell you what; I'll meet you at seven in reception and you can pay for supper."

"You're on! See you at seven in reception." Lyn watched as he climbed in beside the driver and uttered one word before turning to her and smiling that wonderful smile.

Before entering the hotel, she stood in a patch of shade and cast her eyes over what would be home for the next three weeks. The hotel was ultra-modern, seventeen floors of glass and concrete bore down on the little patch of shade that she felt reluctant to leave. Eventually, after releasing a heavy sigh, she grabbed the handle of the heavy suitcase and pulled it towards the gaping dark hole of reception, hoping to God that the lifts were working.

When Lyn had originally made the reservation, she had specified a double rather than a twin-bedded room and as the receptionist guided her through the check-in procedure, she noted, and resented, the knowing looks and words of sympathy as she explained that Mr Fairbank wouldn't be joining her. Relieved at last to see the back of the receptionist, Lyn headed for the eleventh floor, thankful that the lifts were all in working order.

On entering her room, she was particularly grateful to find that the large bathroom contained a bath as well as the walk-in shower cubicle. Before anything else, the bath-plug was rammed home and the taps turned fully on. Everything she'd worn on the journey was heaped in a pile by the opened window; except the money pouch, which was flung on the bed. A scrap of white material, caught in the zipper of the pouch momentarily pulled her attention away from the gigantic effort to get organised; but the sound of gushing water, just yards away, reminded her what was most important.

It was heavenly to sink up to the neck in lukewarm, scented water, and Lyn felt that she might well stay put for several hours. However, after a fraction of that time, guilt began to chip away at the pleasure. She'd promised to ring James on her arrival, just to let him know that she'd arrived safely, but something had got in the way of performing this simple task. There hadn't really been the opportunity to carry it out in privacy, because Andy had been there every step of the way, just as James *should* have been.

With a fluffy white bath-towel wrapped around her clean body and a similar but smaller version wrapped around her freshly washed hair, Lyn spread herself luxuriantly across the king-sized bed and reached for her handbag. On retrieving her phone, she realised the true depth of her resentment towards James, as three words only were punched in as a text message.

I'VE ARRIVED SAFELY

Was sent into the electronic system which linked the distance between Australia and England. Reaching across to place the phone on the bedside table, her eyes were drawn to the money pouch which had clung close to her body, holding her money in marsupial fashion for the duration of the long journey. What had specifically caught her eye was that scrap of white material caught in the zipper. Lazily hooking her foot under the strap she hoisted the pouch and dropped it in her lap. The zipper wouldn't budge. The more she tried to free it, the more entangled it became in what she could now see was tissue paper. Curiosity, frustration and a mounting sense of foreboding struggled for supremacy in the deadbeat environment of a brain that was crying out for sleep. Frustration was the victor. Lyn pulled so hard at the zipper that all the stitches down one side of it gave way, allowing her access. Very slowly and very carefully she lifted out the contents. In place of the 3,000 Australian Dollars and the 600 English Pounds, was a bunch of folded paper-napkins, each stamped with the crest of the Middle-Eastern Airline that had carried her far from home and everything she loved and trusted.

"You Bastard!" she shouted as the pouch hit the far wall with a dull thud.

A cleaner three doors away heard the outburst and the dull thud, followed by an eruption of sobbing. Back in her own country, she would have knocked on the door and offered assistance; but since working in the big cities, she'd learnt that lots of weird things happen in hotel rooms and it was safer to mind your own business.

Lyn awoke to a raging thirst wondering where the hell she was. Within seconds, her fractured memory began piecing together the nightmare of events before she'd fallen into an unconscious, exhausted state; a state that had lasted just over four hours. The room was baking hot; her intention to switch on the air-con had been shelved, like everything else, until she'd had a bath. Cursing this oversight and knowing now that it was only one of many, she rolled off the bed and lay naked and spread eagled on the cooler laminate floor.

Basic instinct kicked in as she remembered the small fridge, disguised behind one of the matching cupboards. A row of miniature bottles of spirits kept cool company with a can of beer, a can of Coca Cola and a small (250ml) plastic bottle of water. She snatched the bottle of water and wrung its neck, flinging the cap over to the bin and missing it by at least six inches. She downed it in one long gulp, knowing this was a bad thing to do and also knowing that it would cost her a fortune in money, money she no longer had. She was near to tears when the final drop disappeared down her parched throat and the bottle was flung in the same direction as the cap, scoring a goal! Without cheering, she grabbed at the can of Coca Cola, rolling its chilled, metal body over her neck and breasts in an effort to check the heat, before ripping off the tab and tipping it down the same chute; this time with moderate gulps because of the effervescence.

As the temperature in the room cooled and hydration brought back a modicum of self control, Lyn began to plan the best way forward; she still had her credit card and passport, so things could have been worse. Rejecting the strong desire to book on the next available flight home, she concentrated on the positive and tried very hard to remember as much as possible about Andy…What was his name? There was a growing determination to regain what had been taken, and for this she needed the help of her former boss and neighbour Vinny Conway. After calculating the time differences, she knew that she'd have to leave phoning Vinny for at least a couple of hours, he wasn't likely to be up at 6am on a Monday, and if he was, he'd be in no mood for shelling out sympathy to Lyn's predicament. Dressed in cotton shorts, sandals, skimpy vest and the all-important sun-glasses, she braved the great outdoors of Darling Harbour, in search of her next priority—a bank.

Smarting from the triple whammy of unfavourable exchange rates, exorbitant bank charges and a nebulous fee for transferring funds, Lyn fully understood why she had been encouraged, especially by Vinny, to bring cash. Checking at least twice that the freshly drawn money was safely in her purse, she wandered around the large, indoor shopping mall, viewing the splendour of the famous harbour through its vast glass windows. She needed to relax; she needed to feel in control again. Tiredness was beginning to descend, and determined not to let this spoil her chance of phoning Vinny, Lyn followed the sign to the third floor where all the refreshment bars were situated.

The aroma of freshly-ground coffee greeted Lyn as she stepped off the slow-moving stairs, but before reaching its source, a large poster, positioned on the far wall, stopped her dead in her tracks. A woman's face, radiant and self-assured, smiled across the space.

Lyn stood motionless, looking into the eyes of the two-dimensional face of Jennifer Beck. From this distance the wording on the poster was too small to read, but there was no doubting that this was the face of her mother. She'd logged in to the artist's web page many times over the last few months; mostly to just look at a smaller version of this very same photograph. Twice she had emailed the woman and once, only the once, she had spoken on the phone: not as a daughter, Jennifer Beck had no knowledge of Lyn Porter's background, but as a prospective client, wanting to purchase a couple of her paintings to embellish the foyer of her business premises. She was suddenly forced to move closer when a family of five, having just travelled the same route up the moving stairs, shoved her out of their way.

Mind and body were now fully alert as Lyn sipped on the large cappuccino, seated directly in front of the larger-than-life poster. The exhibition started on Wednesday morning and would be attended by the artist for that day only. The Exhibition Centre was only a five minute walk from the hotel, much closer than imagined when the hotel was booked. At the time it hadn't mattered; James would have been with her to share any journeys around Darling Harbour, enjoying the sites as they walked it's perimeter or ferried across the water. She tried not to think of James and the exasperation she felt towards him; instead she focused on the woman, who, in her opinion, deserved every drop of her resentment.

Jennifer Beck felt nervous as she packed her suitcase for the two-night stay in Sydney. She had been hoping that they could both attend the exhibition; Pierre had been much calmer, more manageable during the last few weeks, and the change of scenery, she knew, would have delighted him. But overnight, he'd slipped back into the lonely, hell-hole of torment and frustration that ripped at her heart. Whilst in that state, he barely acknowledged her; then suddenly, a spark of recognition would animate his torpid features and he would begin a tirade of abuse. She'd had to ring the nursing home and book him in for four days."No more than four days, darling." She had promised as tears filled her eyes. Pierre had aggressively pushed her aside and for the umpteenth time had shouted, "Cold-hearted bitch!"

He was asleep now in the garden room, surrounded by a wealth of plants and flowers, miracles of nature that were always available for the artist or photographer. For the rest of today she would stay close to the man she had loved since she was seventeen, but tomorrow she would have no choice. The flight and the hotel were already booked and her most recent paintings were already in position at the Exhibition Centre. Regardless of how *she* felt, cancellation was not an option.

Lyn stared at the phone in astonishment, checking again that she'd dialled the correct number; in the meantime she'd been left hanging on and dreading the cost of the call.

"G'day Mate; you've arrived safely then?"

"Hello Vinny, who was that, who picked up your phone before you?"

"He's a bloke helping me out on a job, that's all."

"I thought you couldn't stand foreigners, let alone working with them."

"I've got five minutes before I'm out the door, Lyn, so get to it. You've obviously arrived safe and sound, does 'lover-boy' know?

Lyn gritted her teeth and opened up the folded piece of paper. "James knows I've arrived safely, yes, but he doesn't know I'm phoning *you* and I want to keep it that way."

"Fair enough, I can be as secretive as the next man, especially when it comes to chatting up his bird. Now what has happened and what do you want?"

"You remember your suggestion, about taking my money out in cash? Well it's been stolen!" A loud sniff followed by a disgusting-sound of his throat being cleared, was all Lyn got as a response, before an inpatient sigh brought him back.

"Lyn, I told you to keep it close to your body, I even showed you where you could buy a fucking body belt what…"

"I did use an 'effing body belt and the bastard still got to it!"

"Who's the bastard, who are we talking about here?"

She was close to tears and knew that Vinny could sense it. Both of her hands were slippery with sweat, despite air-con temperatures in the hotel lobby. "The passenger who sat next to me for the whole flight, was a twenty-four year old guy called Andrew Fernley." (The surname had suddenly slipped into Lyn's consciousness only half an hour ago. She'd only heard it once and it had come from the lips of the security officer at Heathrow when Andy had been marched off for searching; but recounting the dream of the tree-fern had crystallised her muddled thoughts.) "He lives somewhere in Kent and I know he has a sister living out here, around Sydney, can you get me as much information as possible about him?"

"I'm a private detective Lyn, not fucking Interpol! Besides, what were you and this young thug getting up to for all those hours? How was he allowed to scour your body for the money belt?"

"Will you help me or not?"

"Give me what you've got, again, and I'll see what I can drag up; but it's gonna cost you, make no mistake about it."

Lyn opened her mouth to respond; but the connection had been cut.

Chapter 13

Monday Morning—Torbay

The sky lightened on a brighter day. Gulls screeched and darted around the harbour, announcing to the local population that it was time to rise and face the day. Someone close by, whistled a merry rendition of Waltzing Matilda, hitting a particularly raw nerve in James Fairbank's fraught body. He'd slept later than usual, silencing his alarm at seven, checking his answer phone for messages and after finding none, climbed back between the still-warm sheets and returned to the oblivion of sleep. Now, he was feeling groggy, grumpy and guilty from lack of self-control. The whistling continued, interspersed with clattering and banging. Annoyance and curiosity drove James to the rear window of his apartment; here, he could see Vincent and Stefan loading tools and wood into a van. He called out from the opened window, cutting off the inane Australian tune.

"Vincent, have a little more consideration for your neighbours. Where are the two of you off to at this early hour, and what are the tools for?"

"How about considering minding your own business,

you grumpy old git. I thought you might be more cheerful today, knowing that your piece of skirt has arrived down under, safe and sound."

"I haven't heard anything."

"Don't give me that, she told me herself that she'd been in touch."

"*You* have heard from her! When? Vincent, don't drive off, I'm coming down!" James gulped the last mouthful of coffee and threw his jacket about his shoulders. He checked his answer phone again before descending the stairs two at a time and heading for the back door. Stefan was already seated in the front passenger seat and the engine was running, spewing foul-smelling diesel fumes into the fresh morning air. Vincent was locking the back door of the van and as James approached he heaved an impatient sigh.

"I'm already late, can't this wait?"

"You said you've heard from Lyn, when was that?"

"Are you fucking deaf? Yes, she phoned me, she told me she'd contacted you, now can I go and do my job? Like I said, I'm late, we'll talk later."

"Why did she phone you and not me?"

Without answering, Vincent pushed past the solicitor and climbed into the driver's seat, closed the door and rolled down the window. "She's in a spot of trouble and there's no point in relying on you for help, you're unreliable mate. Now if you wanna do something useful, renew your cosy friendship with Radcliffe and inform him about Carl's scam. He's bound to cough up how he can be contacted, and then we'll think of a way to flush him out."

"And how do you suggest I do that? Tell Peter how, after

entering his premises and opening his safe, we casually read through his private papers and discovered an anomaly!"

"Think laterally man, use the brains that cost your parents a fortune in education to get developed, do whatever it takes to let Radcliffe know that he's about to be stiffed by Carl. Maybe when *you* have achieved something, then we'll talk some more!" The van shot off with a screech of breaks, leaving James in a cloud of diesel fumes.

For the first time in over a year, James regretted not having a secretary. When Clara went on temporary leave to have her baby, he'd prided himself on managing alone; and by the time the maternity period was over and Clara had decided she preferred full-time motherhood to full, or even part-time office work, James had got quite used to being a one man band. The legal profession wasn't exactly flourishing or popular during such dire economic times, particularly conveyancing, and having recently escaped from the burden of massive debt, he was determined to keep his outgoings as low as possible. But as he sat at his desk, eyes fixed on the overflowing in-tray, he felt overwhelmed with nostalgia for Clara's calm reassurance and down to earth common sense.

The telephone rang, forcing him out of the morose state. It was an anxious estate agent, wondering what had happened to the searches on a commercial property that had been promised over a week ago. James placated him with a promise he wasn't convinced he could fulfil. He replaced the phone's receiver slowly as his mind revolved around a cluster of words the caller had said. "I left two messages on your mobile."

Suddenly animated, James feverishly searched for his mobile. He didn't use it often, it was there mainly as a means of contact when he was off the premises. Lyn had made it quite clear that she wouldn't be using hers as a method of communication, due to the horrendous costs involved. But maybe? He strummed his fingers impatiently on the desk as he waited for the switched on phone to initiate. Suddenly, three messages tunefully made it apparent that they were available to be read. The two from the estate agent were ignored. Lyn's message, eagerly accessed but bitterly disappointing, was read several times over. Just three words, saying nothing about trouble. James slumped back in his chair, wondering what he should do next. His telephone rang again, the brief exchange of words gave him hope of redemption, at least in the eyes of Vincent.

"When you have friends and neighbours, the world is a happier place." Peter Radcliffe sang the words of the old song as he prepared a tray for his morning break. Coffee for James, and, because of doctor's orders, a small pot of tea for himself. He'd just spoken to James by phone, diplomatically relaying to him how he was fully recovered from the unfortunate experience of the day before. James had apologised once again and asked if there was anything he could do for him—walking straight into the set trap. Peter mused at how he'd handled the perfect opportunity, and voiced it to the boiling kettle. "Well, actually James," he said, as he poured the steaming water onto one heaped teaspoon of Darjeeling. "There is one small favour you could do for me. I have a one-page loan agreement which is couched in such convoluted language that it beggars belief and you must witness this sort of thing all the time. Come over for coffee sometime, old chap, and cast your learned eye over it for me." And James, anxious to make amends for the disastrous Sunday lunch, had agreed to pop round immediately.

Peter carried the loaded tray into the sitting room and placed it alongside the signed document from Carl. His timing was perfect, a gentle rapping of the door knocker, told him that James had arrived. "I did it my way!" Was superimposed over the melodious background music of the radio, as Peter waltzed down the hallway to his front door.

Stefan remained silent as Vincent weaved in and out of the rush-hour traffic. Unsecured pieces of wood slid and knocked into the side of the van each time they turned a corner but Vincent's mind was too full of conflict to notice. He had been that way since the phone call earlier from Australia and he had become even more so since talking with James Fairbank. As usual, a woman was at the centre of the heartache, reminding Stefan of his own heartache, Elena. The next day would be his birthday. For twenty-two years, they had always been together or spoken on this special day. If there was no contact from her in the next twenty-four hours, it would confirm his worst fears—she was being held prisoner. He checked again that his phone was switched on and fully charged and then forced his mind back to the job he was being paid for.

They were heading inland to the far edge of a town

named Newton Abbot. Vincent had said very little about the work; but Stefan had filled in the gaps from what he overheard from the two long telephone conversations that had taken up a good portion of the previous evening. An elderly couple, returning early from a four-week holiday celebrating forty years of marriage, had found their home taken over by, what Vincent described as filthy, foreign squatters. There were six of these so-called squatters and they came from Romania. On arriving back at their home, the old couple were shocked to find that the front and back door locks had been changed and the lower windows boarded from the inside. Also, a large satellite dish had been erected in the back garden, breaking a law connected to planning and adding to the crimes already committed. In spite of this, the police were unwilling, or unable, to do anything about these crimes; saying that it was a civil matter and the homeowner would have to gain a possession order and eviction notice.

Unbeknown to the leader of the Romanians, the rightful owner of the house was related to the manager of a Debt Collection Agency, an agency that sub-contracted work to Vincent. Nick, the manager of the agency, had told Vincent what needed to be done; but Stefan would have to wait until they arrived to find out what that was. Stefan's orders were to keep quiet and do exactly as he was told. This suited him. Vincent thought that all people from Eastern Europe spoke the same language, ignorant of the fact that like the rest of Europe, language and culture varied considerably. Vincent thought that being Bulgarian; Stefan would have the advantage of picking up on words not meant for the ears of the English. But Stefan had learned over the years that by keeping the voice silent, *all* language barriers could be crossed; and the language of the body, never lied.

Elena carefully removed all her outfits that were hanging in the wardrobe and laid them across the bed. An idea had crept into her mind and at every opportunity she had fed and nurtured the idea, allowing it to develop into a plan. She needed to get in touch with Stefan, even a text message would do, but speaking with him would be better. It was his birthday the next day and if she was denied this very simple act of love and respect to her brother, he would assume she was in danger. Carl had said that he would take her shopping for clothes on Thursday, the day before the wedding ceremony; she needed to convince him that today or at the latest tomorrow would be better.

The bedroom door opened and Carl's tall, angular body stood between the door-frame.

"What are you doing, Elena?"

"I'm checking to see if I've brought an outfit suitable for getting married in."

"I've already promised you a new outfit when we go into town on Thursday."

"Yes, thank you Carl, I really do appreciate your thoughtfulness; unfortunately I'm not a stock size and there is always a good deal of needlework to make an outfit sit properly on my body. A seamstress will need at least two days notice to do this; so I'm left with the choice of using what I've got or going today…Or tomorrow at the latest."

Elena felt his eyes boring into hers, she held his gaze, knowing that the plan would be lost if she showed weakness. He walked slowly into the room shifting his gaze to the bed and the arranged outfits.

"This is peasant-clothing", he said with a dismissive wave. "When I take you to meet Mother, you will wear the clothes of my choosing; they will be made for *you,* and only *you,* there will be no need of a cheap seamstress to pin, cut and tuck. Come now the tide is at its height, we can watch it from the open window and continue our discussion on family-life."

Elena wanted to point out that having clothes commissioned took much longer than having them altered; but Carl wasn't stupid, he would know this, he simply wasn't in the mood to discuss such a trivial thing. She left the unresolved plan simmering in the back of her mind and took hold of his offered hand.

In the far distance, the sea was a pale delicate blue; a reflection of the clear sky. White frothing waves crashed against the bottom of the nearby cliffs, releasing a regular roar and crash that rumbled on the wind as it entered the opened terrace doors. She reached for her woollen wrap, but Carl's arm was quickly placed around her bare upper arms as she was pulled close into his seated embrace. Nothing was said.

She had come to learn that this was the reliving of memories that Carl had shared with his mother, memories that were important to him. Although his mother had lived amongst the Fjords of Norway for all of her married life, she hated and feared it. She regarded the sea as her enemy;

saw it as a monster, just waiting for the opportunity to snatch her from the safety of the rock, where their house was perilously positioned, and drag her into its cold, deep, watery embrace. From a very early age, whilst his father and older brothers were away on the trawler, Carl, the youngest son of the family was left behind. He had told her that Winter was especially difficult for Mother because the days were filled with darkness and the nights were filled with raging storms. As a dutiful and loving son, he had taken on the responsibility of comforting her at these distressing times.

This comforting took place for several years, until he was suddenly sent away to Denmark at the age of fourteen. Elena was naturally curious, but she knew better than to interrupt his reminiscences. Instead she'd allowed him to stroke her upper-arms and shoulders, probably the way he had when comforting his frightened mother. She also allowed him to sniff around her ears, even though this was a little more unnerving When she'd first arrived at the house, she'd found an unopened bottle of expensive French perfume on her dressing table with a gift card saying, *Please use this every day.* He had later told her that this was his mother's favourite perfume.

Carl had never made sexual advances toward Elena and he'd never kissed her on the lips, but the stroking, sniffing and licking of her flesh put her on edge and even more worrying was the casual way he'd announced "When I take you to meet Mother!"

Chapter 14

The hotel's restaurant and bar ran alongside the spacious, ground-floor foyer. Floor-to-ceiling glass walls separated the clusters of contemporary-style tables and chairs from the reception area, giving Lyn the perfect opportunity to view all the comings and goings through the massive revolving doors. She'd sat at the same corner table for over two hours, initially relaxing with a glass of chilled wine, then after half an hour, ordering a light meal. She was now sipping on a café latte, not caring that it would probably affect her ability to sleep. A part of her, still couldn't quite believe that Andy could have done such a despicable thing, so she had kept to their arrangement, half expecting him to breeze through the revolving doors smiling from ear to ear; but as time moved slowly forward, the truth crushingly hit home.

She'd heard nothing from Vinny, not even an email. After turning on her mobile, three text messages and two voice mails were waiting to be attended to, all from James and all full of concern that she hadn't spoken to him. She'd quickly turned it off and left it off; she was in no fit state to deal with more emotion, right now, all she needed was the company of a friend.

The young waitress approached and Lyn handed her the unfamiliar dollars, which included a 10% tip; this brought a beaming smile to her pretty face and a gush of north-country, appreciative words.

"Thanks a lot, I could tell you were English straight away; hardly anybody leaves a tip over 'ere, whereabouts are you from?"

Lyn wasn't in the mood for chatting, not with a stranger, but after saying that she needed to go and make a phone call, the pretty young waitress offered her some valuable advice.

"If ya' phoning back home, don't use ya' mobile; ya' credits will be gone in no time. Get a phone card and use the public phones, here's the best one for maximum time."

Lyn watched as her beautifully manicured hands scribbled a name across a page from her pad, tearing it off and handing it over, the waitress said. "You can buy one just over there."

Lyn followed the direction of the pointing finger, marvelling at its intricately patterned nail, and then offered her appreciation by helping to load the tray. She was treated to another smile and a gush of genuine warmth.

"It's been very nice meeting you love, 'av a nice holiday."

Lyn tucked the piece of paper inside her purse and headed off into the cooler night air of Darling Harbour.

After calculating the time difference, the newly bought phone card was put into action. The ringing, which was surprisingly loud and clear, resounded seven times and just as she was about to forlornly replace the receiver, a breathless Candy picked up.

"Candy Laverne speaking, how can I help you?"

"You're the one who sounds in need of help, have you been out jogging."

"You know I don't go in for all that keep-fit stuff, my life's active enough, a good rest is what I need. Bear with me a minute Lyn, I've left my case on the landing and I don't want some light-fingered opportunist waltzing off with it." Lyn pictured Candy as the appropriate noises confirmed her returning to her apartment's door and heaving in the large week-end bag. The door was closed and the chain slid into position. A nearby chair creaked under Candy's weight and two clonks hit the floor.

"That's better; those shoes'll have to be given the once-over, they've been pinching my poor feet all morning."

"I'm glad I've caught you Candy, how is your sister? Keeping well I hope."

"She's fine thank you; but I haven't just got back from Blackpool, I've been down your neck of the woods. Something came up suddenly and a friend needed a lift."

"Someone needed a lift, what, all the way to Torbay! Haven't they heard of the rail network?" Lyn suddenly found herself feeling jealous of this unknown friend who commanded such devotion and sacrifice from Candy.

"It's a long story, love, and I'm mindful of you ringing long-distance, incidentally I was surprised, and saddened, to see that James hadn't made the trip with you."

"You've seen James! Have you spoken to him?"

"Yes love; it's all part of the long story."

"I've just bought a phone card which is a very economical way of phoning England, and right now, Candy, I could do with talking."

"Tell you what, love, give me the hotel and room number, I can hear that you're out on the roadside, and I know it's getting late over there. I'll ring you back in half an hour. I'm dying for a pee and a cup of tea, in that order."

"Thanks Candy, right now, you feel like my only friend. Speak in half an hour."

After settling down with a pot of tea, Candy deleted the first of the two messages that were waiting for attention on her answer phone, cursing the fact that unsolicited calls got through in spite of her being ex-directory. The second message however, was listened to several times *and* responded to before she made her promised call to Lyn.

"Sorry I'm a bit later than promised Lyn; I hope it's not keeping you up."

"I'm lying on the bed, so if jetlag carries me off in the middle of the 'long story', blame yourself." Lyn heard the peevishness in her own voice and immediately regretted it.

Candy sensed her turmoil and responded by giving Lyn a brief and factual account of what had taken place since Stefan's anguished call on Friday afternoon. Lyn remained silent until Candy touched upon how she'd had a run-in with James over his resentful attitude and the reason for cancelling his trip to Australia.

"You're wasting your breath; *I* couldn't get him to open up, he's just like that."

"No one is just, like that, there's always a reason. His reason was, on the evening of the lingerie venue, he'd caught sight of you running up to your apartment in tears and dressed like a prostitute! His words not mine. Then you locked the door and refused to speak to him. He'd put two and two together and made five." Silence followed the blunt disclosure; and for a minute Candy thought that Lyn had slipped into a jetlagged state of unconsciousness, until.

"He actually said that he suspected I was on the game!" Lyn's voice sounded so incredulous and so loud that Candy moved the mouthpiece away from her ear.

"I put him straight, naturally, and he was a bit sheepish after that, but I could tell that he was still very concerned about something. After a further little chat, he mentioned the large sum of money that miraculously appeared out of nowhere; allowing you to buy his fancy business premises, cash in hand! You can't be secretive about that sort of thing in a budding relationship, Lyn, it encourages the wrong conclusions.

"We weren't in any kind of a relationship when I came by the money, so as far as I'm concerned, it's none of his bloody business!" Lyn felt the peevishness notching up a level and this time she had no regrets.

Candy softened her voice in an effort to calm Lyn's rising tension. "He suspects that Carl was involved, love, and Carl is the number one enemy in his life at the moment. He's got every right to be concerned, the man's dangerous and unscrupulous. I'm your friend; will you tell me where you got the money?" A long stretch of silence followed and Candy began to wonder if James's suspicions were justified. Eventually Lyn responded in a hesitant manner.

"I…I won it! I won it on the lottery! Happy now?"

Candy laughed; more from relief than humour. "So why the secrecy? Millions of people gamble on the lottery every week I'm sure your family were delighted."

"You're the only person I've told and I'm not a gambler. It's just that I found this bright, shiny £1 coin when I was at rock bottom and I somehow knew it could change everything. I just kept it a secret, and now, well it seems too unbelievable."

"I promise not to say anything when I speak to James; but I hope you'll let him know when you return; it will certainly stop the worry that's eating away at him."

"Why do you need to contact him again?" the peevish voice had returned. Lyn had only been half listening to the earlier account of why Candy was in Devon, her mind had been wandering all over the place.

"I've just heard some very disturbing news from one of my ex-models. She got married to a rich, older man, fourteen months ago. Although he was supposedly fit and healthy, he's recently dropped dead from a massive heart-attack; leaving my ex-model penniless and begging for her old job back."

"I thought you said the man was rich."

"Apparently he owed a lot of money to a financial institution, named V.C. Enterprises; and because most of the man's wealth was held in trust back in Amsterdam, the Westminster apartment, where the couple lived, was seized to cover the debt."

"Well I don't mean to sound unfeeling toward your ex-models Candy, I know how fond you are of them, but unfortunate things are happening all the time. When they agree to marry for financial gain; there's always the risk of it backfiring."

"I'm just giving you an explanation of why I need to contact James again. Carl and V.C. Enterprises are one and the same. Elena and Peter Radcliffe are due to marry in a few days time and this has also been arranged by Carl."

"Beautiful Elena is to marry old Radcliffe! What ever for?"

"Believe me, she only wants to help her family and remove them from a dire situation."

"Sorry Candy, I can't get my head round anything more; I just need to sleep."

"Sleep well love, I'll send you an email sometime tomorrow."

Chapter 15

Monday Afternoon—Torbay

As James strolled back to his office, the sound of a vehicle screeching to a halt, followed by the unmistakable voice of Vincent venting his spleen, brought him to a standstill. At the lower end of The Terrace, two men could be clearly seen arguing about who was at fault behind the slight collision. The solicitor was torn between offering his help and facing Vincent's wrath or ducking indoors to the peace and quiet of his office and feeling guilty. The sudden ringing of his phone, forced the decision.

"James Fairbank, how can I help?

"Candy Laverne, are you free to talk, James, it is important."

"Yes of course, what is it?" James listened attentively as Candy relayed the conversation she'd had with her former model. It was obvious that Carl was pulling the same scam with Peter Radcliffe and Elena, and documents headed V.C. Enterprises would be faxed to him the next day, to prove it. Before Candy rang off, James broached the subject of Lyn and wondered if she'd heard from her.

"Yes, I had a nice long conversation with her earlier; mind you, she sounded a bit weary, and a bit lonely."

Mixed emotions left him uncertain as to how to respond. Without thinking he blurted out "She won't be lonely for long, she'll be meeting up with her long-lost mother in a day or so."

"What do you mean, her long-lost mother? I thought that her parents died when she was a nipper."

Reluctantly, James explained, as simply as possible, how Lyn had come to know about the whereabouts of Jennifer Beck, and how this trip was to include their reunion. After a lengthy pause, he added, "Thinking about it, I'm not sure that Jennifer Beck has any idea yet of Lyn's existence. I haven't had the opportunity to speak with her yet Candy, will you convey my best wishes and tell her that…That I'm thinking of her."

"I'd give you her hotel number, love; but I'd need to clear that with her first, you do understand don't you?"

James responded by changing the subject. "I had coffee with Peter Radcliffe a while ago; thought it a good opportunity to squeeze him for information."

"And, were you successful?"

"Yes and no, I managed to get him to reveal the V.C. Enterprises contract, he even let me take a copy which puts me in the clear legally, but he says that he has no means of contacting Carl, and I believe him."

"Did you point out to him what might happen if he should suddenly drop dead in the next six months!"

"Well of course I did; but his reaction seemed to be that it wouldn't be his problem."

"What a cold-hearted bastard! James we have to stop this marriage one way or another."

"I managed to obtain one of the, the Viagra capsules. I've just returned from dropping it into the local pharmacy for analysis, he happens to be an old school friend of mine."

"I'm looking forward to hearing all about the finer details of how you got him to part with that capsule. It would do us all a favour if he tried a couple out before Friday."

James knew if anything happened to Peter before Friday, Victor Carlson would soon be a very close neighbour.

Peter Radcliffe paced up and down the antique oriental carpet, not caring that he was further undermining its age-worn, fragile structure. He'd owned it for more than thirty years but its existence had begun a hundred and fifty years before then. Running half the length of the sitting room, between the back of the settee and the large rosewood display cabinet, it was usually given a wide berth in preference to the wool rug from Marks and Spencer's that lay across the front of the fireplace; but consideration for a mere floor covering, albeit a very valuable one, was lost amongst the disturbing thoughts that circled around his brain.

The hour spent with James Fairbank had been very revealing. Peter had silently marvelled at the speed in which the solicitor had deciphered the convoluted wording of the contract; but hadn't taken too kindly to James's insistence that he ought to cancel the contract by paying back the loan and having nothing more to do with it. In truth, Peter didn't have a choice. Over half of the borrowed money was already spent on refurbishments to the inside of his property, and the rest would soon follow during the spring when the outside of the building was tackled. Fortunately, there was no need to start repaying the loan until a year after he'd married Elena, by which time she would have found gainful employment, to pay off the instalments of the loan. It was fine and dandy for James, easy for him to pontificate and hand out advice whilst sitting pretty after selling his next door property and still young enough to accrue more money from a well-paid profession.

Still, not everything was fine and dandy for James. A smile creased Peter's lined face as he recalled James's embarrassment when revealing that he needed a little help in the bedroom department; and how Peter suddenly understood, why he hadn't wanted to waste a three week expensive holiday with the lovely Lyn. Excusing himself for a minute, he'd returned from his bedroom clutching one of the precious, bright orange capsules and handed it to James saying "Take this by way of payment for your help; if you need more I'm afraid it will cost. Apparently, they are the best thing on the market for solving problems connected to drooping in the nether regions." Peter had watched with satisfaction as James, still red-faced with embarrassment, had wrapped the blister packed capsule in his handkerchief and slipped it carefully inside his jacket pocket before bidding his goodbye and slinking out of the front door.

Peter wasn't unduly worried about anything that James had revealed. It was the phone call, five minutes after James's departure that had put him on edge, and also threatened to undo all the well worked out plans of the last few weeks.

Vinny felt as taut as an over-wound spring. The whole morning had turned out to be one disaster after another, climaxing into some fucking idiot of a driver running into the side of the van and causing heaps of damage. It would never have happened if Stefan had been beside him; but he'd had to leave him behind at the old couple's house. And, those foreign, squatting bastards would have been dealt with if he hadn't been delayed from setting out.

The door to James's office was thrust open and he marched up to the desk where the solicitor sat filling in the boxes of a form. Unable to contain his frustration any longer, he let rip. "I've had the worst fucking morning since I set up in this place! And it's all down to other people delaying me on the job."

"Sit down Vincent, would you like some coffee?"

"No I don't want any fucking coffee!

"Would you like to discuss what's bothering you?"

"What, you my fucking shrink now?"

"Sit down and stop being so melodramatic; I'm sure you're not the only person alive who has experienced an off-day."

Vinny opened his mouth to continue the tirade but quickly found that he was out of energy. "I've changed my mind about the coffee."

Without altering his expression and without saying a word James pushed away from his desk and headed toward his office kitchenette.

"And don't forget the chocolate biscuits, I'm starving," Vinny called after him, before plonking himself down in the solicitor's chair and scrutinising what was on the form.

The tray was set down between them and Vinny immediately reached for one of the biscuits and slid the whole thing effortlessly into his mouth. After a period of crunching, followed by a series of slurps from the freshly poured coffee, Vinny fired his next accusation. "I suppose you haven't had time to think about how you're going to approach Radcliffe and how to locate Carl. You've probably been too tied up filling out these pointless forms."

"They may appear pointless to you, but its part of my job as a conveyancing solicitor. Now, regarding Peter Radcliffe, I had coffee with him earlier, I put him straight about Carl's illegal contract and I've taken one of the dubious Viagra capsules for analysis. Candy Laverne has also been in touch; she is faxing me a copy of another similar contract issued by V.C. Enterprises which will serve as extra evidence of the man's crookedness."

Vinny reached for another chocolate biscuit and again pushed it whole into his mouth; devouring it along with the snippets of information that Jimmy had just given. "Ok, so let's have the details."

"Oh no, that's not how it works, Vincent." James picked up one of the fast diminishing biscuits, dunked it delicately into the black liquid and after shaking off the drips expertly bit off the small dampened portion."

"What do you mean, that's not how it works?" asked Vinny, disgusted at the prissy way Jimmy ate.

I'll give you everything I know, when you tell me what has happened to Lyn and why she's ignoring my efforts to communicate."

"Oh come on Jimmy, that's a separate issue altogether!"

"Look Vincent, the way I see it, we are in grave danger of having Victor Carlson as a close neighbour within a few months time and neither of us wants that to happen. You need to tell me all you know and especially where Lyn got the money for buying next door. Is Carl with her now? Is that why she refuses to contact me?"

"You know what, you are fucking paranoid! How many times do you have to be told, she didn't get the money from Carl and apart from that first loan, which was done legally, she's never had any dealings with him.

"So where did the money come from?"

"Right, I'm sure you've got a key to her place so get the key, and I'll show you where she got the fucking money! Ok?"

"I can't just go waltzing into someone else's private domain without their permission. And how did *you* acquire a key to Lyn's place; and does she know you have it?"

Vinny reached for another biscuit; but instead of filling his mouth, he walked over to the window with his back to Jimmy. "You forget sunshine, we share the same building; which means, we share the same building's insurance as well as boiler maintenance etc etc and when she's away, it's obvious I need access for certain things."

"Both premises are self-contained, so don't insult my intelligence Vincent. Does Lyn hold a key to your place? Or is this just a, one-way, neighbourly thing?"

"For Christ's sake Jimmy, do you want to know where she got the money or not?"

Vinny stood back and watched as the solicitor slowly and deliberately unlocked the door on the opposite side of the hallway, hesitating before moving into the neat and stylishly furnished office. Out of frustration, he pushed past him and headed straight to a corner desk, pulling open its deep bottom drawer. Flicking through the suspended files he retrieved the one he'd examined in the early hours of Sunday morning. The file contained Lyn's bank statements of the previous two years as well as used cheque books and paying-in books.

Suddenly hands reached from behind trying to tear the file from his grip! "This is not right, if Lyn should find out!"

"If you pull a stunt like that again and rip the fucking page, she's bound to know isn't she? I just need to show you one entry, then we're out of here, so give me a break will you?" He ran through several sheets, checking the dates and taking care not to pull any free from the punched holes. "Here we are, feast your eyes on this Jimmy!"

The solicitor's eyes fixed on the printed figures above the tip of Vinny's chocolate-stained, chubby index finger.

"I can see the entry of £304,060.00; but it doesn't tell us where it came from."

Vinny was already riffling through one of the used receipt books. "Gotcha, take a look at that." Vinny passed over the opened book saying, "Lyn used to work for me, remember, and she was always a stickler for keeping the bookwork in apple pie order. She's even done a photocopy of the winning ticket and stapled it in the receipt book with the entry." The two men sat on the floor by the open drawer: one wore a satisfied grin as he watched the other mouth the words 'Lottery Win Cheque from Camelot in Watford'.

"But why didn't she just tell me? Why all the secrecy?"

"Pride, I'd say. It's much better to give the impression you've got your money from blood, sweat and tears, rather than a stroke of luck. Anyway, you're the most secretive bastard I've ever come across, apart from Carl, so come on, time for you to cough up some info."

"I'd like to know what this trouble in Australia is all about first."

"She's had some cash nicked, thinks it was the young toerag sitting next to her on the flight. She wants me to find out what I can about him."

"Lyn must know his name then."

"Yeah, she knows his name, probably got quite cosy the two of them. Twenty-four hours is a long time when you've got nothing else to do but get friendly with the person in the next seat." Vinny's mobile suddenly blurted out its weird tone preventing him from catching Jimmy's reaction to Lyn's misfortune. "It's Stefan, I need to take this, make sure everything is as you found it, I'll catch you later."

Stefan slipped his mobile and the piece of paper back inside the pocket of his leather jacket. The number 12 bus had just arrived and he should be back at Vincent's place within the hour. There was no need to wait at the old couple's house any longer; he had all the information he needed.

They had arrived at the Newton Abbot house too late. The old man had made the mistake of telling the Romanian gang that help was on its way; it was a natural thing to do, the doors to his own home were locked against him. Knowing they would soon be forced to move on, the Romanian leader had threatened to do all kinds of damage to their home if the couple didn't pay a large sum of English pounds. The old couple had refused, confident that the promised help would arrive very soon.

In the couple's beautiful garden, was a deep pond where large, colourful, Japanese Carp enjoyed a pampered life from the old man. In the constant presence of the old lady, two long-haired lap-dogs also enjoyed a pampered life. The Romanian leader, whilst not fully understanding such devotion to these creatures, took advantage of it. He threatened to net, kill and carry off the fish, for eating later and then place both dogs in the same net and sink it in the vacant pond. Very soon the old couple had handed over what cash they carried and many valuables that were in the house. The gang were gone by the time the promised help had arrived and Vincent had been very angry.

The large satellite dish that the Romanians had brought with them, remained in the garden, and Stefan felt sure that at least one of the gang would return for it, so it was agreed that he should stay behind and wait. Whilst waiting, he asked the old couple lots of questions but because the Romanians spoke only in their own language to each other, he didn't gain much information; but he did gain the leaders name, because according to the old lady, it had caused a bit of an argument.

Before long, Stefan heard and then saw, a beaten up old car pulling a wooden, flat based trailer. It rattled noisily down the road, slowing down as it past the old couple's house, then rattled on for another fifty metres before stopping. Stefan had advised the old couple to stay out of sight and not to answer the phone. He had then slipped quietly out into the back garden.

"Where's Dragos?" He hissed, as a pale-faced youth crept through the back garden gate and headed toward the massive satellite dish. Stefan had caught the youth's arm as he'd turned to run.

"Calm down, me and Dragos go way back, he'd said, adding, Dragos said I could stay here for a few days, where is he? The house is locked and empty!"

"We needed to move quickly, before the heavies arrived, I've been sent back for this," the sullen youth had said as he'd given the dish a half-hearted kick. "Dragomir, I'm not allowed to call him Dragos, treats me like a dog's body, even though I am the most educated. I speak four languages you know."

Stefan had placed an arm around the youth's shoulder. "My friend, when I first knew Dragos, he treated me like a dog's turd. Let me help you load this; but first give me his mobile number."

"He doesn't trust anyone with that."

"He's still as cautious as ever then." Tell me address of next squat, is it far?"

"I'll take you there, He'll flay me alive if he finds out I'm handing out the address."

Stefan's impatience had started to show. "He'll definitely flay you alive if I decide to join another squat! I've got very expensive laptop and good night-vision equipment which he anxious to have, now, I need to go and get gear together first, so do you want help with this or not? If answer is yes, give me address now. I won't drop you in dog's turd, believe me I know how sadistic Dragos can be."

Chapter 16

Monday Evening—Torbay

James needed to get out of here and breathe fresh air. He was back in Lyn's office and the guilt of invading her private space, once again, was no less onerous; but it was the lingering scent of her perfume that was causing the deepest distress.

Vincent's revelations about the lottery win, had left him lost in a mental stupor, unable to carry out the tasks that he'd set for that afternoon. He needed to phone Lyn. Needed to put his mind at rest that she was alright. Knowing that her mobile would now be out of action he went in search of the Sydney Hotel number. It had taken a lot of frantic searching through his own receipts and a forced period of mental calming before he gradually remembered that Lyn had taken care of booking the entire trip, including his subsequent cancellation, which meant all the relevant paperwork would be in her office.

After once again opening up her door, he'd crept across the darkened room like a thief in the night, realising that this was what Vincent had been doing less than forty-eight hours before. Keeping low to the floor, he'd switched on his torch and shielded the glare of its head. The desk top, he'd remembered, had been clear of paperwork and reasoning that what he wanted would be in one of the drawers, pulled open the one which had already revealed a closely guarded secret. Each file was neatly labelled but none had any connection to travel-expenses or holidays. With a slight pressure, he'd pushed the drawer back and drew out the one above. The rush of the familiar perfume had filled his nostrils and all thoughts of finding the hotel telephone number had been temporarily forgotten. Knowing what lay beneath but unable to stop his shaking fingers, he'd lifted the covering of tissue paper, revealing the delicate item from its confinement. The silk camisole and matching knickers, which had been meant as a surprise token of Lyn's love, was laying abandoned in the drawer. Pangs of guilt constricted his chest as his mind flitted to the diamond solitaire ring, also lying abandoned, somewhere in his upper rooms.

After making sure that everything was locked and in place, James stepped out into the evening air and filled his lungs. Instead of the expected fresh, sea breeze, his nostrils were once again assailed by a man-made fragrance. Fried bacon wafted on the air and it was coming from the direction of Vincent's basement apartment. Conversation and a fully-lit room added to the allurement as James realised how hungry he suddenly felt. He walked down the stone flight of steps and rapped on Vincent's door, remembering that he hadn't yet fulfilled his side of the bargain regarding information; and also remembering that Vincent had the telephone number of Lyn's hotel.

Vinny opened the door and made a point of looking at his watch before allowing James to enter the narrow hallway. "As you know, this morning's assignment was a complete, fucking failure, mainly thanks to you; now we've got to leave sharp in half an hour, what do you want?"

"I've come to fill in the details of my morning's efforts; what is that delicious smell Vincent?" Fired with a mixture of determination and hunger, James pushed past Vincent's bulk of a body and walked through to the kitchen where he found Stefan forking out a pan full of well-done rashers.

"Would you like bacon sarnie Mr Fairbank?"

"Thank you Stefan, I would love a bacon sarnie; I notice that working alongside Vincent is broadening your understanding of the English language."

Stefan lifted three rashers and placed them between two thick slices of white bread that had been spread with a liberal layer of butter. "I am learning much about the many layers of culture in this country. This kind of food is usually for builders; am I right?"

"This kind of food is perfect for anyone, when you're starving hungry." James accepted the offered plate and sat on a nearby stool watching as Stefan moved confidently about the kitchen. After the first delicious mouthful James asked. "Has Elena been in touch?" Stefan shook his head and remained focussed on the food.

"How come he's eating before me?" Shouted Vinny as he peered into the kitchen, wondering how much longer his sandwich would be.

"I was brought up to serve guests first," Stefan answered without looking up.

"Well in this house, the one earning the bread gets fed first and just you remember it, and also remember we need to be gone very soon, if I don't rescue my reputation tonight, nobody will be getting fed. And, I want you to leave your mobile phone behind, this is a covert operation and I don't want it scuppered by your phone suddenly going off."

"Leave it with me Stefan," James offered. "If Elena makes contact, I will explain. And Vincent, I'll phone Lyn and explain how tied up you are, maybe *I* can do something to help her situation.

Vinny cursed under his breath; he'd forgotten all about his promise. He grabbed his sandwich and bit an almighty chunk out of it, wiping away a dribble of melted butter with the back of his fist. James watched and waited for his response. Another chunk disappeared into his mouth and it was during the grinding and munching of this second piece that a response was forthcoming. "She doesn't want you to know about the nicked money, so if you do phone her, just say that I've been away on an important job and should be back tomorrow, don't even mention that she was in touch with me, right."

"I promise I won't mention a word about what has passed between us; can you give me the number of the hotel and her room, save me going through a mound of paperwork."

Vinny opened his mouth to say something but instead stuffed the remainder of the sandwich inside and then disappeared into his office. He returned with a scrap of paper, slapping it down on the working surface and saying

"Stefan, give him your phone and then he can fuck off and leave us to get organised."

James, feeling relaxed and self-satisfied, sat in his favourite armchair with a freshly poured glass of wine at his elbow. He waited patiently until his sitting-room's antique clock finished announcing, in melodious chimes, that it was precisely seven o'clock in the evening. As the room fell silent, he began to dial the number that had been hurriedly scribbled on the scrap of paper before him. He breathed a sigh of relief as a ringing tone kicked in on the other side of the globe. Patience endured as the ringing tone continued, until suddenly, catching sight of scribbled words under the number, caused him to jerk with trepidation and accidentally knock his wine to the floor.

Time difference, Sydney 9hrs ahead

He had always been a smart dresser, a legacy from Mother, Father had always been suspicious of well-dressed men. Tonight however, Carl would dress with particular care and attention to detail. He was taking Elena out to dinner. Personally, he had never minded spending time alone; there had been numerous occasions when he'd travelled to remote places for a break from the mental drain of business; absorbing the entire holiday without conversing with or even seeing another human being. Elena, on the other hand, was much needier of human contact and it seemed only fair to go part way in allowing her what she needed. Apart from Mother, he had never felt so magnanimous towards a woman. In only two days, they had become close; understanding each others needs. He felt sure that at long last he had found his life-partner. A partner, who would fill the lonely nights and help to chase away the horror-filled dreams that left him feeling bereft, confused and writhing in cold perspiration. Mother will be delighted. Very soon, she will meet Elena. Very soon, Mother's deep concerns for him will fade away.

He couldn't allow Radcliffe to marry Elena. He wouldn't even allow him to look upon her again. Tomorrow, he would work out a plan where Radcliffe could be disposed of before the scheduled ceremony, after all, the marriage was just a means to what would be the same end; he would soon own the property on The Terrace and Elena would soon live alongside him in that property.

Shelving all thoughts of Radcliffe, Carl turned his attention to the evening ahead. He had booked a table in the name of Andersson (Mother's name before she'd married) at the only restaurant that was open in the area. Monday, was obviously not a popular evening for eating out in these parts, he thought, brushing aside a rising frustration. This was a celebration and Champagne would be enjoyed. The taxi would arrive soon and carry them on their first date.

Elena perched nervously on the edge of the brocade-covered chair. Carl twitched with irritation as he waited for the manager to appear. They'd been guided to a table which was situated in the middle of the near-empty dining room and Carl had indicated, in a forthright way, that he'd prefer to sit in a corner.

"The corner tables are for four people sir," responded the waiter in a quiet, respectful tone.

"On a Monday evening, I doubt whether you will have more than four people in the entire restaurant." Carl indicated with his hand, the only other couple in the room, who also happened to be positioned on a central table.

"Sorry Sir, its restaurant policy."

"Well it's my policy to sit where I like when I'm paying the bill; get me the manager!"

The waiter disappeared from view and Carl led Elena to a discreetly positioned table that was elevated on a raised platform. Elena noticed that all four tables on the raised platform had RESERVED signs on them. This didn't stop Carl from drawing out the chair for her to sit.

"How can I help, Sir?" The manager looked and sounded tired. Elena felt sure that he was the chef with his apron removed and a jacket thrown quickly around his shoulders.

"You can help by allowing us to sit where we feel most comfortable. We are celebrating an important occasion and a little privacy would be very much appreciated."

"Not a problem, Sir; can I take your order for drinks?"

"I'd like a bottle of your finest Champagne."

"Very good, Sir." The tired look momentarily vanished beneath a forced smile, as he dropped a couple of menus on the table and disappeared back to the kitchen.

The meal had been surprisingly good. Carl, having recovered quickly from the earlier incident had been impressed with the quality of the Champagne and had consumed two glasses before any food arrived. This alone, had enhanced his mood and several times he'd referred to Elena as, my darling. *She* hadn't contradicted anything that was said. As far as she was concerned, this was a celebration of her forthcoming marriage to Peter Radcliffe. An arrangement that would soon be legalised and Carl would then be off the scene. The ring of a mobile phone from the other occupied table, reminded Elena of Stefan's birthday. She watched intently as the woman turned off the phone when her partner pointed out the sign that mobile phones were not to be used in the dining area.

"Would you like a brandy, my darling? Or should I arrange for the taxi to take us back? you look a little pale!"

"No, I'm fine really, you have a brandy, I still have Champagne in my glass." Keeping a watchful eye on the other table, Elena pulled the silk wrap tighter around her shoulders and smiled as Carl squeezed her hand. Soon an opportunity presented itself. As the requested bill arrived at the other table, the lady excused herself and moved toward the ladies toilet. Waiting for a minute or so, Elena did the same. She found the lady checking who her caller had been.

"I've suddenly remembered that it's my brother's birthday today and I've left my phone behind; could I be really cheeky and borrow your phone to send a quick, happy birthday text."

The woman hesitated, then with a shrug of her shoulders smiled and introduced herself before handing over the phone "I'll do my replies when I've used the loo."

After a few false starts, Elena forced herself to calm down as each step of the process was done as speedily as possible, pressing, SEND, with a sigh of relief.

"Are you alright darling, you look quite flushed, I think we'll get you home? The bill is settled and the taxi is on its way." Carl finished his brandy and took Elena's coat from the waiter; holding it for her to slip into.

Elena climbed into the taxi; but before Carl had a chance to settle beside her he was stopped by an urgent shout from the woman who had sat at the other table. "Elena, I have something for you!"

Carl turned and headed back to where the woman was waving frantically. Elena froze in panic. How would Carl react to Stefan's response to her call? She couldn't bear to look at the two of them exchanging words.

"I think you must be sickening for something, darling, you have gone quite pale again. Here put your scarf on, you left it in the ladies room. It never ceases to amaze me how women can be so friendly toward each other regardless of the fact that they are complete strangers.

"Thank you Carl. And thank you for such a lovely evening."

"You're welcome, my darling; but the evening is not over yet."

Filled with irritation, Peter Radcliffe marched over to the radio to turn it down but after a seconds thought the knob was turned fully anti-clockwise, plunging his sitting room into complete silence. "That's better," he announced to the furniture. "How is a man supposed to think straight with a row like that going on?" The row that had been cut off in mid stream, was Nigel Kennedy and The English Chamber Orchestra, performing one of the more gusto sections from Vivaldi's, Four Seasons—a piece of music that would normally have had Peter playing role as conductor while flicking his feather duster amongst the ornaments—but the mood wasn't with him this evening. In fact his mood hadn't been good since the phone call from his daughter, earlier in the day.

She'd phoned to inform him that she would be arriving in two weeks time. The flight was booked and she'd arranged a hire car at Heathrow, so no need to worry about arranging a lift for her at the airport. The world-wide economic down-turn, she'd gone on to say, was affecting her and her family particularly badly. Because of this, they were thinking of returning to England for a few years until the boys had gained their A levels, enabling them to go on to University.

"We still hold full British Citizenship, so we are entitled!" she'd informed him in her usual curt manner, going on to reveal that they could no longer afford to pay for decent education where they were.

Peter had tried explaining to her that the major part of his premises was up for sale and the rest was half let to a long-standing tenant, leaving an area which you could barely swing a cat for himself. But she wouldn't let up; arguing that he should think himself lucky to be in such a position when his only living relatives were in such dire circumstance.

Prior to hanging up, she'd said. "My flight arrives at Heathrow on the 16th. I'll phone you from there to give an indication when to expect me. I'm really looking forward to seeing you Daddy, it's been far too long!"

Chapter 17

Tuesday morning—Sydney

Filled with a sense of expectancy, Lyn entered the lift and pressed the button that would transport her to the ground floor. Just across from reception and partially screened from view, was the I.T. Zone, an area which consisted of four computers, each set in its own little cubicle. She'd slept well and risen early; but mindful that this particular hotel was well used by the business sector, she'd showered and dressed quickly.

The rushing had been in vain. All the computers were occupied and two women, leaning against one of the partitioned walls, idly chatting, gave her a look that clearly said, we are next in line. It was barely 7-30, too early for breakfast and too boring to be standing in line behind a bunch of workaholics, so Lyn wandered out through the large revolving doors and headed in the opposite direction to where she'd strolled the day before.

There was no sign of the searing sun, either it hadn't yet risen above the multitude of sky-scraping-buildings or the cloud layer was thicker than it looked, either way, Lyn was grateful, she'd dared to step out without sun-block or a hat. With keen observation, she kept track of the exact route that she'd travelled and soon found that she was on the opposite side of Darling Harbour with the back face of her hotel, which happened to be more impressive than the front, clearly visible across the water. She was surrounded by beautiful waterside restaurants, their outdoor terraces embellished with tropical plants, contemporary sculpture and intriguing water features. This early hour was warm but comfortable, and, having steered away from the main walking route, which was congested by people in suits and cyclists, also in suits, the earlier tension soon began to dissipate. Several times she was tempted to have breakfast sitting amongst tinkling water or the giant scented blooms of the evergreen Magnolia tree; but she resisted, reminding herself that there'd be plenty of time for pleasure when the serious business of finding a thief was out of the way.

Back at the hotel, she was disappointed to find even more people waiting in line to snatch the use of a vacant computer. A familiar voice from behind suddenly grabbed her attention.

"Ayah, after nine is the best time to get lucky with a computer, I'd say you've just about got time for a coffee."

"I need more than coffee, I'm starving."

"Even better. Come on, I'll plonk you on a table where you can just about see the row of computers, I call it the pre-breakfast hot-seat, and it's just become available."

Lyn was ushered over to the table by the waitress she'd met the evening before. "Thanks again for your advice on the phone card; my name's Lyn by the way."

"I'm Crystal, named after some American TV star from the eighties; me mum loves the telly. Me dad said it was the daftest name he'd ever heard of; not that his opinion mattered, he'd slung his hook before I'd turned one."

Lyn was a bit unsure of her ground. She'd never before met a near-stranger who was so up front about such personal information. "Well Crystal, what do you recommend for breakfast?"

"Steer clear of the Full English, you'll be disappointed. They can't quite get their head round the fact that bacon and sausages should be well done. If I were you, I'd break myself in easily on the first day by having fruit and cereals to start, followed by scrambled eggs on toast with grilled tomatoes and mushrooms, and end up with toast and marmalade; or, if you want to be posh, croissant and jam."

"That sounds perfect, leave off the posh end; I'm just your regular toast and marmalade type of person."

The portions were enormous, but surprisingly, Lyn demolished the lot, and then helped herself to a second cup of coffee to help the mass to settle. It was nine twenty but there was still a steady stream of would-be computer users, eager to take up any vacant slot that became available. Crystal appeared with her tray "I don't suppose you want anything else, apart from an available computer."

"Why don't they just go to the office and do what they have to there?" Moaned Lyn, as she surreptitiously massaged her lower abdomen.

"I reckon it's to do with, Melbourne Cup, I wasn't 'ere last year so I can't say for sure, but there are a lot of business types booked in for just one night and there's certainly a lot of fancy hats being shown around."

Lyn's face must have indicated total confusion. Feeling obliged to explain; Crystal perched on the seat opposite and gave a vivid account of how a particular horse-race, held in Melbourne at 3-00pm on that afternoon, would bring the whole city to a virtual standstill. She hooked her thumb in the direction of the computers, "I bet this lot are social networking their plans for the day and evening. She leaned forward and lowered her voice. You know, I shouldn't be on duty this morning; but I'm covering for Kate who's having her hair done, a manicure, pedicure and leg wax, all for the sake of a horse-race. It's also cost her twenty-five dollars for a hat that's barely more than three blue feathers and a bit of ribbon."

"I take it that you're not a horse-racing fan."

"No way, apparently me dad was a compulsive gambler, that's why things didn't work out between him and me mum. You never know what's going to be handed down from your parents, so I just stay well clear of that sort of stuff. I know it's mainly a bit of fun with the Melbourne Cup, but you'd be surprised how serious the Ozzies are about it, and, it has to be said, they do like their gambling. So what are *you* doing today?"

The question caught Lyn by surprise "Probably walking this off," she rubbed her lower abdomen again only this time more openly. "Do you have any suggestions other than the Melbourne Cup? I must admit, horse-racing is a non-runner for me." Both women groaned good-naturedly at the pun.

"Well, if you enjoy sight-seeing on foot, today will be good because according to the weather forecast, cloud will dominate all day." Crystal walked a few yards to where a stand was overflowing with tourist information, and after plucking out one of the pamphlets she returned to the table and opened it out to reveal a large-scale, well-detailed map of the area. "Follow this path which takes you right round the water's edge to the Harbour Bridge." Lyn's eyes followed the route of Crystal's elaborately painted-finger-nail. "There's the Opera House. There's the Botanical Gardens. Along here at Circular Quay, there's plenty of ferries that will carry you across to: Taronga Zoo, if you're an animal lover, or Manly, if you're a beach lover, or…"

"Manly, what's Manly?" Lyn was almost certain that this was what Andy had said to the taxi driver as she was dropped at the hotel. Manly, yes she was sure of it!"

"Manly, is a lovely place across the water from Sydney Harbour; its biggest attraction is Manly Beach; but I like to shop there because it has a lot of smaller shops and they're reasonably priced."

"I met someone on the plane who plays in a bar at Manly. Maybe I'll pop over there and try to find him. Do you know the name of any bars where a guitarist plays?" Lyn's heart quickened at the thought of finding where Andy hung out.

"There's dozens of bars in that area, and any number of them would have live music on certain nights, besides, wouldn't it be easier to just give him a ring? I don't hold much store with all that, wanting to surprise someone, it rarely works out like it does on the telly and besides none of the bars will be open until the evening, everyone will be watching the Melbourne Cup, remember. Quick! Quick! Look there's one there!"

Lyn jumped to attention and followed Crystals excited arm movements. And sure enough, a computer had at last become vacant.

"Done already!" Exclaimed Crystal, surprised to see Lyn return. "They haven't crashed, have they? It wouldn't surprise me after all that frenzied key-tapping."

"No, the computer's fine, I was expecting an email concerning my business, it'll probably arrive tomorrow, I just popped back in for the map."

Crystal folded the pamphlet into its original compact state and handed it to Lyn.

"What line of business are you in? If you don't mind me asking?"

Laden with disappointment and the need to get moving Lyn was in no mood for elaborating on how she earned a living; but anxious to avoid appearing too secretive, especially after all Crystal's help, she said simply. "I'm a Florist."

"I suggest that you head straight for the Botanical Gardens. The colours and smell of the flowers will blow your mind, and there'll be no sign of Melbourne Cup revellers there to spoil the experience."

Lyn checked her watch and found that she'd been walking for over half an hour, barely aware of anything that she'd passed. The disappointing hurt ran deep and she was torn between how best to bring about a solution to ease its corrosive influence. There'd been no contact from Vinny and she'd begun to doubt whether he'd had any intention of even trying to help. As soon as she reached Circular Quay, she could ferry over to Manly and begin her own search for the thieving bastard. But then again, if Crystal was right, what were the chances of finding him during the day?

There had been two emails in her inbox; the latest from Candy urging her to contact James because he was worried about her. Well he should have come with me as planned, thought Lyn, dismissing James from the equation and returning to the problem of today.

Sitting on a nearby wall, she removed a bottle of water from her bag. Taking several long swallows, her up-turned face locked on to an amazing sight. The magnificent span of Sydney-Harbour Bridge was directly above. As she squinted at the detail of the ironwork, she could just about make out a long row of strung-together walkers, looking more like ants from this distance, climbing the high-arching, metal-causeway. Watching those ant-people, experiencing the pleasure of their unique surroundings, helped her to decide how best to spend the rest of the morning. The second email had been from Jill and, as well as urging her to keep in touch regularly about how things were progressing with meeting her mother, it was a reminder to take lots of photographs of the Australian flora. Lyn decided to head to the perfect place for photographs and leave the murkier world of thief hunting until the evening.

Thanks to the Melbourne Cup, traffic was unusually light as Jennifer Beck's taxi made its way from the airport to her hotel. She might well be forced to return home sooner than the planned three days, so any time spent at the gallery today, before the big opening ceremony tomorrow, could ease any later pressure. A wave of nostalgia interrupted her train of thought as the taxi passed by sites that were particularly poignant. She adored this city. Always had and always will. So many of her happy memories were born here.

After his career was cut short in London, Pierre had taken advantage of the ten-pound assisted passage that was on offer during the 1960's and from the minute he'd stepped off the boat, after the six-week-long voyage, he knew without a shadow of a doubt, that he'd made the right decision. The Immigration Welcome Centre, at Coogee, had been bursting at the seams with families from all over Europe, eager to take advantage of a fresh start on the huge island where the sun never stopped shining. The atmosphere and camaraderie had made it very easy to make friends, and some of those friends were still kept in touch with today. Pierre had worked unstintingly, giving art and English lessons as well as working a ten-hour day at a local factory. His overriding aim was to provide a home, no matter how modest, for his woman and child.

Jennifer had arrived nine months later on a similar assisted passage. Unfortunately, their baby had to be left behind in England with Jennifer's mother. A chest infection had left the child very weak and the doctor warned that a six-week sea journey could prove fatal.

Jennifer forced her thoughts away from the sadness of having made that decision and shifted back to the happy memory of meeting Pierre at the docking point at Sydney. Three days later they were married and five weeks after their marriage they were ready to move into their very first home—a tiny rented apartment close to where Pierre worked. Jennifer had been only eighteen, but soon found work cleaning for the better-off in the local community, saving every penny so that she could return to England and bring back little Fleur.

"Here we are lady." The taxi stopped at the foyer of Darling Harbour's most expensive hotel.

"Would you mind waiting? I need to go on to the Exhibition Centre after checking in at reception."

"No worries. Give me a chance to listen to the race, see if I've got something to celebrate!"

Chapter 18

The heart of Sydney had slowed to a pace which could only be described as, barely ticking over. No doubt this happened early on Sunday mornings, bank-holidays and Christmas; but today was Tuesday, it was the middle of the afternoon on what should have been an ordinary working day. Lyn had emerged from the lush greenery of the Botanical Gardens looking for a suitable place to have a long, cold drink. She walked across wide roads devoid of traffic to an area dotted with pavement cafes. The cafes, whose owners had made it obvious that a television set was available, were stacked out with customers, their faces locked in one direction. After choosing one of the quieter establishments, Lyn soon found, with mounting frustration, that the staff had disappeared to the nearest screen showing the Melbourne Cup Race. Determined not to be held hostage to a bloody horse race, she noisily scraped back the chair she'd settled in and headed for a parade of shops she'd remembered seeing near Circular Quay station.

With an ice-cold bottle of coke and a large packet of crisps tucked under her arm, she marched toward an empty bench on the quayside; a bench that stood well away from any cafes and bars, because the screaming of the gulls was preferred to the manic commentary of the race. The protective shield of cloud, promised for the whole day, was beginning to thin and break-up, causing the afternoon temperature to rise into the high twenties. After quenching her thirst and finishing the bag of crisps, Lyn decided a ferry across the water to her hotel would be a much more sensible and enjoyable option than the long walk she'd taken that morning.

Twenty minutes waiting for the next ferry to Darling Harbour gave her the opportunity to run through the photos that she'd taken in the Botanical Gardens, intending to send Jill a couple of the best shots when she finally got round to answering her earlier email. As she flicked through the dozen or so frozen scenes, she was transferred back to the sheer beauty of the place. A stand of Jacaranda trees, arching overhead and dripping with blue blossom, was a perfect contrast to the white clouds above it. Several swathes of green-leaved, golden-headed Cannas, competing for attention with the same species of crimson-headed purple-leaved variety, were also a particularly good composition which she knew Jill would love. An irresistible third choice was a large group of fruit-bats, inverted and suspended from a tall tree that towered above a grouping of fan-palms. Lyn promised herself a return trip to the gardens during sunset; just for the joy of watching the bats take flight to their feeding grounds.

After boarding the ferry, the camera was tucked reluctantly back inside her bag; the battery needed to be recharged so any more shots would just have to wait for another day. In no time at all she was back on dry land mounting the steps on the harbour which led to the area of her hotel. She stopped suddenly in her tracks! The door to the Exhibition Centre was open and curiosity got the better of her.

From where she stood, Lyn had only a partial view of Jennifer Beck's work, which had been displayed at eye level along the north-facing wall of the spacious gallery. She took several steps through the open doorway and a broader span of the paintings was revealed. She moved closer, hardly believing her own eyes.

Since the unexpected discovery, nearly twelve months ago, that Jennifer Beck her mother, was still alive, Lyn had accessed her web site many times in an effort to find out all she could about the famous artist. But lack of personal data had always left Lyn feeling frustrated. However, admiration for her work and the desire to own a piece of it had grown. Unfortunately, there was no sign here of the beautifully executed, still-life floral paintings that Lyn had imagined embellishing her studio wall in Torbay. Jennifer Beck's latest work was completely at odds with Lyn's expectations. Her brow furrowed as she stared at a particular 80x80cm painting. It seemed like she was looking at a floral display through a fractured mirror. It was confusing and disturbing.

A cough from behind caused Lyn to turn in surprise! Jennifer Beck, the woman who had given birth to her, the woman who had abandoned her as a babe in arms in order to follow her own dreams in the sun, was standing approximately ten metres away with a large folder in her hand.

Jennifer Beck placed the folder on a nearby table then turned to face the woman who had wandered through the door; reaching out her right hand as she slowly and gracefully walked toward her. "I'm so sorry to have startled you. The exhibition isn't officially open until tomorrow but please feel free to wander; you can barely move around on opening day and that's mainly due to the complimentary glass of wine."

Lyn remained silent; unsure how to respond. There was no doubting that this woman before her was the artist in the life-size posters; but in the flesh she looked older and there was an aura of sadness about her that obviously hadn't been apparent in any of the photographs that Lyn had seen. Her clothes and makeup were impeccable. She wore a stylish, mint-green linen suit and colour matched sandals which complimented her trim figure and tanned skin. Looking down at her own crumpled shorts and comfortable walking shoes, Lyn suddenly felt embarrassed and blurted out. "Sorry for barging in; the door was open. And I was curious."

"You're obviously English, are you on vacation?"

"My name's Lyn Porter, you probably don't remember, but I phoned you last month."

Jennifer paused for a moment before a beaming smile broke forth. "Of course, I knew I'd heard that voice before; you're the florist from the south west of England."

Without warning, both of Jennifer Beck's hands were touching her! The right one had somehow managed to take hold of Lyn's left and was squeezing gently in a hand-shake whilst the other rested on her left shoulder. The woman was talking to her; but the words weren't registering. Lyn looked into her eyes, smelt her perfume, witnessed her smile, which made the tiredness disappear, but even if her life depended on it, she couldn't recall a single word that was said since feeling her mother's touch.

Flushed with confusion and a sudden rising resentment, Lyn turned back to the paintings, abruptly cutting the physical contact. "Is this exhibition only showing your latest pieces?" She waved a dismissive hand across the area where the paintings were hung."

"Yes, and I can sense your disappointment Lyn. If I remember correctly, you wanted to buy a piece of my work for your studio."

"I was hoping to choose two, actually; I admired the purity and honesty of the paintings that are shown on your web site; but I don't like these at all! I find them disturbing!"

"I have a steady following of collectors and they've been making overtures for some time now that I should branch away from images that are too naturalistic. Images that can be reproduced from any good, high-pixel camera. Don't get me wrong, I'm not looking to use them as an excuse, I too have found it quite stimulating to diversify and express feelings and mood instead of just capturing the pure beauty of the bloom."

Lyn forced herself to look at the woman she was criticising "I'm sorry, I know art is subjective but as I said, I find them disturbing."

"Maybe my life *is* disturbing at present and *you* have a well-developed intuition." There was no sign of sarcasm in artist's words; but a hint of the previous sadness, shifted across her elegant face.

The trilling sound of a phone echoed through the high-ceilinged space, and Lyn noticed a wave of panic disturb the artist's features even more. Jennifer Beck retrieved a neat, mobile phone from the slit pocket of her A-line skirt and flipped open the top. "Excuse me, Lyn, I need to answer this; why don't you run through the folder of my earlier work, I'll be back soon."

Footsteps were barely heard as Jennifer Beck retreated to a room in the far corner of the gallery. Lyn tried hard to calm her hammering heart as she sat at the table and opened the folder.

The artist closed the door on the gallery and perched on a window seat that overlooked one of the Harbour's magnificent water sculptures. Her order book still lay open on a nearby table where she had been bringing her paperwork up to date. The sound of footsteps in the gallery, had put paid to that. She hadn't thought for one moment that someone was about to take flight with one of her paintings; but she had been trusted with the keys to the gallery and felt duty bound to honour that trust. Before returning the call she'd just missed, she watched a small boy splashing his bare feet in the cool running water of the child-friendly water sculpture. His look of delight and the squeals of joy brought a mixture of pleasure and pain.

"Pauline, how is he?" Jennifer listened carefully to the owner of the nursing home, learning that Pierre was being very difficult. His aggression, apparently, was upsetting the others and Dr Sanderson had been informed. Jennifer knew what was coming; but this time she was determined. "I understand your concerns Pauline; but try explaining to him that I'll be back tomorrow. I'm sure he'll calm down once he realises he's only there for the one night. I'll put in an appearance here tomorrow morning and catch the afternoon flight back. Sedation only leaves him more confused and alienated; and it's this that Pierre fears more than anything." Jennifer's body relaxed as Pauline agreed to calm him verbally before doing anything else. "Thank you, Pauline, I'll speak to Pierre this evening by phone if you think it will cam him. I am very grateful for all your help."

She slipped the phone into her pocket and made her way back to Lyn Porter, whose head was bent in deep concentration over the folder.

For the second time Lyn was startled as Jennifer Beck suddenly appeared beside her and asked "Have you seen anything that's more to your liking?"

"All of it, especially this!" Lyn had opened the folder at random and before her was the picture of a blond-haired toddler who was the image of her own grandson, Martin, except for the fact that this child was about a year older. In the picture, the toddler was holding a red rose by its stem. The stem of the rose, which was dotted with sharp thorns, had punctured his thumb and caused him to cry. A tear, rolling over the child's chubby cheek, reflected the head of the rose at a given point and it was at this given point that the composition was frozen. Lyn had fallen in love with the image, the moment she saw it.

Jennifer had been mentally running through the changes she needed to make to her reservations, until she saw what Lyn was engrossed in.

"How on earth? I'm sorry, Lyn; but that's been put in the wrong folder. It's not my work. It's a photographic piece done by my partner."

"It's beautiful. Is it for sale?"

"No! No, this is just a small copy of the original that was produced over thirty-five years ago."

Lyn wanted to ask who the child was but sensed that this was not a good time to start gathering personal information. "Look, I've taken up enough of your free time. Which will be the most convenient of the three days to run through your folder? To see if there's anything else that I find irresistible?"

Jennifer groaned inwardly. This woman had flown halfway around the globe to purchase a piece of her work and circumstances dictated that she could only be in Sydney for half of the opening day. "Are you and your partner staying nearby?"

The question caught Lyn by surprise. "Yes, a five minute walk away; but I'm here on my own actually; James's had to cancel, his work commitments changed."

Jennifer sensed the woman's disappointment and was reluctant to add to it. "My circumstances are also a little fraught right now and unfortunately I can only stay for the morning of tomorrow. I don't want to presume what your plans are but if you take the folder back to your hotel and peruse it without me breathing down your neck, I promise to find time during the morning. Or, if you have no other plans for this evening, join me for dinner and if you've discovered a piece that you'd like, I'll do the paperwork after we have eaten."

Again Lyn was taken aback, but quickly realising that this might be the only opportunity to discover answers to questions she'd become obsessed with. She asked boldly. "Which hotel, and how do I get there?"

Filled with relief that the embarrassment of letting down a potentially new client had been overcome, and happy with the thought that she wouldn't now be dining alone— a situation that always filled her with dread—Jennifer took hold of the folder and walked with Lyn to the front entrance of the gallery. "You see that delightful fountain?" She pointed out the lavish reception to Darling Harbour's most prestigious hotel. "That is the entrance to my hotel. I'll meet you there at 7-30." Jennifer handed Lyn the folder, squeezing her hand again. "I'm really looking forward to getting to know you better."

Chapter 19

Tuesday Morning—Torbay

James resisted the urge to let his frustration get the better of him. If there was one thing he'd learnt over the years, since qualifying as a solicitor, no matter how bad a situation, no matter how slowly a case was progressing, nothing was to be gained by losing one's temper. He had just replaced the receiver of his phone after speaking, for the third time with Natasha, the receptionist at the hotel where Lyn was staying. James sensed Natasha's disappointment at not having been successful in coordinating a time for him to speak with the woman he loved. He'd thanked her for trying and asked if she would give Ms Porter the simple message "Please forgive me."

A light tap on his office door and the smell of cigarette smoke propelled James to his feet. He'd never hidden the fact that he disliked the smell of tobacco in his office or rooms and to prevent his no smoking rule being broken he marched over to the door and snatched it open. "Stefan, good morning. I believe birthday greetings are the order of the day?"

"Thank you, Mr Fairbank. Today is my birthday, yes."

"What is it Stefan, you don't appear to be filled with birthday cheer? I would have thought that Elena's, Happy Birthday, text from last night, would have eased your concern."

"How far away is Lyme Regis from here Mr Fairbank?"

"Stefan, we are friends aren't we? Please call me James, and tell me what's happening at Lyme Regis." James ushered the gentle giant of a man through his door and offered him a seat. Stefan remained standing.

"I speak frank with you Mr Fairbank. Last night, as you say, I have text message from Elena." Stefan held up a hand to prevent James from interrupting. "Is good yes, she text me for saying Happy Birthday; but is not her phone, the number is strange to me. I send two messages asking where she is. She no reply! One hour ago I ring this strange number and lady in Lyme Regis say she let Elena use her phone to send message. This lady tell me, Elena and tall man with golden hair and light blue eyes are eating in same restaurant as her. This is the man, Carl, yes?" Stefan fell silent waiting for James to respond.

"It sounds like Carl, Stefan, and Lyme Regis is not a large town; but how on earth do you intend to find Elena?"

"I *will* find her; but I need car. Can I use your car Mr Fairbank?"

"That would be against the law Stefan."

"I have proper licence, from when I work in London and if I have map to follow."

"It's a question of the Insurance, Stefan; can't you drive over there with Vincent? He's the one with the skills for ferreting out leads on finding people" James sensed that there'd been a disagreement between the two of them and asked when he'd need the car.

"For the afternoon only, I promise I good driver and leave no scratches on car. I leave this as my bond" Stefan dug deep into the inside, zipped pocket of his leather jacket and pressed a silver pocket watch and chain into James's palm. "This was my father's and his father also, is very precious for me; but Elena more precious."

"I will keep it safe for you Stefan and I'll phone my Insurance Broker and get him to change my policy to allow you to drive legally for twenty-four hours. I would come with you but I have two appointments this afternoon; what's Vincent up to today?"

Stefan shrugged, it was obvious he didn't want to give anything away; but a favour had been granted and everything had its price. "He's trying to put right, the damage to his reputation and we disagree on the best way for him to do it."

Vinny heard Stefan entering the front door He shut down the computer and pushed Lyn Porter out of his mind. He had enough on his plate without running around after the stupid bitch. After all, it wasn't his fault that she'd allowed some young punk to circumnavigate her body, discovering a wedge of money on route, the lucky git. It was going to be one of those weeks, he could feel it in his bones. He was already well out of pocket; what with the damage to the van and not getting paid for the squatters job. Stefan had proved to be invaluable where the Eastern Europeans were concerned. He knew what made them tick, and, he knew just the right method to retrieve what was taken, without involving the law and without anyone getting hurt. Trouble was, Nick, from the Debt-Collection-Agency, also thought Stefan was a boy wonder and had asked Vinny for Stefan's mobile number. Vincent had obliged before Nick (the slippery bastard) then went on to ask if Stefan was looking for a regular job. Vinny had spun him a yarn that the lad was only here on holiday and due to return to his job after the next weekend; and in the meantime he was just helping out for a bit of holiday cash.

Then out of the blue, Stefan wants to use the van for the afternoon. Well, you don't have to be fucking brain of Britain to work out the fucking obvious, and if Stefan's taken on by Nick, there'll be less fucking work coming this way!

Stefan came into the office carrying two mugs of steaming coffee and placed one in front of Vinny.

"The milk is finished, Vincent, and bread is also finished. I go to shop for supplies, yes?"

"We've got at least a dozen security locks to fit this morning, so I suggest the shopping is done this afternoon."

"I have other plans for afternoon Vincent, I don't expect for you to pay me when I not working, but I need to make journey."

"You can't make a fucking journey without fucking transport and I need the van. Understood?"

"Mr Fairbank say I can use *his* car."

Stefan watched as Vincent, in response to his announcement, grabbed the mug and took a large gulp. The freshly made coffee, containing only a tiny dribble of milk, was hotter than usual. Vincent danced around the office—eyes watering, hands flapping and his face turning a deep shade of red—looking desperately for somewhere to expel the burning liquid. Eventually, it was spat, at considerable force, into the metal waste-paper bin, before he marched out of the door and slammed it behind him.

Without bothering to knock, Vinny stomped into the solicitor's office to find him relaxed in his leather swivel chair with the phone in one hand and a pen poised over a blank pad, in the other.

"No, I don't mind holding." He heard Jimmy say to the mouthpiece, in his usual, annoyingly courteous way, whilst gesturing to him to sit down.

He was too pent up to sit down! His mouth was burning like mad, he felt like he'd been had-over by his best client and the two men whom he had regarded as friends, were colluding to stiff him. After impatiently marching the width of the office space several times, a marked shift in the solicitor's body language coupled with the loud outburst of "How much?" helped Vinny to focus on something other than his own immediate discomfort.

"But it's only for a few hours," continued the solicitor, pen discarded and pad shoved to one side. Vinny felt sure that before too long he'd pick up what was suddenly rattling the man; but unfortunately Jimmy's final sentence before slamming down the phone wasn't enough of a clue. "In spite of his age, that quote is bordering on daylight robbery! Now I suggest you do your job properly, and trawl through a few more companies until you find a more reasonable one.

"I'll bet that was a sixty-year-old granny with arthritis who you've just torn to shreds. Shame on you!"

"Vincent, how many times do I have to remind you that in a civilised society, it's customary to knock before entering another person's office. How can I help you?"

Realising that he wasn't going to gain anything from Jimmy's phone call, Vinny ploughed straight in "Why are you lending Stefan your car this afternoon."

"There's obviously been a disagreement between the two of you but you can't expect me to take sides, Vincent."

"Take sides, take fucking sides, you do know where the ungrateful bastard's going and after all I've done for him?" Unable to control his anger at the perceived treachery that had occurred, Vinny spewed out his worst fears; interlaced with a good measure of colourful language.

"Let me get this straight, Stefan asked to borrow the van for the afternoon but you didn't actually ask him what he needed it for?"

"Are you fucking deaf? I know what's going down! He didn't need to spell it out."

James heaved a heavy sigh. His attention skipped between the aborted telephone conversation and what Vincent had just revealed. "Would you like a piece of helpful advice Vincent?"

"Not really; but I know I'm going to get it anyway!" He slumped into the chair opposite his adviser but turned his head defiantly toward the window.

"I'm sure that you are aware that today is Stefan's birthday, and, in spite of your name calling, I know you happen to be quite fond of him." Vinny's head swung round and he glared at the solicitor; he was about to let rip in defence of his sexuality but Jimmy continued in his maddening, preaching way. "As a happy birthday treat, why not offer to accompany him on this journey, that he needs to take. Not only will you learn the truth behind its necessity but it will bind your friendship and heal your differences. I'm not a bad judge of character, Vincent, and I think Stefan is too honourable a man to be taking advantage of you behind your back."

Vinny unconsciously patted his still-tingling lips as he thought through Jimmy's proposal. Then changed the subject completely "When you next speak to Lyn Porter, tell her that there's sod-all I can do from this end; in spite of the fact that she now knows where to find the thief. And whilst on the subject of advice giving, I could do with a holiday; maybe you'd like to cover my expenses and I could fly out to Oz and give this guy a good hiding for her." He stood to leave just as Jimmy's phone rang again. He watched, as the solicitor listened to the voice on the other end, interrupting after just a few seconds. "No, that is still far too much; I think we'll forget the whole thing. Goodbye!"

"Come on Stefan, we have work to do," shouted Vinny as he walked into his own office. "As a special birthday treat, we'll take the afternoon off and we'll head off to wherever you like."

"I'd like to head off to Lyme Regis my friend; and I'll explain why as we drive there." Stefan's face beamed with satisfaction. His little plan had worked well.

Candy Laverne picked up her phone, dialled a number then replaced the receiver before any ringing could commence. This was the second time she'd procrastinated. She'd gained snippets of information, from several sources, on a subject she'd found intensely interesting and she wanted to know more; trouble was, the snippets were hearsay and Candy preferred information straight from the horses mouth, no exaggeration, no watering down, just the simple honest truth.

The subject that had intrigued her came to light after James Fairbank let slip that the main reason for Lyn Porter's visit to Australia was so that she could meet up with her, long-presumed-dead mother. As far as Candy knew, it was a three week romantic holiday in the sun and an opportunity to visit and purchase a couple of paintings from an artist whose work Lyn admired.

Earlier, she'd had a long conversation with Jill, Lyn's partner, who was keeping the business ticking over whilst Lyn was away. Jill was very free with information, and Candy had been brought up to date regarding Lyn's one and only email sent to her partner with a few photographic attachments. According to the email, Lyn was having dinner that evening at the artist's hotel. There was no mention of emotional reunions, tears of happiness or any indication that Lyn had even mentioned the word, Mother. During Jill's conversation, she had hinted that Lyn was anxious to check out any siblings that might think Lyn was a gold-digger, looking to cash in on any future inheritance, but just how this was to be achieved was anyone's guess.

186

Candy had sent the promised fax, the document headed V.C. Enterprises and signed by Carl, to James Fairbank over half an hour ago and assumed he would have responded by now. His response, especially if it was by phone would give her the perfect opportunity to find out what was going on in Sydney as well as what was happening in Torbay. With gritty determination the number was dialled a third time. Who cares if he thought her a nosy old bat, she'd survived worse things in her life.

The ringing continued for seven rounds before the answer phone kicked in. Frustration and disappointment caused Candy to cut short James's well mannered, beautifully spoken excuse for not being available.

James knew it was his phone that was ringing; but he was on a mission and turning back, unlocking the office and reaching his phone just in time to hear that his Insurance broker had miraculously found a company who wasn't run by the Shylocks of this world, wasn't going to aid him in that mission. He was on his way to the local chemist, to pick up the typed analysis of the Viagra-type-capsule from his pharmacist friend. And if the analysis was as damning as Stefan had predicted, this,coupled with the fax that had arrived from Candy Laverne, there should be enough evidence to stop Carl in his vile and corrupt tracks. By the end of the day, the whereabouts of Elena should be known, giving her brother a chance to bring her up to date with Carl's deadly intentions, and, Peter Radcliffe would have been given the true facts surrounding Carl's intentions regarding The Terrace property.

He wasn't sure how Peter would react to the cancelling of his imminent marriage to the young and beautiful Elena; James would have to tread carefully, feeding him the information a little at a time.

Peter Radcliffe frantically pulled back the top and bottom bolts, breaking his finger nail in the process. Kicking his daily newspaper to one side along with a scattering of mail he released the mechanism on the five-lever-lock and yanked open his front door.

"Damn and bugger", he cursed in the chill of the mid-morning air. He'd caught sight of James Fairbank from his upstairs window heading toward town and had realised there and then that this was the man who may well get him out of his current situation; but he hadn't acted fast enough, the solicitor was already twenty yards or so past Peter's property, marching like a soldier on parade.

The last couple of days had been full of anxiety. He had tried rationalising. His life was bound to be stressful, he was about to marry a woman a third of his age; but would he be up to it? The evening before, he'd decided to experiment by taking one of the magic capsules and emptying its contents into a glass of orange juice. Then with pencil and paper at the ready, pyjama bottoms removed and his dressing gown gaping open, he'd settled down to a CD of enchanting music to record timings and results. But after taking the first tentative sip, a scratching sound and a slight movement in the corner of the log basket by his feet, caught his attention. Keeping his eyes fixed on the area, Peter reached behind for his glasses, knocking over the potent elixir and sending it crashing to the floor. A startled mouse shot over Peter's bare foot and headed into his kitchen where it disappeared from sight.

Realisation had gradually begun to dawn. The dream, the promise of excitement and fulfilment which Carl had said was there for the taking, was losing its appeal. He needed to find an escape route! And once he'd accepted that this was not what he really wanted, he'd begun to feel less stressed. But Carl and Anna were real enough and out of the two of them, the latter was the biggest headache.

He sifted through the mail, dropping most of it in the waste bin and positioned the postcard from South Africa on the mantelpiece—a second reminder of Anna's arrival— as if he could forget. He decided to prepare a pot of coffee and sit glued to the window and await James's return, hoping that the solicitor wouldn't be long.

A smile crept over his face, rearranging the wrinkles into an interesting pattern, as the head and shoulders of his neighbour came into view over the brow of the hill. He dashed to the door and waited.

"Good morning James, I've just made a pot of fresh coffee, will you join me?" Peter beckoned to his neighbour and took hold of his arm once he became level with his front porch.

"That's decent of you Peter, save me the bother when I get back to the office." James had been looking for an excuse to knock on Peter's door. The analysis on the capsule was indeed very dangerous for a man of Peter's age. The pharmacist had insisted on knowing the age of the recipient before giving James any information.

Each man courteously allowed the other to sip on their respective coffees before broaching the subject of why one had been invited in and the other had gladly accepted without a minutes thought to time and the working day. Suddenly, they both spoke at once; a double apology was followed by yet another period of silence.

"I take it you need a little more advice Peter?" James leaned back into the sagging cushions of the armchair and took another sip of coffee, his eyes remaining fixed on the older man's face.

"And I take it that you are more than happy to give it."

"I am a solicitor Peter, and giving advice is how I earn my living. But as neighbours, I'll do what I can, within reason, and time is ticking away." James made a point of checking his watch, and was horrified to see how late it was.

"I want you to advice me on the best way to disentangle myself from this, this arrangement with Carl. Can we escape on the grounds that the contract is somehow illegal; you intimated that this might be the case."

"The contract, it's true, does contain anomalies, and any solicitor worthy of his title would have advised you against signing it; but sign it you did and the two weeks, which is the usual timescale for allowing one to change their mind, has long passed. What I would suggest you do, is write to V.C. Enterprises and inform them that due to unforeseen circumstances you would like to pay back the loan in full straight away, including any interest due, and just see what happens."

"I've already spent over half of the money, man! I needed it to refurbish this place, you know that already."

"Oh come on Peter, you must have stocks and shares, bonds or property with land that you can sell; you've been a successful accountant for most of your working life."

"During my so-called successful years as an accountant, I paid a small fortune into a pension fund which could have bought me several properties; it's now worth only a third of the amount promised, and the only asset, apart from my home, is a miserable strip of land that runs along the back of six near-derelict shops. It's used as allotments and brings in about five bob a week. I took it on as a bad debt years ago, after realising that I wasn't going to see a penny of the enormous account that was owed."

"Do you have the deeds and full rights to the land?"

"Well of course I do, I'm not a complete moron; but take it from me, it's not a wide enough strip for building on, unless you were a family of Pygmies. I haven't been down there in years. My last visit ended in a row with the three belligerent old boys whose lives consisted mainly in growing the biggest marrows and gaudiest coloured dahlias. I respectfully suggested that an increase in the allotment rent was way overdue. I think a lot of in-breeding went on down that end of town; they chased me off waving spades and hoes At the time, I was thankful they didn't own a shot gun! Suffice to say, I haven't been back since."

"So you still have half of the money you borrowed, and this strip of land?" James waited for confirmation but Peter looked uncomfortable and squirmed a little in his seat."

"No, not exactly half; on the day of the marriage, I've agreed to hand over twenty thousand pounds, in cash, to Carl. A colossal amount, I know, but…"

"Do you still intend to go ahead with this sham of a wedding?"

"No! No I can't! My circumstances have changed you see. Anna, my daughter, is arriving in a couple of weeks; but the twenty thousand is non-refundable, Carl made that absolutely clear. I've been thinking James, now that things have cooled between you and the delightful Lyn, perhaps you would like to take my place. Elena is a couple of decades younger than Lyn and these Eastern Europeans are such hard workers, you could dismiss any domestics you currently employ and even train her up as a secretary; and, as far as the problems you were having in the bedroom department, I'd throw in the dozen Viagra capsules. What do you say?"

The incredulity of what Peter was suggesting left James lost for words. Taking his silence as a positive, Peter continued the pressure. "In three days time James, you could be happily married to a young and beautiful woman. The twenty thousand covers all the paperwork and even the gold ring, its very tempting don't you think?"

Keeping his opinions of Peter's ridiculous proposal to himself, James silently withdrew a folded piece of paper from his jacket pocket. "I thought you might like to read the analysis on those wonder pills of yours. In a man of your age and condition, one dosage could trigger a fatal heart-attack; thank you for the coffee, Peter. I'll see myself out."

Peter's eyes fell on the decreasing patch of dampness on the rug and knew he was right. He just had to find a way out of this mess!

Chapter 20

Tuesday—7.00pm—Sydney

Lyn was ready to go, had been for the last ten minutes; but Natasha was determined and she knew that if she stepped out of her room before seven she would be caught out. She'd been pounced on as soon as she'd set foot in the hotel. James, according to Natasha, had been trying desperately to contact her since she'd arrived two days ago.

"Please call him back!" The receptionist had whined, as if her life depended on it." Lyn had told her that she needed a new phone card and wasn't prepared to pay the exorbitant tariff imposed by the hotel, but Natasha had persisted. She'd pushed the reception phone under Lyn's nose, jammed her finger down hard on the key to activate an outside line and said "At least let the poor guy know that you've arrived safely, you have my word that the call will not go on your bill."

Lyn had jammed the keys just as hard, easily remembering the code and James's number. After listening for a while, strumming her fingers in earshot of Natasha, she'd spoken into James's answer phone. "Hi James, it's Lyn.

Obviously you're not at home right now; I'll catch you another time. Bye for now."

But Natasha hadn't given up. "I'm on duty until seven and he's bound to phone again; I take it you'll be in your room?"

"Natasha, I haven't come all this way to spend my evenings sitting in a hotel room. If I'm there, I'll answer, if I don't answer, it means I'm out, got that?" She had then marched off to the bank of computers to check her emails.

Her inbox had been empty. Disappointment, frustration and anger rose like an uncoiling snake from the pit of her stomach. She'd checked her address book, just to make sure that she'd got Vinny's email address right, knowing in her heart that she had. Infuriated, she had typed in the words *Thanks for your help. I'll deal with it myself…* Then pressed SEND, quickly, before she had had the chance to wither and change her mind. After checking her watch, she had moved quickly on to Jill. Realising that there wouldn't be much time for forwarding all the photos and a lengthy email; she'd typed the brief message. *Been invited out to dinner! Will fill you in tomorrow.*

Twice, during what should have been her leisurely preparations for the evening, her room phone had rung. The first time, she'd been in the middle of washing her hair and totally ignored it. The second time had been just a few minutes ago. She could easily have answered, she was barely three feet away applying makeup; but, something had stopped her from connecting to the man she thought she had loved. All Lyn wanted right now, was to sit quietly in the hotel's bar with a relaxing drink. Just a little Dutch courage before dining with Jennifer Beck.

It was ten past seven before she finally ventured from the room, using the back stairs which conveniently avoided reception. Within a few minutes, she was sitting at the empty bar, dry martini and tonic water in hand and Jennifer Beck's folder opened before her. She had already scanned through a couple of times, from the privacy of her room; but now there was a little time to look carefully. Drawn once again to the copy of the tearful child holding the rose, she carefully removed it from its plastic protector. On the back, words as sharp as the rose thorns, read.

Life can be so bloody cruel.

After leaving Jennifer's folder with the immaculately-dressed doorman, the two women were escorted to a window table overlooking the splendour of Darling Harbour. The sky was dark; a perfect backdrop for the myriad of bright lights. The hotel restaurant was very busy but a calm assurance of wealth and status permeated the air. Conversations were low-key and although there were plenty of smiling faces, the spontaneous laughter that Lyn had become accustomed to hearing since arriving in Sydney, was nonexistent.

"What would you like to drink, ladies?" asked the handsome young waiter as he flicked open the white linen table napkins and laid them across each of their laps.

Jennifer Beck spoke first. "I'd like a sparkling mineral water with a twist of lime, please." She turned to Lyn and explained that she never drank alcohol the day before taking a flight, adding, "But please, you have whatever you like Lyn."

"That's fine for me too." She had already downed two martinis in quick succession and was anxious to keep her wits about her.

The food was superb—three courses which were easily managed due to the well thought out, digestible amounts. Conversation mainly revolved around the paintings and if Lyn had seen anything in the folder that would suit her. She'd answered by saying that she'd like to run through them again in Jennifer's presence. Lyn's earlier anger and frustration had calmed. The martinis had helped; the luxury and the ambience of this hotel, compared to the bare-bones, business like atmosphere of her own had also helped; but what had helped most of all, was the sensing that all was not well in Jennifer Beck's life. Up close, small personal things that had been overlooked earlier stood out. Several stray hairs on the artist's lower jaw and between her eyebrows were screaming to be plucked. Slightly chipped nail polish, on hands that would surely, under normal circumstances, be well-manicured, told of a hurried departure and a need to get back home.

This was confirmed as they moved into the lavishly furnished lounge for coffee. Jennifer had just retrieved her folder from the desk and her order book from her bag, when a smart-suited gentleman appeared by her side and whispered into her ear.

"Sorry Lyn, we are interrupted again by a phone call; but I do need to take it!"

On her return she looked pale and preoccupied. Lyn poured coffee from the pot and pushed it toward her. "Not bad news, I hope."

"I asked them not to. I told them it only makes matters worse, why on earth don't they listen?" For a while Jennifer Beck seemed unaware of Lyn's presence.

"I'm a good listener; it's the least I can do after such a lovely meal." Jennifer Beck needed to unburden and Lyn was more than happy to oblige.

There was slight resistance; but Lyn soon learned that Jennifer's partner, having been placed in a nursing home whilst she was attending the exhibition, had taken a turn for the worse and had been given drugs that played havoc with his condition. Jennifer didn't actually say what that condition was, only that he was deteriorating.

Curious about this partner who had produced the intriguing photograph of the blond haired boy, Lyn asked "How long have you and your partner worked together?"

Jennifer looked confused. It was only after several moments that the meaning of Lyn's question hit home. "He's my partner in the truest sense. Pierre is my husband. He is my soul-mate! We've been together since I was seventeen, he was my first love and I've never loved another!"

Lyn was shocked into silence! It suddenly dawned on her that they were talking about her father! Unlike her mother, there had been no picture of him in Gran's chest of drawers and there had been no mention of him on Jennifer Beck's website. She'd just assumed that he'd either died or moved on to some unknown place. He was alive! And by the sound of it, he could be dead pretty soon! But right now he was alive and Lyn was determined to see him before it was too late.

Feeling relieved, Jennifer closed her order book and tucked the folder out of the way. For a while she had been under the impression that Lyn Porter had wanted commissioned work for her studio in England; but a series of small paintings— executed to celebrate the New Millennium—had really excited her. This series had been based on The Secret Meaning of Flowers. Twenty-one blooms—each picture measuring thirty centimetres square—had taken almost three years of continual hard work. The research, the gaining of permission from various people and organisations to quote wording from the history of associated meanings, had been laborious; but eventually, when all the necessary correspondents were in place, putting paint to paper had been its own reward. Just as well; to date, she had only managed to sell three from the series. 'Young and Beautiful'—a red rose bud—was bought as a christening present for a couple's first granddaughter, 'Woman's Love'—carnation—was sold as a gift from wife to husband on their wedding anniversary, and 'Passion'—yellow iris—was bought anonymously.

Jennifer had unconsciously begun to relax; her work was her solace and when she was involved, nothing else penetrated. "The Sweet Violet, which represents, Modesty, was the first painting in the series, and my personal favourite; I'm so pleased that at last someone else likes it enough to want to buy it. My inspiration for it came from a Floral Border in an ancient Book of Hours. Peach Blossom too, was a delight to paint; but I think its meaning 'I Am Your Captive' was taken too literally for the modern woman. How would you like them sent Lyn? Unframed would obviously be cheaper and less vulnerable."

Lyn sensed the lowering of Jennifer Beck's guard. "There are two more that I might be interested in, but I'd like to see them first."

"These samples are done by high-resolution photography; I promise you, if you like the photos you'll love the real thing."

"Nevertheless, I'd like to stand back and view the full-size painting; it will help me to visualise the placing of them in my studio. Are they available from a Sydney gallery?"

"I'm afraid not, they're at my studio in Twin Waters."

"Well, I'll just have to travel to Twin Waters, wherever that is, I really do want to return to England with the paintings, and as you say, unframed and placed in a tube would make that possible."

Jennifer was at a loss for words. She wanted to sell her paintings, naturally, but since the onset of Pierre's illness, she'd discouraged any invasion of their privacy. "Lyn, Twin Waters is in Queensland, a three day drive from here or an internal flight away, I can't expect you to go to those lengths."

"My booked arrangements included an internal flight. James and I had intended to see more of Australia than Sydney; I might as well put to good use what's been paid for. I'm sure you'll be able to recommend accommodation in the area and I promise not to be a burden on you or your time."

Jennifer flushed with shame and embarrassment. "Of course you may come if that's what you want. "I'm leaving tomorrow on the early afternoon flight to Brisbane, I'll check availability for you and if possible we can travel up together. I'll also give Martha, my daily help, a ring, and ask her to prepare one of the guest rooms for you. I'll see you at the exhibition tomorrow morning, to finalise the arrangements, goodnight Lyn and thank you." Jennifer stood and offered her hand. She smiled; but behind the smile, Lyn sensed a deep concern.

A nervous excitement propelled Lyn up the steps and through the revolving doors of her own hotel; but as she headed for the lift the calling of her name stopped her in her tracks.

"Ms Porter, excuse me, are you Ms Porter?" A middle-aged man with a slight limp, hobbled toward her waving a piece of paper in his right hand.

"Yes, I'm Lyn Porter, is there a problem?" It took a few seconds for the man, who according to the badge on his lapel was named Mark, to find enough breath to answer. Eventually, Lyn learned that she would be receiving a phone call at 10-00pm, on the dot, and that Mark would patch it through to her room. He then went on to apologise for his slowness on the job as he'd been in a motor-bike accident and was only released from hospital two days ago. Lyn had a sudden image of the young and energetic Natasha. This ailing night-receptionist had easily succeeded in a task that had brought her nothing but failure and frustration.

It was almost ten o'clock by the time Lyn was propped comfortably on her bed and resigned to having a conversation with James. Her feelings for him stirred and warmed as she concentrated on the good times they'd shared. She made up her mind to tell him everything that had happened since her arrival, including the chance of meeting up with both of her parents.

She picked up on the second ring "Hi, sorry I've been so difficult to get hold of."

"No you haven't; after getting the number from Jill, I found it remarkably easy to get through; and you sound so clear, you could be in the next room. So how are you enjoying the land of plenty Mum…Mum, are you still there?"

"Sorry Sarah, I was expecting the phone call to be from James."

"I thought James was there with you."

"No, something came up, you know how it is."

"No, not really, if Fergus and I make up our mind to do something, we just do it."

Lyn wasn't in the mood for a battle of wills with her daughter and lurched into a description of the places she had visited so far, which wasn't many, and then told her of the next days intended flight to Brisbane in Queensland. She left out any mention of Jennifer Beck and her partner; because Lyn was determined to scrutinise the artist's personal background before she even mentioned her existence to Sarah.

"Oh Mum, if I'd known I would have come with you, I'm so looking forward to seeing Queensland. I've heard that it's the place to be in Australia if you're into horses!"

"Sarah, how could you possibly have come with me to Australia, little Martin is only what…eight months old. How is he by the way?" Lyn felt as though she was out of synch with the conversation and desperately tried to realign it.

"Fergus's mum has him a lot of the time, he adores her,

besides, we'll be back and forth a lot in the next twelve months so he'll get used to it."

"Get used to what, what are you talking about?"

"Didn't I say? We've decided to move to Australia! Fergus's family have had connections with the TBA for years and *they* recommend Queensland as well.

For several minutes Lyn remained silent as Sarah filled in the gaps behind this alarming news. The TBA, which stood for Thoroughbred Breeders of Australia, was founded ninety years ago and is recognised by the Australian Government as the main industry body for breeding race-horses. The Executive Officer from the Queensland division was liaising with the three-generation-Irish-family, to locate a suitable farm and homestead, where the youngest members of the clan could settle.

"And what about my grandson, when will I see him?" Again, that feeling of being out of sync.

"Whenever you like Mum, you've only visited us here in Ireland twice since he was born. You're over there now, and for what, to buy a picture for the wall in your new house, wasn't it? The world's much smaller than you think, Mum. Remember all those years ago when Dad wanted to emigrate to Oz and you and Gran crushed his dreams? Well don't try to crush mine! This is survival for the family business. Ireland is going down the tubes, like the rest of Europe. Land and property prices have nose-dived and we are haemorrhaging money. Fergus has made up his mind, and as his wife, I am right behind him. I have to go now, you can tell me what you think of Queensland next time we speak. Buy Mum. Love you!"

Chapter 21

Tuesday Afternoon—Torbay

James's in-tray was beginning to overflow with unfulfilled promises. Today had been set aside to deal with the most urgent paperwork; but as yet, nothing had been done to diminish the pile. After Peter Radcliffe's interesting revelation, that he owned a strip of land, known only as 'the old allotments', James's attention had been focussed on nothing else. On returning to his office, he'd phoned John Haydon, a long-standing client of his who had purchased Vincent's failing florists. The strip of allotments ran along the back of some of the derelict shops that John had been given permission to demolish and redevelop, and James had been eager to find out what this small margin of land would be worth.

John Haydon's first reaction to James's probing was coy and non-committal, asking only for the name of the land's owner; but after James reminded him of, client confidentiality, he'd been more forthcoming. With growing excitement, John had revealed that he'd been trying to find out who owned this strip of land for years. Ownership hadn't been recorded on Land-Registry-Files and the old boys, who had paid a pittance of a rent for growing their vegetables on it, were all dead and buried.

"Even as we speak" John had blasted into James's ear, "Those bastards in London are trying to acquire it through some abandonment law. They are sucking up to all kinds of local officials; offering half-baked promises for the area if they hand this strategic piece of land over to them! James, I've got to have that piece of land! It will solve all my access problems, and those bastards know it. Incidentally, have you any idea of Carl's whereabouts? I haven't been able to reach him on the number he gave me."

Wanting to keep focussed, James pressed for an approximate value on the allotment site, and asked if John was prepared to move fast on this.

"Damn right I am, and if Carl is sniffing around and edging up the price, don't agree to anything without consulting with me first. Got that James! And I do appreciate you ringing me on this."

John's final statement, gave James good reason to smile, and, a further reason to ignore the mountain of paperwork.

For the third time in as many hours, Peter Radcliffe flushed away the contents of his fluttering bowels. It wasn't only the frequency of visits, which in itself was causing soreness and discomfort, it was the flatulence that was painful to hold onto but extremely embarrassing to release. He knew that this had been brought on by the constant worry and lack of sleep. He'd had only a little warm soup for lunch, hoping that it might settle his stomach, but in his heart he knew, only one thing could do that.

A knock on his front door sent Peter shuffling to the window for a peek at who might be calling. It was the time of year for charity collectors and it was pointless wasting precious energy unbolting the door. But a look of delight and a slight twinkle in his rheumy eyes transformed the wizened features and dissipated his concern.

"James, come in dear boy, I just knew you'd reconsider." Peter led the solicitor into his sitting room. The blast of air-freshener that he'd squirted before opening the door was still apparent and caused them both to sneeze simultaneously. "Now James, let me get you a brandy, or if you prefer, I have a ten-year malt that'll keep the germs at bay."

"Thank you for the offer but I'm in the middle of a working day, and, in a hurry. I'd like to see all the documentation you have on The Old Allotment site."

Peter took a minute or two for James's words to sink in. "I was rather hoping that you might have reconsidered my earlier offer. Still, he muttered huffily, I need a moment or two to think where the paperwork might be after all this time."

"Surely, it will be in your safe!"

"The paperwork in my safe, James, is only connected to things of value, like I said, I've never gained anything from that particular transaction, except a good ear-bashing from my wife. God rest her soul!"

"Peter, providing the documentation proves that you are the rightful owner of this land, this might well be your chance, your only chance, of reversing your financial situation."

A fountain of hope sprung from somewhere deep within Peter's tired and aching body pushing him from his chair. Within seconds he was rifling through his file cupboard, not caring that he would have to spend the rest of the afternoon putting them back in a neat and orderly fashion. Suddenly a sound, a strange mix of elation and relief, left the old man's tight lips as his bony fingers plucked the shabby envelope from a box file marked, *Miscellaneous.*

Peter's elation and relief began to waver after James, having spread all the pieces of paper—some going back to the turn of the century—studied them in silence for over twenty minutes. In spite of several interruptions, his eyes remained glued to the faded, musty papers and his expression gave nothing away.

Peter had almost given up all hope when the solicitor, all of a sudden, shuffled the papers back into their shabby envelope and abruptly said "Well, the papers seem to be in order. Do I have your authority to sell this piece of land Peter? We both know that time is of the essence, so we can't mess about advertising or shopping around."

"My dear fellow, you must do whatever it takes, just point me to where I have to sign; and James you are my greatest friend, I want you to know that."

As James opened the front door to leave, Peter caught hold of his arm. "If possible, I'd rather the money didn't pass through my account, James." Peter tapped his nose, "I'd like to keep this quiet from the Inland Revenue boys; don't want what few benefits I get to be taken away and of course, I'll need Carl's money in cash."

They'd travelled in virtual silence; but once they'd turned onto the main coastal road, Vinny asked, "So what's at Lyme Regis, apart from a load of old fossils?" From the confused look on Stefan's face, he knew that the word 'fossil' was new to Stefan and *he* was in no mood for explaining. Exasperated, he tried again. "Why the fuck, are we driving all the way to Lyme Regis when we could be having a happy-birthday-pint down the local?"

Stefan's attention remained fixed on the road as he checked the next sign against his map. Satisfied that they were heading in the right direction, he turned his head. "We are going to this place, for finding my sister!"

Vinny slammed on the van's brakes and skewed into a lay by, which turned out to be a fortunate move because this particular road was a clearway and a police car cruised by them a few seconds later.

"Right Stefan, I'm fucking pissed off at being kept in the dark! I want to know everything before I move another inch. I know Fairbank knows; but muggins here," a fat finger was prodded in the centre of Vinny's chest, "knows sod all about what's happening!"

Anxious to get moving Stefan yielded; telling how he'd phoned the mystery woman again before leaving and asked which restaurant Elena and Carl were in the evening before. He'd also found out that they'd taken a taxi back to wherever they were staying.

Vinny said nothing as he listened to Stefan's simplified way of giving him the facts. He admired the way this Eastern European could stay calm and in control under stressful situations and wondered if that would change when confronted with Carl! Carl was a force to be reckoned with all right. And, it seemed more than likely that the reckoning would be happening today while Fairbank was sitting on his arse, doing nothing but filling in fucking forms.

"You got a fag, mate?"

"Yes, but I no give one for you, is better you not smoke after being strong for long time"

"Just give me a fucking fag and stop being a nurse-maid!"

In spite of the opened windows, the smell of smoked tobacco filled the interior of the van as each man returned to their own thoughts and their own fears.

Without warning Vinny was caught off-guard as Stefan asked, "This man Carl, you think he would rape Elena?" The young man's features were fixed in their usual composed way but his eyes had taken on a cold hardness and his fists were clenched tight.

"I don't think he's interested in women for sex! Don't get me wrong, he's not, you know, bent." Vinny gave a limp-wristed flick to demonstrate his meaning; but something happened one night that was really weird." As Vinny recalled the weird event, a churning deep in his gut, reminded him of what could be in store.

"It was about eighteen months ago, Carl was my best buddy back then and we'd met in the Gym's club bar for a couple of beers. These two girls, both tasty, decided to sit at our table and naturally allowed us to buy their drinks. After several vodkas, the tastiest of the pair made it more than obvious that she had the hots for Carl. As far as I remember, he had only got as far as stroking her bare arm and shoulders, whereas I'd progressed to a squeeze of the other girl's tits and a tongue-exploring kiss. Impatient to catch up with her mate, Carl's girl suddenly reaches into the groin area of his trousers. Well, he went berserk! He slapped the girl so hard that she landed on the floor—spilling a table full of drinks on the way down! Carl then marched out of the club and I, naturally followed. Don't forget, he was my best buddy back then and after witnessing that slapping, well there was no point in staying, my manhood had shrunk to the size of a chipolata. As we'd walked across the car park, Carl suddenly stops alongside a black Mini Cooper (I knew it was the tasty bird's car, she'd bragged about it most of the evening) and runs a coin along the full length on the driver's side, leaving a bright silver scar across its newly polished black surface."

"And you say nothing?" interrupted Stefan.

"What was the point, the damage was done! But that's not the end of it. I happened to bump into the tasty bird a few weeks later. After allowing her to run off steam—my God her language was worse than an Irish navvy's—she told me that Carl had nothing in his trousers. Her precise words were. "He's got balls, but nothing that could satisfy a woman!"

Vinny checked his rear view mirror and started up the engine. "Right, lets get this over and done with, Stefan." He flicked the cigarette butt out of the window and pulled quickly onto the road in front of a slow-moving tractor. The tractor driver blasted his horn and Vinny responded with an upturned finger.

They drove at a snails pace down the narrow high street of Lyme Regis. They'd asked, and had been told, exactly where the restaurant was; but they had also been warned that parking close to it was almost impossible.

"There it is!" pointed Vincent; stopping without warning, in front of a double-fronted building; not caring that the motorist behind was pressing on his car horn.

"In and out as quick as you can. I'll pull down further and let this wanker go by."

Mindful of Vincent's instructions, Stefan laid aside all emotions and concerns for his sister. It was obvious that Carl was a very dangerous man; but if he was to succeed in rescuing Elena, he would have to keep control of his feelings.

Seven tables were occupied in the restaurant; three of them seated families with young children. A harassed-looking waiter, darting from kitchen to tables, glanced over as Stefan stood waiting for attention but made no attempt to communicate. On his third entry from the kitchen, carrying a tray loaded with hamburgers and chips, Stefan intervened.

"Excuse me Sir, I see you very busy but I need the name of taxi people who take my sister home from here, yesterday in the evening." Looking even more burdened by having to work out what had just been asked of him, the waiter turned to head back to the sanctuary of the kitchen. But Stefan caught his arm. "Please, what my sister left in taxi, is, how you say, sentimental?"

Without saying a word, the waiter pushed past Stefan, grabbed a menu from the bar and flicked to the back page.

There, inserted and protected by clear plastic, was a small leaflet advertising the taxi firm used by the restaurant. The leaflet contained name, telephone number and address, with a convenient little map showing its exact position in the town. Stefan looked at the name and thanked the waiter; but after he'd disappeared back to the kitchen, the leaflet was pulled from beneath the plastic and pushed into his pocket.

"What fucking kept you? That bastard is only three cars away." Stefan looked in the direction that Vincent nodded. A traffic warden, diligently marking down information on his pad, was edging his way up the hill. As Vincent pulled back onto the narrow street, he called out to the warden. "Your mother must be very fucking proud of you!"

After studying the leaflet and taking a right at the bottom of the street they were pleased to find they could park immediately outside the taxi office.

"Let me deal with this one Stefan, we haven't got all fucking day!"

The taxi office was empty, apart from a greasy-haired man of about forty who was sitting behind the counter reading a newspaper. Stefan stood to one side allowing Vincent the space directly in front of the man, who continued to read. Vincent was impatient and in a voice loaded with sarcasm he said. "Sorry for interrupting your tea break, mate, but we need some information."

"Tourist Information Office is down the road, turn left," said the man without looking up.

Vincent drew himself up to his full height and pushed back his shoulders. The man continued to read. Stefan knew what would happen next but he remained calm and impartial, watching every move and every step in this fascinating dance. Strip away language and culture, and you find men are the same the world over, he thought.

"We haven't got all fucking day!" Vincent's voice had lowered to a snarl as he reached to snatch at the newspaper.

The other man's reflexes were sharper; and the paper was pulled easily to one side, folded and placed safely out of reach. He rose from the wooden stool and faced his opponent, who was at least four inches taller. In spite of the difference in height and age the man was not intimidated. "You've got my full attention, mate, what's the problem?"

In sparse detail, Vincent explained what was needed. The man very quickly replied that it was more than his job was worth to give out where a fare had been dropped, then added, unless of course you're the cops but I can smell them a mile off. With a heavy sigh, Vincent delved into his pocket and slapped a £20 note on the counter.

The man scratched at his greasy head and then said 'Buena Vista', sliding the money toward him as he spoke. This time, Vincent's reflexes were sharper. He pressed his clenched fist firmly on the note and pulled back, regaining the money's lost ground.

"Benny who; what kind of a fucking address is that?"

With an admirable amount of patience, the man went on to explain that 'Buena Vista' was Spanish for 'Beautiful View', an elevated property which stood alone, hence it had no number or street name. He scribbled directions on a piece of paper and offered it with one hand whilst taking hold of the £20 note with the other and shoving it into the back pocket of his trousers.

"I can give you more information about the place if you want it."

"Not if it's going to cost!" Vincent fired back.

"Just hear me out first." The man went on to say that this secluded premises was mainly rented out to writers. The owner of the property was himself a writer who spent the colder months in Spain. Understanding the need for peace and solitude, but aware of the vulnerability of the properties situation, he had removed the land-line telephone and installed a secure, metal-gated entry to the sweeping drive, which, according to the taxi driver, was the only way up to the property.

"And you just happen to know the code that opens the gate."

"That's right. My brother just happens to be the postman for the area."

Vincent's lower jaw twitched with the tension of his cornered situation. He looked over for the first time to where Stefan was standing. A slight nod of the head gave Vincent cause for another heavy sigh. "How much will it cost me?" he asked, with contempt.

"Another one of them will do." The man tapped at his back pocket and Vincent slapped another note on the counter. Armed with the four digit code, they set off on the final part of their journey.

As Vinny drove the van through the narrow rutted lanes of the east Devon countryside, his stomach lurching and his heart pounding, he wondered what the hell they were going to do. Neither had said a word since they'd left Lyme Regis, Stefan just silently pointing, each time a change of direction was needed. He'd give anything to just turnaround and go back, but he couldn't do that. Stefan had become more than just temporary casual labour. Fairbank was right, he had become fond of him, fond in a brotherly sort of way. He had no doubt that Stefan would do whatever it took to free Elena from Carl's hold on her, even if it meant killing the bastard! Trouble was, Vinny was shit-scared!

The large imposing property was built into the side of a steep hill, providing shelter from behind and fantastic views over the distant coastline from the front. Several sign posts had made it easy to find and the rising disappointment made Vincent realise just how much of a coward he was. As a precaution, they parked the van in the gateway to a small electricity power house and walked back the couple of hundred yards.

The code was entered and the recently-painted, wrought iron gates, swung open on well-oiled hinges. As they both made to mount the steep incline of the curving driveway, which at this angle, was out of site of the property, Stefan placed a hand on Vinny's shoulder.

"No my friend, I need you to keep watch here. If I need you, I call, like this". Stefan cupped both hands to his mouth and made the loud piercing call of…some creature, but whatever it was, Vinny couldn't mistake it.

Filled with relief at being left out of the action, He sat on the stump of a felled tree surrounded on three sides by evergreen shrubs. Out of sight from the drive and the nearby road he waited, engrossed in the antics of a spider. The spider, having caught an insect twice its size in a web that stretched nearly three feet across, was closing slowly and deliberately in for the kill. Before the two insects combined, He heard footsteps walking without stealth down the drive. He shrunk back to tighter cover and then saw it was Stefan; alone and hands free from Carl's blood.

"The house is empty, I must return tonight!"

"It'll be pitch-black out here at night, besides Carl's probably moved on to somewhere else."

"No, garage is open for his return, I use ladder from there to look into windows, I see Elena's things in one of the rooms."

"Well there you go. I think we're jumping to conclusions about her being in danger, mate, I think she's going along with this quite happily."

"She being sold like piece of meat to old man, I cannot allow it! I will not allow it!"

Chapter 22

Tuesday—late afternoon

Unaware that his secluded Lyme Regis hideaway had been discovered, Carl led Elena into one of Dorchester's town centre cafes. They'd spent the afternoon shopping for clothes and several bags of expensive finery had already been deposited in the trunk of his car. Shoes were the only thing remaining on the long list of items that he'd promised to buy for her; but they both needed a break. Carl was feeling happy and relaxed. Everything was slotting neatly into place.

While Elena had been engrossed and occupied with an assistant, who was helping her choose her outfit for Friday, Carl had slipped out to the telephone booth, across the road from the boutique, and contacted Peter Radcliffe. His original plan, had been to turn up unannounced, set the trap that would cause the old man's demise, then disappear without anyone knowing that he'd been there. But, he needed to be sure that Radcliffe would be at home and not stuck in some hospital reception room, waiting and hoping for any positive news on the state of his declining health.

The old man had picked up on the third ring, sounding nervous and agitated. It soon became obvious why. Amidst a gush of excuses and a fair amount of stuttering, Radcliffe had dropped his bombshell.

"I do appreciate all that you've done for me, Carl, but I've decided against the marriage. Naturally, I intend to pay back the loan, and of course any interest that's accrued, but taking on such a commitment at my time of life, I…I'm sorry, but I just can't go through with it! I think I mentioned that I have a nephew. Funny really, I haven't seen him in over twenty years and suddenly out of the blue, I've received a letter from him saying he's coming to England to pay a visit and…Well it's all just too much."

The simpering whine of Radcliffe's voice, grated, but Carl remained focussed. He'd had no intention of allowing this marriage to go ahead anyway; Radcliffe's cowardice was just making it easier. "Naturally, Elena will be extremely disappointed. I suggest you write her a simple note stating that, you can't go on with it, no need to complicate matters with personal details. I'll arrive tomorrow at midday. And Peter, don't worry, we'll sort things out over a couple of drinks; but remember, we must continue to keep this to ourselves." Carl smiled as he replaced the receiver. With that simple little note to Elena, his accidental death becomes a suicide.

Elena stood in front of the mirror in the ladies toilet, her cheeks flushed with the activities of the afternoon. It had been exciting choosing whatever she wanted regardless of price; but she was growing more worried. There were only two more days of this strange captivity. Two more days of pretending to be interested in the life of a man who was obviously mentally ill. She'd wanted to talk about her approaching marriage to Peter, but whenever she'd so much as mentioned his name, a look of cold hatred had flashed in Carl's ice-blue eyes, and his mood would change from friendliness to sullen silence. A silence that could last for several minutes or even several hours. She'd played along with everything he'd wanted to do and everything he'd wanted to discuss, sensing that to disagree would be dangerous. No one knew where she was and there hadn't been any opportunities for her to contact Stefan or anyone else. She'd thought about sending a letter to Candy; but even if she'd managed somehow to buy a stamp, how could Candy respond? A rising panic sent her eyes searching for a way to make an escape; but the only door from the toilets led to the main body of the tea shop, and Carl was seated facing it.

Splashing her face with cooling water calmed her. Carl had used the telephone booth on the high street while she was trying on outfits. She wasn't meant to see him so there was no point in asking who he'd phoned; but it told her one thing, he still wasn't using his mobile.

Elena returned to her seat in time to see a tray of tea and scones being delivered by a waitress dressed in a dark blue dress and white apron.

"As we are visiting a quaint old English town, I thought the right thing to order would be tea and scones, am I right, darling?"

"Of course, you are always right." Elena saw the look of satisfaction as he relaxed back into his chair. Determination took hold as she pressed her advantage. "There's only two more days left for sharing this exciting and mysterious holiday, what shall we do tomorrow?"

Carl remained silent until the waitress had walked away then leaned forward and took hold of Elena's hands. "Sweetheart, we have the rest of our lives for excitement! I intend to show you the whole world with all of its mysteries; but tomorrow morning I need to leave you alone for a little while." There was a subtle change in his expression as he continued. "In the evening, we'll dine out somewhere really special, there'll be much to celebrate. First of all we will visit my homeland. Mother will adore you, she always knew that one day I would find someone special. As you know, I have four brothers and they will be very impressed, when they meet you. Unlike you, Elena, I've never been close to my siblings. Mother and Eric, my oldest nephew, are the only family members I can trust and the only ones that I care to communicate with. Eric, unlike his father, is handsome, intelligent and destined to do far better than wasting his life hauling fish from the sea."

Elena was only half listening. The fact that he was leaving her alone the next day sent a wave of relief coursing through her body. Careful not to let it show, her mind feverishly explored any possibilities of finding a way to contact Stefan while he was gone. She remembered seeing a public telephone about two kilometres from their isolated property; if only she could reach it! Carl would never leave her alone without locking the doors; but if she could escape through a lower window…

"You look very engrossed, what are you thinking?" Carl's hands gripping her own brought her attention back to the Dorchester tea room as he waited for her answer.

"I was just thinking about how the time alone will give me the perfect chance to sort out my new wardrobe, and do all the little things that women need to do in order to look and feel attractive. By the time you return, all my pampering will be done and I'll be ready for whatever you have in mind for the evening."

Chapter 23

Before leaving the office, James flicked through his briefcase to make sure that he had all the necessary paperwork and his cheque book. He'd been ready to leave over half an hour ago, anxious to get the deal with Peter signed and sealed; but the unexpected phone call from Clara, his former secretary, had been well worth the delay.

After her designated period of maternity leave, Clara had made the decision to remain a full time mother, at least until her daughter started school. At the time, this hadn't been too much of a blow for James—property sales were spasmodic and Lyn was in close proximity for helping him with various things connected to secretarial work. But out of the blue, Clara's husband had been made redundant from the civil engineering company that he'd worked for since leaving school. This sudden change in circumstance, which included a moderate cash settlement, had given the redundant new father, the opportunity to start up as a consultant working from home. It had also given Clara the opportunity to seek part time work, as a back-up measure until the fledgling business got off the ground. James had thanked her for ringing him first and told her that he would be happy for her to work sixteen hours per week, knowing that this would be more than enough time for keeping his office running smoothly again.

He had spent most of the day, transferring the documentation and ownership of the allotment land to J.L. Holdings, his own, newly formed company. These were difficult times and one needed to plan for the future, and, an opportunity like this was extremely rare. He had searched his conscience and was content with the conclusion. Peter had jumped at the offered price, so long as the transaction could be completed straight away.

Without knocking, the front door was swung open as James mounted the steps to Peter Radcliffe's porch.

"Come in dear boy, I expected you sooner, I've held off from having supper so you'll have to excuse my rumbling stomach."

"I do have other clients Peter. I got away as soon as I could, and, I have been extremely busy on your behalf."

"Forgive my impatience, I've got so many things on my mind, and the worry of it is taking its toll. Can I offer you some refreshment?"

The stifling heat coupled with the strange smell that permeated Peter's sitting room was overbearing and claustrophobic. "Thank you, but I'd prefer to run through the paperwork, get the necessary signatures and then leave you to enjoy your supper in peace. We will need an independent witness for counter signing the document; is your dentist-neighbour available?"

The old man looked aghast "I have no intention of allowing that…That snake-in-the-grass to know anything about my private affairs!"

"Peter, I am paying you £100,000 for a strip of land that you hitherto regarded as worthless. As this money is coming from my own bank account, I insist that the transference of the documentation is done legally. Which means it has to be witnessed! So unless you have someone else in mind I suggest you give your neighbour a ring. Besides, the only page of the document he will see; is where he witnesses our signatures. Unless *you* decide to tell him, how could he possibly know anything?"

With a heavy sigh, Peter made the necessary phone call. By the time James had run through the paperwork, handed over his cheque and laid out the document in such a way that privacy and discretion were respected, the retired dentist was lightly tapping on the front door. Before allowing him entry, Peter scooped up the cheque and deposited it in the top drawer of his writing bureau; then cast a wary eye around the room as he moved towards the porch.

The signing and witnessing was finished in a matter of minutes and as James walked the elderly neighbour to the door, embarrassed that Peter hadn't offered him a drink, or even barely given him thanks, James offered him a £10 note for his trouble.

"Helping out a neighbour is no trouble at all" said the retired dentist, as he shook James's offered hand. "And to accept money for such a small thing would be quite wrong." Lowering his voice he continued. "Peter doesn't look at all well; putting his affairs in order is a wise move."

James gathered the paperwork and placed it quickly in his briefcase, the loud click of its closure signalling that the transaction was complete. He wanted to be out of here; but protocol dictated otherwise. Peter moved towards the drinks tray and poured a dribble of brandy into a glass and handed it to James before taking up a half empty glass of water.

"Sorry I can't seal the deal with something more appropriate; but like I said, I do appreciate what you've done for me James. And the remainder…? The cash for Carl? When will you…?"

"Don't worry, you will have the money by tomorrow afternoon. I need to arrange it with my bank first."

"Any chance you could make it in the morning dear boy; I hate to press you, but I've had a phone call from Carl. He's calling on me at midday tomorrow. I just want to be rid of him and this whole sorry business. If he should demand the money there and then…What I mean is, I don't want to give him any excuse for returning."

The fear in the old man's eyes was unmistakable and James unconsciously took a step backward, in order not to be caught up in its contagion. "Victor Carlson is actually coming here tomorrow at midday? Am I right in assuming that Elena will be with him?" James downed the brandy in one swallow in the hope that it would help him to keep a dispassionate focus on what Peter was saying.

"No, no he'll be alone! I've told him that I can't go through with the marriage. He sounded quite amenable, in view of the short notice, but even so, I find him quite intimidating. And, he's obsessive when it comes to secrecy. I would deem it a massive favour if you could deliver by late morning; but do phone me first. Heaven knows what the man would do to me if he found out I'd spilled the beans."

Vinny flicked the last half inch of a smouldering cigarette into the gutter and pulled himself up from the chill of the stone step. James Fairbank, in his smart business suit and carrying a leather briefcase, was just arriving back from, God knows where.

"Hard day Jimmy? I notice there's a slight crease in the left side of your trousers and is that a speck of ink on your thumb? There are times when I feel really sorry for you and your ilk."

"Oh hello Vincent, was that you smoking? I thought that you'd given up months ago."

"I had, but it's not easy when there's another smoker under your roof. I'll be glad when I can get my life back to normal. I'm knackered, I could do with a holiday but I don't have the wherewithal. Where've you been? Your average working man would only dress like that if they're up before the magistrate!" As usual, the solicitor remained secretive. Vinny caught sight of Stefan, walking purposefully up the hill with a bag of groceries in each hand. He was starving hungry and ready for a beer. "Here comes my buddy with the dinner. Apart from the lack of sex, it's like being married. Better go and lay the table."

"How did you get on in Lyme Regis, Vincent?"

"Complete waste of fucking time, and money!" Turning back to the solicitor, Vinny gave a brief account of their afternoon, happy to unload the pent-up frustration. Then he added. "Stefan is insisting on going back tonight; but I've told him straight, he'll have to get a taxi. Carl and his sister are staying in a large isolated property. There are no street lights and in the dark any vehicle approaching the place, would be spotted a mile away. Besides, it seems too cosy a set-up if you ask me. I reckon they're working as a team to rip off Radcliffe; but Stefan won't have a word said against her."

Vinny changed the subject as Stefan got closer. "How is Lyn getting on in the land of sunshine, Jimmy?"

His question was completely ignored as Fairbank turned to Stefan. "I hear the afternoon in Lyme Regis didn't go too well Stefan."

"For me, it was success." Stefan shot a sideways glance at Vinny before continuing. "I know now where my sister is, and tonight, I go for rescue her."

Vinny let out a rolling groan which was meant to be under-the-breath; but the sound, akin to a wounded animal, was easily heard by the other two men. Feeling pissed off with the pair of them he headed for his front door, but was suddenly halted by the solicitor's next words. He was advising Stefan to postpone the night time run because Carl was paying Radcliffe a visit the next day, without the company of Elena. A heavy vehicle passed by and the continuing conversation was lost in the noise of its engine. Livid, Vinny marched into his flat, looked into each empty room and then marched back to the front door. "Come on Stefan, I'm fucking starving! Jimmy's probably booked into some posh restaurant for *his* dinner."

"Is good, no!" Stefan watched as Vincent ran the chunk of bread around the plate, mopping up the last of the tasty sauce. Money was tight and mindful of this fact, Stefan had bought provisions from a newly-opened Polish store, saving at least twenty-five percent on the total bill. Vincent had frowned at some of the food; but Stefan knew that he'd be fine once he'd tried it. Everybody felt happier with good, hot food inside their bellies.

"Yes Stefan, the food was fine, just like you said it would be. Now, I'd like to know what's going down with Carl and Radcliffe. You've obviously changed your tune about returning to Lyme Regis tonight. Or is this a big secret between you and Fairbank?"

"Is no secrets, Vincent. Old man Radcliffe is, how you say, having cold feet! He tell to Carl that he change his mind about marriage to Elena. Carl is coming to see him tomorrow, for money I think. While he is here, I go for rescue my sister. Is simple!"

"Stefan, I know this guy, and believe me when it comes to Carl, nothing is that fucking simple! For starters, how did the old git miraculously manage to contact Carl to tell him that he'd changed his mind? Carl never gives out his number, especially if he's about to scam you. No, I reckon Carl phoned Radcliffe. He needed to discuss the final arrangements and as you say the old man got cold feet and blurted out that he couldn't go through with it. I also reckon, and you won't like what I'm about to say Stefan; but it needs to be said. I think that Elena is more involved than you think. What I mean is…"

"I understand what you say Vincent; but you wrong!"

Stefan collected the empty plates and placed them in a bowl of hot, soapy water. He didn't blame Vincent for thinking the way he did; Stefan had known lots of women and many of them would happily sell their souls to link up with the likes of Victor Carlson; but not Elena. Elena had suffered and experienced too much to get involved with such a dangerous man. Tomorrow he would do his best to persuade her to return home. Is true, Bulgaria is much poorer than England and crime is all around; but at least it was much easier to separate the bad guys from the downright wicked.

Candy Laverne eased her Jaguar into the large parking space. There were spaces closer to James Fairbank's building; but she felt the walk, although short, would do her good. Her body still felt heavy from the hotel dinner; she'd left a good portion of the main course and had declined dessert, knowing that she'd suffer the consequences if she retired on an overfilled stomach. Alice, her eighty-two-year-old sister, was down in Torbay on her yearly jaunt to one of the two star, all-inclusive hotels. She'd been doing it for years. Back when she'd first retired and still living in her own bungalow, there were fourteen of them, all women and all retired teachers, and according to the testament of several of the coach drivers, they were wilder than a bunch of teenagers. Now, only five remained of the original bunch. Nevertheless, this five, all in their early eighties, were still more than happy to clamber aboard a stifling coach, which would take virtually all day, to arrive at their modest accommodation. Several times Candy had offered to arrange something more up-market; but Alice wouldn't hear of it, pointing out that the daily excursions and the evenings playing bingo or having a waltz, to a third rate duo, was all part and parcel of this yearly pilgrimage. Memories of their old friends and colleagues were brought back to life during their four-night-stay, keeping faith to a vow that would continue until every last one of them had passed away.

As Candy approached the solicitor's front porch, she heard voices coming from the flat below. The voices, although muffled weren't difficult to make out but she cocked a deaf ear to the clipped-English of Stefan and the brashness of Vinny's responses. She was in no mood for argument. The sole purpose of her journey to Torbay, apart from hoping to share the odd cup of tea with her older sister, was to try and talk Elena out of making such a terrible mistake.

She wrapped her fur stole about her shoulder and waited for a response to the push bell which resounded behind the solid wooden door. James Fairbank, looking relaxed in his cable knit sweater, smiled warmly and stepped aside to allow her entry.

"Thanks for allowing me to call on you at such short notice James, hotels are such lonely places during the dark evenings."

"I thought you said your sister was holidaying down here."

"She is, but not with me, and as it's her evening for bingo, well quite honestly, I'd rather watch paint dry. Oh, no offence to you James."

The solicitor indicated that Candy go up to the sitting room while he shut down his computer and closed up the ground floor office. He'd been anxious to finalise all the paperwork and correspondence between himself and John Haydon before Clara moved back into the secretarial seat.

Candy accepted the glass of red wine and settled into the comfortable leather armchair. The room was warm, too warm for James she noticed, as he peeled off the heavy-knit sweater.

"I'm here for the sole purpose of trying to put a stop to this farcical marriage between Elena and that selfish old goat. I know she's happy to go along with it but she can't possibly know about the skulduggery that lies behind the contract."

"Are you quite sure of that Candy?"

"I'd stake my life on it! Knowing that she will never have children of her own, thanks to the brutality of a gang rape she was subjected to when she was first brought to this country, Elena's family mean everything to her. All she wants, is to provide security for them, by sacrificing a few years of her own life taking care of a much older husband."

"Well, you'll be pleased to hear that the selfish old goat has changed his mind and the wedding, as far as he is concerned, has been cancelled. Victor Carlson is paying Radcliffe a visit tomorrow, alone, so its anybodies guess where Elena heads from here."

"Does Stefan know?"

"Yes, but I got the strong impression he wasn't reassured."

James's words hung in the air. Candy took a sip of her wine, swirling the remaining contents absentmindedly as she tried to envisage what might happen next. "I'd like to see Stefan; but there was an argument in progress when I arrived." She raised her eyes from the glass and found James's clear green orbs fixed on her face. His expression, though friendly enough, held a concern that mirrored her own; but she was in no doubt that his concern was linked to preventing Carl from taking possession of Radcliffe's property. *Her* one and only concern was to prevent Elena from being dragged into any further danger; and she was convinced that the argument in the flat below was reflecting both points of view.

"Will you involve the police?" asked Candy, already knowing the probable answer. Carl had obviously brought about the early demise of the Dutch Industrialist, to further his own ends, and there were bound to be other incidents that the law enforcers would be keen to follow up. As a solicitor, James had little option; but he would have to make very sure that the evidence against Victor Carlson was water-tight, and from previous experience had learned that that was easier said than done.

James lifted the bottle to replenish her glass but her hand stayed him. Without hesitation, he replenished his own. "I've come to the conclusion, Candy, especially in matters like this, that finding redress in justice is often quite different from redress in law. Victor Carlson is allowed to act with impunity within the latter, and there's very little one can do about it, or so it seems. Maybe it's time to give justice a helping hand and allow those that have been wronged, to settle the score!"

Chapter 24

Wednesday—3-30am

The sound of his own anguished voice, piercing the silence of the night, woke Carl from the nightmare. He was drenched in sweat. The bed sheet, clinging and twisted around his lower limbs where he'd writhed and kicked out to free his body from rough, powerful hands, was damp from the tainted perspiration that had oozed from his overheated flesh.

A cool hand touched his shoulder, and the soothing sound of a woman's voice fragmented the horrific scene that was still pressing to be made conscious. But Carl wouldn't allow it. He had to be strong. He had to keep the terror of that night buried where it belonged. There was a time, many years ago, when this nightmare was a regular visitor; but, with the help of Mother and her hypnotist friend, he had learned how to suppress the constant intrusion from his sub-conscious mind. Gradually, the panic-filled horror of his disturbed nights had dwindled then disappeared altogether, leaving Carl a firm believer, in taking total control of the mind.

He turned in the direction of the women's soothing voice and in a cracked, husky tone that sounded alien to his own ears, he asked, "What was I saying?"

Before answering, Elena switched on the bedside lamp and offered up her half-filled glass of water. "Here drink; it will soothe your throat."

Carl ignored the offer. "Tell me," he insisted.

With reticence Elena tried. "You were calling out in your native tongue. I couldn't understand it all but…You seemed to be begging for your mother to help you. Followed by much cursing and kicking out. I'm sorry, I couldn't understand more; but you seemed very frightened. Would you like to talk about it?"

"There's nothing to talk about. It was only a bad dream. You must have them occasionally, everyone does."

Elena looked at him searchingly before saying. "My bad dreams are always connected with bad things that have happened. I welcome them. They are there to help me to come to terms with the trauma."

"I have my own way of dealing with bad things; turn off the light and go back to sleep."

Carl slid silently from Elena's bed and returned to his own room. He knew from past experience that sleep wouldn't be possible without help; but if he succumbed to the temptation of sleeping tablets, the plans for the day ahead could be jeopardised. Elena's offer of talking was well meant; they had spoken of much in the last few days and apart from Mother, she was the closest anyone had come to knowing Carl. But how much did he know about himself and what really happened before he was sent away to

Denmark, at the tender age of fourteen? Mother's version wasn't exactly in accord with his own memories, or the content of the nightmares. It was readily accepted, at least by his family that facts that are too horrendous to bear will distort until they become more credible and easier to accept. But since meeting Elena and discussing each others family-life, dreams had started to return—nothing as frighteningly violent as tonight—but nonetheless they were dreams involving his early teens. Carl was beginning to wonder where the blurred line between truth and fiction lay.

By the end of the week, he would be in the company of Mother. As always, she would plead with him to leave well alone; but with a conviction stronger than anything he'd ever felt before, he intended to rake over the past and extract from her every detail about what happened on that fateful night. Elena was right, the truth, no matter how shocking, needed to be faced.

With the minimum of noise, Elena had stripped down her bed and replaced the sheets. Her body was desperately tired; but even the luxury of the cool fresh linen against her skin couldn't override the tension that was keeping sleep at bay. As quietly as possible, she headed down to the kitchen, hoping that a warm drink might help.

Sitting at the breakfast bar clutching a mug of cocoa she could hear the ocean pounding against the cliffs and wondered, not for the first time, what life would be like living at The Terrace with Peter Radcliffe. Peter, old and sick, was looking for companionship and help with his day to day life and she was happy to oblige. She'd been assured that he wasn't interested in a sexual relationship and this suited her. She was damaged; damaged in a way that wasn't apparent to others. She would never be able to bear children and doubted whether she could ever make love again. The brutal, perverted rape that she'd suffered, when first arriving in this country, put paid to that.

Carl was damaged too, psychologically; but it was difficult for her to empathise. He frightened her! This was the second night that he'd climbed into her bed in the early hours, wrapping his arms around her from behind and spooning his bent legs into hers. *She* had been disturbed into wakefulness while *he* had slipped into restful sleep. He'd apologised the next morning, saying that bad dreams were bothering him, and all he needed was the comfort of another person to cling to. There were no sexual advances from him, just the feel of his fingers stroking her arms and shoulders and the heat of his breath on the back of her neck. She shuddered now at the memory of it.

After rinsing out her empty mug, she wandered through to the large utilities room, which housed the boiler and laundry facilities. She moved over to a window that was partly obscured by an ironing board. The window, like the rest in the house was locked; but its key was protruding from the lock, making it convenient to open when the steam from the laundry or heat from the boiler demanded easy access to fresh air. She removed the little key and slipped it into her dressing gown pocket, before climbing back up the stairs to bed.

Chapter 25

Lyn Porter and Jennifer Beck emerged from, Arrivals, at Brisbane Airport and headed for one of the waiting taxis. The flight had been relatively short, compared to the long-hauler that Lyn had endured only several days before. And the palaver that she and Andy had experienced, as they'd passed through several queues of security checks at Sydney Airport, was conspicuous by its absence. This ease of passage was undoubtedly due to it being an internal flight; and as a novice traveller, Lyn felt compelled to store this information at the back of her mind for any future eventualities. Thoughts of Andy, and the determination to right the wrong he had inflicted on her, was also pushed to the back of her mind, for now.

After giving instruction to the taxi driver, Jennifer removed her mobile from her shoulder-bag and checked for any incoming messages. There were none; and it was again slipped away. The phone, it seemed, had been her main companion on the journey—keeping it switched on until the very last minute before take-off and barely able to wait to switch on again the second the plane landed—and even during the flight, it was held and looked at obsessively on several occasions. There'd been very little conversation between the two of them, which had disappointing Lyn. She had hoped to learn more about Jennifer's immediate family; but apart from the odd perfunctory one-liner about the weather or a passing scene, she had gained nothing of interest. Determined to broach the subject, she tried a different angle. She had begun to talk about Sarah and her husband's desire to move to Australia. She'd pointed out how disappointed she would feel about missing out on seeing her eight-month-old grandson growing up. Either, the one-sided conversation couldn't penetrate through to Jennifer's troubled mind, or, she had been completely disinterested. She'd handed Lyn a magazine from her bag and excused her lack of conversation on a headache, apparently brought on by the cabin's air-pressure. Lyn had accepted the magazine, opened the first page and closed her eyes to retreat back to her own thoughts.

As the taxi moved easily along broad, tree-lined roads, Lyn caught a sideways glance of her mother and tried to analyse her feelings towards her. But she felt nothing. There was only an emotionless hole, devoid of any memories! She'd asked Gran on several occasions, when she was growing up, what her parents were like? Gran had always responded in the same way, (*You lost your mother and I lost my only child. There's no point in raking over memories that give rise to pain. Leave well alone, Lynda.*) Jennifer caught sight of her gaze and smiled briefly, saying they were only a couple of kilometres from her home.

"Has your headache eased, now that we're back in the fresh air?" asked Lyn, at a loss for anything more to say and wondering how the next few days would be filled.

"Yes, thank you, I do feel better. I am sorry that I haven't been much company. My husband's illness has been playing on my mind. I should never have agreed to mount the exhibition. I should have known better."

"Well I'm glad you did, sounds selfish I know, but I am looking forward to seeing some of your earlier work. With a view to purchasing of course; but I will understand if you feel my presence in your home will be a nuisance. I'm sure there are hotels not too far away where I could stay for a few days." Lyn held her breath as she waited for Jennifer's response; and she made up her mind there and then that if Jennifer Beck reneged on her promise to have her as a house guest, she would never speak to her again!

"No. No it's quite alright for you to stay. We have plenty of room. I may have to leave you a couple of times to visit the nursing home, which is only a ten minute drive away, so you won't be completely left to your own devices. And please, feel free to use the telephone to let your family know that you've arrived safely."

Apart from Sarah, Lyn hadn't told anyone where she had headed so there was no need to inform anyone about anything. She'd kept her hotel room, with most of her clothes still hanging in the wardrobe, informing reception of a possible return date of three days time; but naturally, that depended on how things developed between her and her estranged parents.

The clicking of the cars indicator intruded on Lyn's

thoughts, and arrested her attention. The taxi turned right onto a long, gravelled driveway and then scrunched to a halt. It was 7-20pm, local time, and the sun, hanging low in its cloudless domain caused long shadows to form from anything that lay within its path of brilliance. Clusters of tropical trees and blossom-laden shrubs, formed jagged patterns of darkness as they reached across the immaculately tended gardens. A green painted post box, blending easily with its surroundings, displayed the name of the property—***Calm Waters***. A flock of parrots, disturbed by the slamming of the vehicle's door, took flight to a neighbouring tree, squawking their disapproval at being disturbed. Lyn looked about her and couldn't fail to be impressed. Even the distraught birds had quickly settled in the calming atmosphere of this beautiful setting. No wonder Jennifer Beck was anxious to return home; compared to the hustle and bustle of Darling Harbour, this place was a paradise of tranquillity. Lyn felt an overwhelming desire to explore the garden; but she held that desire in check.

A short, plump-faced woman greeted them at the front door and was introduced as Martha, the daily help. Lyn followed Martha's lead through the luxurious two-story, building. A broad flight of polished sandstone steps led to the guest wing at the far right of the property. The bedroom was large. Too large for one person and for a fleeting moment she imagined James sharing the room with her. But the intrusion of pressure, felt in the area of her chest, reminded her that she already had too much other emotional baggage to deal with.

Martha's voice intervened. "The air conditioning is set to cut out at 10pm; but you can leave one of the doors open slightly, provided you keep the mesh doors closed."

Lyn walked over to where Martha was pulling on vertical rods which opened the floor to ceiling drapes, revealing sliding, glass doors. The doors led onto a balcony that supported two loungers and a table with four chairs. Martha demonstrated how the doors worked, reminding Lyn again to make sure that the mesh doors were always closed behind her.

"Is that to prevent the parrots from flying in, Martha?" Lyn had read all about the poisonous snakes and spiders of Australia; but didn't think they could be a problem in this elevated situation.

"No my dear, it's the mosquitoes, nasty little devils they are. As you can see we are surrounded on three sides with water, and Mrs Beck suffers terribly if she's bitten; so it's a house rule never to allow them entry. They have the habit of hiding in the drapes, and then in the dead of night, they make their blood-sucking attack on any exposed, warm flesh. Just one mosquito, given the chance, will attack in several places. I remember one summer when Mrs Beck was made really uncomfortable from three bites which caused her leg to swell like a balloon!"

Lyn wasn't about to neglect this useful advice, she too suffered terribly from mosquito bites. "Don't worry I'll be careful; I find mosquito bites affect me badly too; but thanks for the warning."

"I've left a light supper for the pair of you; but I'm sure Mrs Beck will want to pop along and see her husband first."

"Martha, what's the nature of Mr Beck's illness; is he terminally ill? I don't wish to be any more of a burden to Jennifer than I can help and knowing what I'm up against will forearm me against saying or doing the wrong thing. Incidentally, what hours do you work here?"

"Usually afternoons only, but I remain flexible. Mrs Beck has a great deal to contend with. What with…"

A light cough from behind, where Jennifer Beck stood framed by the open doorway, silenced Martha in mid stream.

"Thank you Martha, I'm sure your cats will be ready for their feed. It was kind of you to prepare us a meal, I'm sure Lyn is ready for supper, the food offered on the flight wasn't very appetising." Turning to Lyn, she said. "I hope you'll be comfortable in this room Lyn, it's quieter at the back of the house."

"It's beautiful! I can't imagine anything disturbing the tranquillity."

"The parrots can be a problem early in the morning; but you'll be fine at the back of the house, we've removed the trees that harbour them." Lyn felt a pang of disappointment at these words, she had been hoping to sit on her balcony and enjoy watching them feed. She'd only managed to get a fleeting glance of them on arriving and was looking forward to zooming in and catching them on camera.

The three women descended the stairway with Lyn at the rear. Martha headed to a side door off the kitchen where Jennifer bid her goodnight. Then turning slowly, she asked Lyn if she minded eating at the breakfast bar. Lyn's eyes followed the indicating hand. A single place setting was neatly arranged on the sandstone breakfast bar.

"I don't mind waiting to eat if you want to visit Pierre first, in fact, I don't mind coming with you, if you'd like the company." From the look on Jennifer Beck's face Lyn realised her offer had been a mistake. Jennifer's features, already pale and drawn from the pain of the headache, appeared to crease first, into a look of curiosity, followed by a hint of disapproval, and finally into a scowl of dislike. "But, I don't mind eating alone if that's what you prefer."

"I've already phoned the nursing home. Pierre is sleeping peacefully so naturally it's better for all concerned that he's not disturbed at this late hour. I will visit first thing in the morning, alone. Taking along a complete stranger to visit wouldn't be helpful at all."

Lyn felt stung by her last remark and mumbled an apology which she didn't sincerely feel. She wasn't wanted here. She'd never been wanted as a child, so why should anything be different now. Jennifer Beck was a selfish cow whose only concern was to herself and her beloved Pierre. Soon, she would learn the truth, that Pierre was Lyn's father and she had every right to see him, and see him she would. Even if it meant falling foul of the famous artist. With her back to Jennifer Beck, She took a seat at the breakfast bar and poured herself a glass of wine.

Jennifer Beck was livid. How could she have been so easily duped, so easily drawn into the fictitious tale that Lyn Porter was only interested in buying one or two of her earlier pieces of work. The constant questioning should have warned her;

even Martha had been targeted. A true collector of art would be more interested in the paintings; the ideas and concept behind each piece, the development of the work. Lyn Porter's interest and fascination seemed only in the background and personal details of the artists' and no doubt what she could glean from their present day existence.

She paced the floor of her studio growing more and more agitated. She'd arranged to bring Pierre home from the nursing home next morning; but an excuse would have to be made. How could she expose him to this lying, conniving woman? How could she break a promise made during such a traumatic episode in their lives? Both had agreed, never to let a journalist cross the threshold of their home, ever again.

There had been a time, many years ago when the media had been their greatest ally, helping to propel the artists' from relative obscurity to the warm and welcoming heights of celebrity status. All was fine and dandy until that fateful day when tragedy struck. Overnight, their lives were changed forever. It wasn't enough that the horrible death of their only child brought such heart-rending suffering. Their pleas to be left alone, to grieve his loss, were totally ignored. Even after allowing a trusted journalist into their home to give an account of what had happened. The growing curiosity of the nation had been hell-bent on knowing all the gory detail and the minutiae of the case that followed. And the media had been determined to satisfy this warped, insatiable curiosity. Every day for weeks on end, crowds of journalists trampled across their private outdoor space and circled the surrounding neighbourhood like marauding sharks, hoping to gain any snippet of information or to flash their cameras as Jennifer and Pierre left their besieged home.

She shuddered as she recalled the worst period of their lives; and was determined never to allow such intrusion again. Pierre's condition, she believed, was connected with the trauma that was visited on them when Henri was so horribly killed. Had he been allowed to grieve in the normal way, guilt and blame would have taken its natural course instead of being suppressed, emerging years later coiled amongst the ravings of unintelligible language.

Jennifer heard noises in the kitchen which indicated that Lyn Porter had finished eating her supper. Plates clattered as she rinsed them under running water, despite the fact that Martha had pointed out the dishwasher. Knowing that she would have to make conversation, and determined to sell the pieces Lyn Porter had shown interest in and then be rid of her, she braced herself for what needed to be done.

As Jennifer headed toward the kitchen, Lyn Porter was pouring the remains of the half bottle of wine into a second glass, which she carried, one in each hand, to search out her host. The two women almost collided as one entered and the other left the kitchen.

"Oh, I'm so sorry Jennifer; I didn't mean to startle you! Martha opened a bottle of wine; which I'm sure was meant for the two of us." Lyn handed Jennifer the glass whilst she brushed a few droplets of the chilled white wine from her top. "The food was delicious, I've covered the rest and placed it in the fridge for you to eat later, when your appetite returns."

Having been put momentarily at a loss for words Jennifer accepted the glass and turned in the direction of her studio. Lyn followed. They entered the large, airy space, well-lit with halogen lamps. Eight hessian blinds were rolled down against the darkness outside. During the day, Lyn noted, as her eyes moved from wall to wall, this space would be flooded with light.

Jennifer placed the untouched wine on the first surface that came to hand, a glass table that held a beautifully arranged bowl of red roses, and with a wave of her arm said "This is my sanctuary Lyn; I know it's getting late, but I'm sure you're eager to see the originals of the paintings that interest you."

Lyn didn't answer at once, she seemed wrapped up in the bowl of roses. Which was to be expected, thought Jennifer, the newspapers, having managed to get hold of a copy of 'Henri in Tearful Pose with Rose' had had a field day concocting the whys and wherefores of the Beck's obsession with blood and roses. The simple truth was, if anyone had bothered to ask, it happened to be Jennifer's favourite bloom and because of this, Pierre had always given them to her on anniversaries and birthdays. Martha had kindly taken on what Pierre was no longer capable of doing, and as another important date had been ticked off the calendar they were here waiting for Jennifer on her return.

"The roses are beautiful. Are they flown in from England?" Lyn asked.

"I believe Holland is where they are produced now for the international market; but this particular variety did originate from England; but of course you would know that being a florist. You did say that's how you earn your living?" Jennifer heard the sarcasm in her own voice.

Lyn's face creased with concern. Jennifer seemed in a strange mood. She hadn't eaten a thing on the flight and to Lyn's knowledge, since she'd arrived back. There must have been a marked deterioration in Pierre's condition; but it was a devil of a job to get her to open up. The glass of wine remained untouched on the table as they moved towards a pair of free-standing easels that supported the paintings she'd shown interest in. Jennifer kept several paces behind and to the right, where she could watch, in profile, the other woman's reactions.

Lyn studied them for a while before her eyes moved beyond the easels and focussed on a low chest of drawers that was against the far wall of the studio Arranged on top of the chest were a collection of framed photographs. Pride of place in the collection was a large image of the child she'd seen holding the rose. There were no sign of tears in this picture; he sat happily on the lap of his father (it had to be his father, the likeness was uncanny.) Both looked beautiful as they smiled easily into the camera, their suntanned arms locked in an embrace, their sun-bleached hair crowning faces of bounding health. Realising that this was probably a cherished photo of the Beck's son and grandson, caused that, all-too-familiar, tightening of the chest. She was too far away to see the detail of the other framed images and as she unconsciously moved to take a step closer Jennifer's voice broke the momentum.

"Well, are the paintings to your liking?" Jennifer had been aware of Lyn Porter's interest in the photographs; the marked change in her body language had given her away. "I have a suitable tube that will make transporting them back with you very easy, and, if you present my invoice at the airport, you will be refunded the G.S.T. which I'm sure you'll appreciate."

Lyn turned, needing clarification of what was being said, and Jennifer explained that G.S.T. was a similar tax to England's V.A.T. and could be claimed back if you were a non-resident of Australia.

"Yes, I like them very much, but it would be nice to see them in natural light, along with your studio."

"Like I said earlier, I won't be around much tomorrow and the studio is always locked when Pierre and I are out. I'm happy to roll them in tissue and place them in a tube; you can view them in your room in the morning. There's absolutely no obligation to buy if you find that daylight shows them to be less pleasing to the eye."

Tissue paper and a cardboard tube of the perfect size, had been placed in readiness at the far end of a working surface, miles away, it seemed to Lyn, from the intriguing photographs. Knowing that this might well be her last chance to be allowed within this space, she agreed to have the paintings wrapped and while artist's attention was engrossed in the wrapping, she moved back to the chest of drawers.

Before Jennifer could do anything about it, the interloper had taken hold of their most precious item, an image of a happy moment showing father and son, captured on the day before Henri's tragic death! Filled with a smouldering resentment, Jennifer abandoned the tube and strode purposefully across the room eager to retrieve the photograph and determined to expose this impostor once and for all. A part of her remained calm enough to be grateful that Pierre wasn't here to witness what was taking place in his very own home. His very own sanctuary.

"Is this a photograph of your son and grandson?" asked Lyn Porter, without an ounce of shame.

"How dare you, you heartless bitch! You wheedle your way into our home under false pretences, just to satisfy the idle curiosity of a section of society who have nothing better to do than prey on the misery of others. Get out of here and leave us alone!"

Lyn flinched at Jennifer Beck's abusive words. "Hang on a minute, I only asked if the picture was of your son and grandson?"

Insulted even more, Jennifer held the framed photo close to her chest and spat her response. "You know full well that we have no son or grandson, I can see through your plan, and it won't work. I will not give any more interviews and you will not be allowed to see Pierre, is that clearly understood! I want you out of my house by the time I return tomorrow afternoon. Goodnight!" Jennifer held the door open for her to leave the studio; but before doing so the woman turned and confronted her.

"You're wrong about me being a journalist Jennifer. I have no idea about your life since you moved to Australia, except what is displayed on your website. Yes, I did have an ulterior motive for coming to Queensland, apart from genuinely wanting to buy a couple of pieces of your work. Pierre is my father, and as such, I feel that I have every right to see him, especially as his health is failing!"

Chapter 26

James Fairbank had gone to great lengths the day before in order to make sure that this morning would remain relatively free. He'd carried out and completed all the necessary paperwork on acquiring the allotment strip, leaving the transferring of it to John Haydon, until after discussing terms at a meeting in two days time. He'd arranged with his bank to collect the cash, insisted on by Peter Radcliffe, and which he'd pick up at 11-00 o'clock. And Clara, bless her heart, had arrived half an hour ahead of schedule to get started on sorting out the back log of his office paperwork.

But all was not going to plan. His mind was in complete turmoil; had been since first thing that morning while trying to reach Lyn at her Sydney hotel. He'd got used to the fact that she'd always been out when he'd phoned, accepting these, brush-offs, as punishment for pulling out of their arranged holiday; but to be told that she'd moved on, without leaving a forwarding address or number, seemed very odd and was extremely worrying. He'd promptly phoned Jill, Lyn's business partner. The two of them were in constant communication, so she should know something. Unfortunately, she too was in a quandary. Since Lyn's arrival in Australia, the only brief message she'd received, and this was via email, was that Lyn had a dinner date on Tuesday evening, which Jill was promised details of the following day. She'd heard nothing, and concluded that she'd probably met a rich and handsome Australian who had swept her off her feet, then added, before putting down the phone to tend to her demanding sons. "Let's hope he's more dependable than you!" With growing unease, James had then phoned Candy Laverne; but as half expected, her mobile was switched off. He left a brief message voicing his concern, sent it and then regretted burdening her, with what was after all, his problem.

Checking his watch, he was surprised to see that it was not yet 9-15. He'd promised Vincent that he wouldn't disturb him before ten o'clock but James was too agitated and troubled about Lyn's whereabouts, to allow forty-five minutes to make a difference.

After the second round of knocking the flat door was opened by Stefan and the waft of freshly made toast and fried sausages accompanied his welcoming smile.

"Good morning Mr Fairbank, would you like breakfast?"

"No he fucking wouldn't! This isn't a soup kitchen for hard up solicitor! Tell him to come back later."

James caught a glimpse of Vincent peering round the bathroom door, a towel wrapped around the bottom half of his bare body. "I'm not interested in food Vincent, I just want to know if you've heard from Lyn, apparently she moved out of her hotel yesterday and no ones heard from her since!"

"Shit, stupid cow!" This wasn't meant for the solicitors ears; but having heard it he bounded up to Vincent in three long strides and demanded to be told what was going on."

Without saying a word, Vincent led his neighbour to the switched on computer and brought up Lyn's last message.

Thanks for your help; I'll deal with IT myself!

"What does she mean? What will she deal with herself?"

"Your guess is as good as mine. I'm not a fucking mind reader, or a miracle worker! The only way I can help is to fly out there, and the expenses will be down to you pal; but may I make a suggestion?" Vincent didn't wait for James's response. "Get the fuck out of here and allow me to get dressed and have my breakfast; then come back at the time we arranged so that we can sort out the more pressing problem of stopping Carl from becoming our fucking neighbour. He caught Stefan looking his way. And, returning this man's sister to her family." Vincent grabbed at the towel which had shifted downward when he tapped Stefan's shoulder.

Recognising the sense of deep concern in Vincent's words, James gave a barely perceptible nod and retreated out of the front door.

Vinny plonked himself onto the nearby stool, shoved half a sausage into his mouth and bent to tie up the laces of his black, leather trainers. Whilst chewing the sausage, he gave Stefan advice on 'how not to allow the likes of Jimmy, to walk all over you'. "They use their posh accents to intimidate; but it doesn't fucking wash with me," he said brushing a fine spray of ground up pork from his jeans before lifting his head and reaching for another sausage which was pushed inside a slice of toast. "And, I'll bet you ten quid Stefan, when we discuss how to deal with Carl; he'll start fucking spouting on about the law and what we can't do. Well let me tell you, Carl is a law unto himself, and very soon now, Fairbank will find that out!"

Stefan had said nothing whilst eating and drinking his coffee; but after clearing the table he asked. "Vincent, why would you want to go all the way to Australia for helping Mr Fairbank's woman?"

"You don't miss much, do you Stefan. Look, when all this is over with Carl, I'll not be hanging around waiting for the shit to hit the fan, no fucking way! You'll be ok, hot-footing it back to Bulgaria and James will be safe in his law-protected ivory tower. I, on the other hand, intend to get away—I mean right away, for two or three weeks until things settle down again. Now I've never been to Australia but I do know that at this time of year it's particularly lovely; but it's fucking expensive and I don't have the money. Fairbank's woman needs my help and expertise; which I'm more than happy to provide, at a price. And Stefan, do not repeat what I've just said to anyone. Right, now let's get down to the more immediate business and check over the weapons."

At ten o'clock precisely, Stefan opened the front door once again to James Fairbank, offering him coffee as he was led into Vincent's office. The solicitor declined. The room became charged with expectancy as the three men seated themselves. Laid out openly on view, in the direct line of vision where the new arrival had been seated, were four items: a baseball bat with rubber-grip handle: a sheath-knife, measuring approximately thirty centimetres long: a ball-peen hammer and an item, which to most people, was not recognisable—Stefan had commandeered this item from the gang of Romanians two days ago. On noticing the items, the solicitor, as expected, left his seat to inspect them and, as expected, shook his head in disbelief.

"Vincent, please reassure me that you will not be taking this lot with you when we confront Victor Carlson; and what on earth is this?" The enquirer pushed around, with one reluctant finger, a black, torch-like object which he was informed was the Eastern European version of a stun-gun—a weapon used in several countries—for what purpose, James Fairbank was loathed to ask. "I am a solicitor; I can't be party to a confrontation where people are tooled up to the back teeth with an arsenal of weapons! Aren't you also forgetting, Vincent, that we intend to meet and discuss this in the home of a sick old man in his seventies; he could well collapse with a heart attack at the site of this lot!" James waved his hand contemptuously at the haul and moved back to his seat.

Vinny's face collapsed into a sneer "Meet and discuss; you're having a laugh. Carl doesn't meet and discuss with anyone unless it's on his terms. And as far as Radcliffe's concerned, his fate of a heart-attack is already sealed, unless we intervene!" Vinny's outburst caused a film of perspiration to break out across his red, chubby cheeks.

In a much calmer, but insistent voice, the solicitor continued. "Believe me, I can fully understand your fears. By all accounts, Victor Carlson is a dangerous and despicable person, but we can't just charge in there brandishing weapons or making threats of tickling his knee caps with a hammer or using that electrode gadget on his nether regions. It lowers *us* to his level. I have documentation which proves, beyond shadow-of-doubt, that Carl has committed serious crimes."

Vinny had heard enough. His fist slammed down on the nearby surface causing tremors and halting the solicitor in mid-sentence. Pens and pencils, spilling from their container, were the only noise disturbing the long silence that followed. Suddenly, Vinny jumped to his feet and marched the length of his short office, before sitting again. "What did I tell you Stefan? He'd try to bamboozle us with a few fucking posh words!"

Stefan had watched both men carefully. *His* agenda was fixed and unshakable; but he also needed these men to play their part. "Don't worry Mr Fairbank, Vincent will be taking only two of the items; the baseball bat and the hammer, and both will be concealed on his person, only for use to intimidate. I take other things for me to Lyme Regis. I maybe find Carl leave Elena with body-guard. I promise you, no unnecessary violence. Is why we display these things. Is good, no, that you see for yourself. Now we need to talk of times and how you and Vincent can be in old man's house before Carl arrives. What is plan?"

Looking disinterested, Vincent left his seat again and began slowly to replace the spilled objects while the solicitor kept centre stage.

"As we already know, Carlson's expected to arrive by midday. I've promised to drop something in for Peter by 11-00, and at that point I'll discuss the final details with him. I take it that you'll be leaving at about that time Stefan to hopefully make contact with Elena. I think that's all I can say at this point."

Vincent swung round, spilling the collected pens once again across the desk "Bullshit! If I can't be in on the discussions, then you can fucking well go it alone! And what is this 'something' you've promised to drop in to Radcliffe. We've been above board with you; what're you keeping from us?"

"My eleven o'clock appointment with Peter is completely unrelated to what we are discussing here, it's confidential, and I was merely suggesting that I take the opportunity…"

"You've suggested enough! Now what *I* suggest," Vincent made a point of stabbing his index finger in the middle of his chest as he positioned himself just inches from the seated solicitor, "At eleven o'clock, Stefan takes my van, with whatever he needs inside, and drives out to Lyme Regis. You *and* me, meet up with Radcliffe. You can carry on with your, private confidentiality crap, while I set the scene. And remember, you need to keep this appointment short. Then we talk about how we handle Carl. If we are hiding behind the scenes, Radcliffe needs to be warned against drinking anything. I also intend to set up a couple of bugs, maybe put one on his phone, whilst you're having your confidentialities. This is serious and dangerous stuff and it needs to be properly organised!"

Rained lashed against the kitchen windows of the secluded Lyme Regis house but this didn't dampen Carl's happy mood. Nor had the discovery of the missing window key, bringing to light Elena's attempt at escape. His smile broadened at the ingenuity of the set trap—did she really think he was that naïve—even so, he would have to take extra precautions when he left her alone. Working methodically, he hummed the tune from a song that was a particular favourite of Mother's, a song that they used to sing together on stormy nights when the two of them were at home, alone. In a few days time with Elena beside him, the three of them will sing together and happiness will flood back into his life.

It was ten minutes after ten and Carl needed Elena to be awake; but after checking on her a few minutes earlier, she had still been curled beneath the duvet, with the unmistakeable breathing of the deep sleeper. Taking hold of a lid from one of the large stainless steel saucepans, he held it above his head and let it fall onto the tiles of the kitchen floor; making a crash and clatter sufficient to wake the dead. "Careless me", he said with a smile, and continued with his task.

He sniffed the single rose on the prepared tray of orange juice, croissants and coffee, Elena's favourite breakfast. The coffee might have proved a problem, but the strength of the sedatives lacing the orange juice, would ensure that, enjoying the effects of the caffeine was never reached. It would also ensure that she would be non-functional for most of the day. There was quite enough to think about and arrange without worrying about what Elena might be up to.

On entering her room, he was relieved to see that she was stirring and apologetic for having slept so late. "I'm sorry Carl, I was wide awake two hours ago, and I should have made an effort to…"

"Shush, my darling it's quite alright. I disturbed your sleep last night and for that I'm sorry, now I must leave you shortly; but I've made amends by preparing you breakfast in bed." As Elena pushed herself into a sitting position, Carl arranged her pillows before handing her the orange juice. "Drink up my darling, I'm sorry I have to leave you; but I'll be back as soon as possible."

Elena gulped thirstily on the refreshing drink; stopping when the glass was approximately half empty. She frowned a little and lay the glass down but Carl, smiling and insistent, returned it to her.

"You are looking peaky sweetheart. You need plenty of vitamin C; I can't present you to Mother with a cold now can I? I shan't leave until you've drunk every drop!"

As Elena's eyes drooped and then closed, Carl removed the untouched croissant from her slackened grip and replaced it on the tray. "You will soon be mine," he whispered as he kissed her quiescent face. "And Mother will be content."

Checking his watch again, Carl's attention turned to Radcliffe. His twelve o'clock appointment with the old man was bound to have been written down somewhere in the pensioner's house and there was no guarantee that Carl could remove all that was checkable by the law enforcers. He would have to surprise Radcliffe by arriving early; then before the appointment became due, the deed would already have been carried out. Everything rested on Radcliffe being home and alone when Carl arrived unexpectedly at his door.

Rain continued to fall from the leaden sky as he activated the rolling garage door, he mentally ran through everything he needed. The contents of two of the special Viagra capsules had been emptied into a grip-top, polythene bag and slipped in his jacket pocket. His mobile phone, which he hadn't used for days and was still minus its sim card, was stored in the glove compartment, to be used only in an emergency. He would phone Radcliffe's place when he was approximately fifteen minutes away from Torbay. It would be disastrous to arrive fully prepared, only to find no one at home.

Chapter 27

Jennifer's mind reeled from Lyn Porter's revelation. The thought of Pierre being her father was ludicrous. But was it? Hadn't she noticed several times, how the bone structure of Porter's jaw, and the shape of the nose, were very similar to that of her husband's. Wasn't it this very coincidence—which was noticed straight away when they first met—that had helped to lower her usual mistrust toward strangers? No. No, how could it possibly be true. The colouring of Porter's eyes, skin and hair, were nothing like those of Pierre. She should try to sleep, take a pill if need be, and tomorrow with the woman gone, all would be well. But Jennifer knew she wouldn't sleep. Her mind was being pulled too hard in the direction of the only period in their lives when Pierre could possibly have slept around.

There had been ten months, back in the nineteen sixties, when Pierre was in the Australian Immigration Welcome Centre at Googee. Jennifer had been in England, giving birth and then waiting for their baby daughter to become

259

strong enough to join her on the long sea voyage to Australia. In the event she'd had to return alone. Fleur had developed a chest infection and had to be left behind temporarily with her mother. Ten months is a long time for a healthy young man to abstain from having sex, thought Jennifer, as she remembered the many young and attractive women that attended Pierre's classes. And guessing the approximate age of Porter seemed to support her fear. She remembered his promises, of how he'd remained faithful to her during those months; but the demons of doubt that lurked in the dark hours, sneered at the earthly sentiment of mortal words. Was it possible that Pierre could have been having an affair? No, she couldn't see it, or bear it. Maybe not an affair; but it was possible that he'd had the odd fling, it only took one night of unprotected intercourse.

What was she to do? Asking Pierre to corroborate any of this was out of the question; on most days he couldn't even remember his own name. There was no alternative. If the woman could prove paternity, Jennifer would have to pay. After all, that's what this was all about—money. If the media got hold of this, they would have a field day and their lives would be made unbearable! She had no choice but to hammer out a deal with Lyn Porter.

Having made up her mind on this course of action, she set her alarm and swallowed the sleeping tablet. She needed to sleep, she also needed to eat but the glass of milk drunk earlier would have to sustain her for tonight. Any solid food eaten now, would make her physically sick.

Lyn stood motionless, a lone figure silhouetted against the silver-grey glow of the moon. The late evening was warm and a light breeze tugged playfully at loose strands of hair that had escaped from her pony-tail. Below, the garden, shadowy and mysterious, was alive with activity. The snuffling, rustling and chirruping, creating a symphony of alien sounds, periodically interspersed with the plopping noises of rising fish from the dark water beyond. Large-winged moths and other unknown insects, attracted by the pools of light from two outdoor lamps, flitted about in the heavily scented night. It was an earthly paradise and everything seemed perfectly in balance with nature. Except for Lyn, who felt miserable and excluded. She stepped back into her room, looking for something, anything that would distract her from the gaping void that she felt inside. The bed was strewn with letters and photographs—contents from the brown envelope that she had hoped, at the opportune time, to share with her mother. But disappointment, humiliation and tiredness had drained the impetuous from her, and the evidence of who *she* was lay scattered like rubbish across the bed.

"It's not going to work." She said in a low, dispirited voice. "I was stupid to think that it would. Gran had been right." (D*on't try to dig up the past, Lynda, it will only bring you pain.*)

If it hadn't been for Jill, keeping on about the reuniting of Mother and Daughter and how it was Sarah's right to know that she had a grandmother living in Australia, her life would have gone on as normal. If only she hadn't found the two letters and the photograph, caught at the back of Gran's chest of drawers, she wouldn't be here now. She wouldn't be suffering the humiliation and the rejection that had grumbled beneath the surface since finding out that her mother was still alive.

Absentmindedly, she reached for the three inch square Polaroid photograph and looked at the strikingly beautiful woman holding a baby. The woman, who was unmistakably Jennifer, wore a powder-blue suit, its hemline way above the knee. The baby, almost hidden beneath the white lacy shawl, was held lovingly in her arms. The last time she looked at the photo, Lyn had kissed the image of her teenage mother; but she had no desire to do so now. Flipping the snap over in her hand, she revealed the one line of neat handwriting, written in faded black ink. Again, she read the few words.

Spring 1962 My Beautiful Flower

Keeping a firm hold on the photo, Lyn sifted through the rest of the papers and retrieved the two letters, before returning everything else to the large, brown envelope that was slipped in her bag. Part of her wanted to tear them to pieces and never think of them again; but Jill had been right, Sarah deserved to know the truth, especially as she was intent on settling here. The first envelope, which contained a single sheet of tissue-thin paper, was spotted with age but bore a clear postmark.

New South Wales-Australia November 3 1962

Most of the address, although faded, was still legible. It had been sent to Gran, where she'd lived in London and was written in the same neat writing as on the photo. Lyn removed the fragile piece of cheap writing paper and read again the few short lines.

Dear Mother,

Pierre has at long last secured a good job; making it possible to rent a place for the three of us. We will soon have enough money for a trip to London and to get married. We are really looking forward to being reunited with our 'little flower' and can't thank you enough for all your help.

Hoping to see you before Christmas, your loving daughter

Jennifer

Unlike the second letter, there was no forwarding address to reply to, although, knowing Gran, neither would have been answered, even if it had been the Queen of England who had written to her.

Without thinking, Lyn held the page to her nose and breathed deeply; but there was no trace of the familiar scent that surrounded Jennifer Beck and which seemed to permeate her home. She returned the page to the envelope where it had lay, folded, for more than forty-five years. Again, she wondered whether it would be better to destroy it. She wouldn't want to put Sarah through the same heartache that she was suffering. And God knows how much Gran must have suffered; no wonder she was reluctant to drag up the misery and discuss it with Lyn.

The second letter, which was typed on good quality paper, bore the name and address of a firm of London Solicitors, the postmark was over a year later.

London December 14th 1963

```
Dear Mrs Cartwright,
We have been instructed by Mr and Mrs P Beck of
Sydney, Australia, to seek out and make contact
with you.
 Please telephone Mr David Markham as soon as
possible in order to arrange, at your convenience,
an appointment at our Liverpool Street Office.
        Yours sincerely
            Robert Markham Senior
```

This letter had baffled Lyn, and with the help of Jill, they had spent a foot-slogging day of research trying to make sense of it; but the firm of solicitors had long since disappeared from that particular part of London.

Thinking of that few days spent in London, when fate had smiled down on her and improved her prospects, brought a fresh wave of weariness and despair. What on earth possessed her to come all this way? She should have been content with what she had.

She thought of James, suddenly needing to hear his voice more than anything else. She reached for her mobile phone, knowing but not caring that the call would cost a fortune; she punched in his office number. The phone rang several times causing her to calculate again the time difference. He should be in his office, she thought, and he usually answered straight away. She cut the line and dialled again, this time more carefully. Confusion filled her head when after only two rings the phone was answered by a well-spoken female. "James Fairbank's office, how can I help you?"

"Eh, can I speak to James, I mean Mr Fairbank." Lyn struggled to connect a face to the voice. It certainly wasn't Helen, James's sister, they'd spoken many times. Besides, this woman sounded quite at home there.

"I'm afraid he's in a meeting; maybe *I* can help you or can I get him to call you back, sorry I didn't catch the name."

"Just tell him Lyn phoned. I'll catch him some other time." The phone, along with the paperwork on the bed, was pushed away, allowing a space for Lyn to lie down and close her eyes against a world filled with hurt and uncertainty.

Chapter 28

As Carl nears Torbay, rain lashing against his windscreen, a growing sense of unease begins to nag. His meticulously timed operation has been messed up, thanks to the incompetence of one lorry driver who had jack-knifed on a tight bend and caused a two mile tail back of traffic. He checks his watch again. Ten minutes to eleven and there are still six miles to cover—miles that would be fraught with traffic lights and queues. Knowing that he couldn't possibly make it in ten minutes, he has no alternative but to phone Radcliffe as soon as possible.

A sigh of relief escapes as he stops alongside a public telephone kiosk. On entering it, an odour of piss assaults his nostrils; but it's the telephone receiver, suspended from its anchorage, that gives Carl the greatest concern. Snatching at it and tapping wildly on the phones mechanism reveals his worst fears. Rage surges within! Both hands coil around the defunct receiver and its plastic body is smashed against the kiosk's metal shelf. He checks again for any sign of life. When he finds none, he rips the damaged hand piece from its housing, throwing it into the gutter before driving off in a scream of burning tyres.

After a mile of frenzied driving, He gradually bridles his anger and calms his fears. Stopping in a quite parking bay, he reaches for his mobile phone and replaces its sim card, pushing aside his feeling of vulnerability to exposure. A few more days and I'll be back in my homeland, he reasons, quelling his feelings of unease. I have enough money and property to settle anywhere in the world. Soon, I will be married and Mother will be able to spend the rest of her days living with her favourite son and his new bride.

Radcliffe answered on the second ring with a shaky "Hello… Is that you Carl?"

"I'll be there very soon Peter; but I can't stay long. Have the letter for Elena ready, and of course a drink would be nice to show there are no hard feelings in the changing of our plans." Carl cut the connection before Radcliffe had the chance to delay him any further. Placing the phone on the passenger seat, he closed his eyes and allowed himself a few minutes to harness all his forces of concentration before carrying out the final stage of his plan.

The ringing of his mobile phone suddenly pierced through the sound of soft rainfall and intruded on Carl's concentrated state. Outraged that the senile old git had had the audacity to phone him back he snatched up his phone to turn it off; but saw that the call was from Eric, his nephew. Eric, Carl's oldest nephew was the only member of his family who was trusted with his phone number, Mother couldn't be relied on anymore to keep the number from his brothers. "Eric, what has happened?"

"I've been trying to reach you for two days, Uncle Victor, but your phone…"

"What is wrong Eric? Tell me."

"Grandma died yesterday."

Carl was stunned into silence for several seconds. "No! No I don't believe it! She can't leave me, not now!"

"I tried hard to reach you before she slipped away. She wanted so much to speak to you. She said she needed your forgiveness. I'm so sorry. The funeral is tomorrow. She is to be cremated and her ashes scattered over the sea, just like Grandpa. Can you get back for the funeral? Please say something, Uncle Victor; I really did try to reach you… The cancer won her over; at the end it was a relief to see her suffering come to…"

Carl turned off the phone. He couldn't bear to hear any more from his distressed and sobbing nephew.

James couldn't believe how quick and easy it had been to purchase a flight to the other side of the world. He'd passed the travel agents on his way to the bank. Its window was filled with famous scenes of Sydney, all beneath cloudless, vivid blue skies, tempting anyone who was already tiring of the bleak months in England. But James was not a man for shirking his responsibilities so he'd continued on to the bank. Surprisingly, he'd been dealt with straight away, by the bank manager, himself. *He*, evidently aware of James's healthy financial state during the last twelve months, was now curious and concerned about hefty sums of money being withdrawn. James had left him still curious.

Leaving the protection of the travel agents doorway,

drizzle developing into rainfall, James opened his briefcase and slipped the ticket within its protective leather walls before unleashing the strap on his large black umbrella and pushing it open.

"Hey watch it, you nearly had my fucking eye out; and why isn't your phone switched on; doesn't it ever occur to you that emergencies happen in the real world?"

"Good morning Vincent, I am a solicitor and I have no desire to broadcast snippets of my private conversations to all and sundry. That is the reason, behind my free choice, not to switch on my mobile phone whilst in public places. Now, what is this emergency that can't wait for ten more minutes until I get back to the office? And who told you where I would be?" James had told Clara that he was off to a meeting, nothing more.

"Radcliffe's crapping himself! Carl phoned him at ten to eleven; said to expect him soon."

"Is that all he said?" James looked at his watch and instinctively propelled his long legs into a march.

Struggling to keep pace, Vincent caught hold of his neighbour's sleeve. "Carl had said more, yes, but the old boy's not saying. He'll only talk to you. Candy found him arriving on your doorstep in his dressing gown; she's walked him back and she's still there."

"And Stefan, has he left for Lyme Regis?" With each stride James could feel the adrenalin pumping through his body. Victor Carlson almost cost him his home and maybe his future with Lyn. The time had come to put an end to the vile corruption of this evil man.

"Stefan won't budge until he knows Carl is here; he's

keeping a low profile and watching Radcliffe's place. Jesus H. Christ Jimmy, slow down I've got a fucking stitch!"

Twenty yards away from Radcliffe's property, Vincent left the marching solicitor and headed up the side road which led to the back entrances to The Terrace, here he would find Stefan, concealed behind a shed waiting for any sign of Carl's appearance.

James boldly walked up to Peter's front door and rang the bell. It was opened immediately.

"Thank God you've arrived before Carl!" Peter Radcliffe took hold of James as though he was greeting a long lost friend, dragging the man's ear toward his gasping mouth. "Did you manage to get…You know, the cash? Carl phoned over twenty-five minutes ago, giving the impression he'd be here very soon. I'm a nervous wreck!"

Peter Radcliffe was obviously shaken; but at least he was now fully dressed and looking relieved since James had tapped his briefcase to reassure him about the money.

"Tell me exactly what Carlson said when he phoned." Pressed the solicitor as he brushed Radcliffe aside, eager to move into the sitting room, away from the chill of the porch and Peter's foul-smelling breath.

It was Candy Laverne who answered. "Carl asked Peter to have a simple note to Elena ready, saying that, *he could no longer go on with it*, and also, to have ready, drinks for toasting the change of plans. I think it's very fortunate that we happen to be here."

James took charge as the next few minutes were filled with creating normality in Peter's sitting room. He and Candy concealed their presence by hiding in the kitchen's large pantry; but not before Peter was given instructions on how and when to switch on the small voice recorder, slipped inside his cardigan pocket. Silence prevailed as everyone remained motionless.

Twenty minutes later and everyone was still motionless. Suddenly, a tap on the back door, followed by Vincent's "It's only me, I'm coming in," caused the other three to groan with released tension. James rushed to the back door.

"Vincent, your actions could well have caused disastrous consequences!"

"He's not coming, it's fucking obvious he's not coming; when Carl says soon, he means ten, fifteen minutes, tops."

Looking confused, Peter Radcliffe wandered toward the voices. "Mr Conway isn't it? What are you doing here. And who the hell are you?" Stefan had joined Vincent, ready for action but lost for words.

The solicitor explained that they were extra security, just in case things turned nasty with Carl. Candy had already explained to Peter what Carl was capable of, adding to his anxiety. In spite of this, Peter felt compelled to confront Vincent.

"You mind your language, Conway, whilst under my roof; especially in earshot of a lady. Now, what do *you* propose we do? Sit around all day and scratch our arses, sorry Candy, nerves talking."

Candy made the suggestion that Peter should ring Carl "Be forthright and ask him where he's got to; tell him you have a doctor's appointment after lunch and it's important you keep to it. Peter took a little persuading, and then informed them all with a sigh of relief, that unfortunately he didn't have Carl's number.

"I have," said Candy. "I know it's a long shot, but it's worth a try."

Peter Radcliffe sat in his favourite armchair, slowly punching in the number that Candy had supplied. Twice his shaking hands had made an error; but his third effort, produced the sound of ringing.

"Eric, did you manage it?" brought confusion to all five faces grouped tightly together. Candy made encouraging signs for Peter to respond.

"Oh, hello Carl, is that you? How, how long are you likely to be? You see, I have an appointment with the doctor soon…And…And.

"She's dead! Got that, she's dead! Nothing matters anymore! Now get your decrepit, whimpering voice out of my ear and fuck-off to hell!"

Silence fell as the gravity of Carl's words hit home. Stefan was the first to break from the cluster of bodies. Checking that his weapons were tucked in place he headed for the back door. "Hang on Stefan, I'm coming with you." Vincent made a point of looking at the solicitor and tapping the two bulges on the inside of his oversized, camouflaged coat, before turning to follow his friend.

"And what if Victor Carlson shows up here after you've left?" shouted James, catching Vincent's attention before he slipped out of their sight.

"Wave your, beyond a shadow of doubt, documents at him, what else?"

As Vincent drove Stefan towards the isolated property in Lyme Regis, without a word spoken between them, Carl was heading in the opposite direction towards Heathrow Airport. Once the death of his mother had truly sunk in, Carl had phoned Eric and asked him to go on-line and find him the next available flight to Oslo. Nothing else mattered anymore!

Stefan kept his face fixed in the direction of the side window; but he saw nothing. His eyes were closed tight, struggling to hold onto to a reservoir of tears. He'd held his dying father in his arms and promised him that he would keep Elena, his only daughter, safe. And now, after all she had come through, after all Candy's help and support, some Scandinavian piece of shit, had stolen her life. Both hands kept a firm grip on the weapons in his pocket. Stefan vowed to avenge his sister; even if it meant spending the rest of his life behind bars.

Vinny screeched to a halt, the front bumper of his van almost touching the wrought iron entry gate. He entered the four digit number and strummed impatiently on the dashboard as the gate glided, ever-so-slowly inward. Stefan had bolted from the van and was halfway up the steep slope of the driveway before Vinny had been able to inch his way through. The van's engine whined in protest as he pressed his foot to the boards in first gear; slamming to a halt in the mouth of the open, double garage. He heard a loud crash of breaking glass and arrived, on cue, as Stefan opened a door to the back of the property. Nothing was said. No words needed to be spoken. Each man retrieved their weapons from concealment and entered the property, one covering the ground floor, the other mounting the carpeted staircase.

Vinny sensed there was nothing to be gained here. Everything seemed normal and in place; even the kitchen was clear of used dishes. It was too late, the car had gone and so had the occupants. If violence had been done, it hadn't happened here. His heart went out to his friend.

Suddenly he heard Stefan cry out. "Vincent, up here!"

Adrenalin pushed Vinny up the stairs, two at a time. Stefan was stood in the doorway of one of the bedrooms; staring at the soft rounded form lying beneath the quilt. It was obviously his sister, incapable of hearing the breaking glass, incapable of hearing anything ever again! Stefan remained rooted to the spot, unable or unwilling to face what the monster had done to his precious sister.

"Let me…Stefan, offered Vinny in a small voice."

"No, no I must do it! Is my fault, I should have come last night."

Vinny stood motionless as Stefan moved over to the side of the bed and gently stroked the mound of golden hair that splayed across the pillow. Tears pricked his eyes, as he watched his friend slowly roll back the quilt to reveal a female form, in pink pyjamas.

There was no sign of violence. Stefan lifted her limp hand and pressed it to his lips. Vinny turned and stepped from view, allowing his friend some privacy. Brushing aside a drop of rain that rolled down his cheek; he wondered what he should do next.

Suddenly, he heard Stefan's agitated voice. "Elena… Elena wake up!"

Vinny ran over to his side, taking his shoulders to lead Stefan away from the grief-stricken scene. Thoughts of brandy and strong, sweet tea tumbled around his head alongside the need to phone the authorities. But Stefan pulled away from him and knelt down by Elena, sobbing and gently shaking her upper body.

"Vincent she still lives! I can feel pulse dancing in her wrist. I think she drugged only! Please, go make strong coffee, my friend."

Elena's head was thumping with pain and no matter how hard she tried to open them, her eyes were tightly locked. Strong arms under her armpits struggled to help her walk; but her knees buckled on each attempt before thankfully being allowed to sit down on a soft surface. What she really wanted was to lie down and drift out of this disturbing dream; but the strong arms wouldn't allow it. One kept her upright, while the other tilted a container of warm liquid against her mouth—more of the vile liquid she had tasted earlier. She tried to keep her teeth clenched; but some of the liquid found its way down her throat, causing her to cough and splutter before another deluge of the stuff was poured in, unimpeded.

In the distance, a familiar voice, "Candy, will you take Elena with you to London." A pause, and then, "No, I wait here for bastard to return. Phone me when you get to Lyme Regis." Elena felt the cup once again grate against her teeth. She wanted to push it away; but her arm, heavy and unresponsive only managed to move an inch or two from her side. Maybe she had died—drowned in the disgusting liquid that was filling up her body. Panic took over and with the next deluge of the foul-tasting liquid; she summoned all her willpower and spat it back. The impetus of this movement caused her eyes to flutter open and she was staring at a strange man with chubby cheeks that dripped with the vile, black fluid. Both screamed in unison; bringing the familiar voice closer. Listless with confusion and fear at what was happening, she reached out to the familiar voice and soon found herself locked in the arms of her brother. And here she was anxious to remain.

Chapter 29

Early Thursday morning—Queensland

Alien raucous sounds penetrated into the depths of Lyn's sleep, splintering images and disengaging her subconscious wanderings. Before opening her eyes, she tried hard to recall the scenes that had brought about an emotion of irretrievable loss; but the deafening racket which filled the bedroom, aided its dissipation. Propping herself on both elbows she raised her upper body, allowing the memory of where she was and how she had fallen asleep, fully dressed, to focus in her muddled mind. Unabated, the deafening din continued as she dragged her resisting body in the direction of its source. Her waking brain, reasoned that parrots were the most likely cause, and this was confirmed as she slid open the terrace doors, startling them into silence for a few wonderful moments. Standing where she'd been the night before, she craned her neck to catch sight of the avian feeding frenzy; but soon realised that their tree was beyond her vision on a neighbouring property. Relief mingled with disappointment.

Five twenty showed on her wristwatch, which felt tight

from the puffiness of sleep. She stepped back into her room and caught sight of the cardboard tube and two paintings, reminding her of Jennifer Beck and what had passed between them. Her mind then flitted to the memory of her failed attempt to speak with James; bringing on the all-too-familiar tightening in her chest. She forced the thoughts to move elsewhere. Out in the garden there was still a riot of activity, and beyond, gliding effortlessly across mirror calm water, a man in his boat was enjoying the relative cool of the early hour. Slipping on her sandals, She decided to explore.

Stone steps led down from the corner of the terrace to a winding path below, heading in the direction of the water. From what Lyn had seen of the gardens at the front—neat and immaculately tended—it was a great surprise to find that in this section of the garden, nature had been allowed to reclaim the upper hand. Shrubs, almost concealing a high fence to the neighbouring property, were desperately in need of pruning, and the winding path, which was almost obliterated in places, was sprouting weeds between the cracks of the paving that remained. Mindful of the diversity of Australia's wildlife, and the poison that lurked in many of them, Lyn proceeded with caution until suddenly, her progression was halted. A tall metal gate, its large padlock rusted with age, barred her way. Shrubbery, on the other side of the gate, concealed any view of the water, although Lyn could smell its nearness and hear it's lapping presence only a few feet away. Feeling frustrated, she thought about climbing over the wrought ironwork; but the closeness of the gates upper spikes would have made it impossible, especially for anyone wearing sandals. Frustration turned to deep disappointment as she retraced her steps along the path looking for another way to reach the waterside. She found none. At some point in her exploration, the parrots had finished their early morning antics and flown away, without her having seen a single brightly coloured feather.

Jennifer Beck, like most Australian women, rose early during the hot months in order to complete her chores before the ascending sun made it too unbearable. These days, apart from her painting, there weren't many chores to do, thanks to Martha and the gardener. But old habits die hard, even when a good night's rest hasn't been possible without the aid of pills. In spite of the turmoil that she'd carried with her into sleep; she'd woken feeling calm and in control of the situation. She'd ordered Lyn Porter to be out of her home by the time she returned from the nursing home; but she would need to make sure that that didn't now happen. Tearing a sheet of paper from the telephone pad she wrote.

We need to talk before you leave. I'll be back soon. J.B.
Jennifer knew that Porter was up and about, she'd heard her opening and closing the terrace doors, but she had no wish to face the woman, not before she'd had a chance to see Pierre. Maybe, just maybe, if he was experiencing one of his more lucid days, she could glean a little information and try to help prepare him for the intrusion. First of all, she would need to phone Martha and ask if she'd mind coming over until she returned. She couldn't possibly leave

Porter in her home, alone. She checked her watch and decided to wait ten more minutes before phoning Martha; she knew she'd be up and about, but ringing before seven seemed a little disrespectful.

Lyn stood beneath the head of the power shower hoping that the tingling pressure of the hot water would go some way towards removing the melancholy that was threatening to overpower her. What should she do now? What she'd like to do, was return to England as soon as possible and get on with her life; but she knew that wasn't possible. For starters, she needed to fly back to Sydney and God knows when the next available flight would be. And once she was there, would she be able to bring forward her flight to Heathrow without incurring huge charges? And, would she live to regret running away from this one and only chance of meeting up with her father? A mix of unanswerable questions continued to rise with the steam, only to swirl and dissipate down the drain of the marbled wet-room. Stepping from the spacious enclosure, she wrapped a towel around her dripping body and padded into the bedroom, trying at least, to get her head around what to wear from the few items of clothing that she'd brought. A piece of white paper, shoved under the bedroom door caught her eye and halted her.

The sound of a car's engine, backing out of the garage, told Lyn that she had the place to herself. She'd read the curt note and shoved it into the pocket of her shorts before heading down to the kitchen. Here, she found the breakfast bar laid out with croissants, cereals and fruit. Halfway through a bowl of muesli, the sound of a key turning and then the front door being pushed open, caused her to freeze, a spoonful of oats suspended in the air.

"Good morning Lyn, it's only me," called out Martha in a bright friendly voice.

A tremor of relief shot through her as she responded. "I'm in the kitchen Martha, I'm just having breakfast."

Martha breezed in and asked her if she'd prefer tea or coffee with her cooked breakfast? Lyn answered with a question. "Didn't you say you only worked in the afternoons?"

"That's right, my dear, but as Jennifer's guest, she didn't want you fending for yourself the whole morning, especially as you're strange to these parts. What will it be then?"

"The cereals and croissants will be sufficient thank you; coffee would be nice, but only if you sit and have one with me."

By the time Martha had placed two steaming cups of freshly ground coffee on the breakfast bar, she had eaten her fill. They chatted amiably about the local attractions and which could be visited given the time available. Lyn was eager to explore the area, on foot, and Martha had promised to seek out a local map for her. The friendliness of this woman, coupled with the food and good coffee fuelled Lyn's determination to make the best of this given opportunity

"Martha, is Pierre dangerously ill? I can understand Jennifer's reluctant to discuss it but I do need to know. I have come a long way."

Martha was looking at Lyn intently. She suddenly blurted out. "You're a relative, aren't you? The likeness is there; not in your colouring but certainly in the bone structure." Martha's excitement was clearly visible; until a frown banished the effect. "But Jennifer said that you were a client, here to purchase a piece of her work; she didn't mention anything about you being related to Pierre."

"I was only a baby when Pierre decided to emigrate here, and this is my first trip to Australia. I didn't even know that he was still alive until…Well until I got here. Surely you can understand how anxious I am to find out how he is."

Martha's smile returned as she placed a comforting hand over Lyn's and squeezed it gently. "Jennifer and Pierre are very private people, and as their employee I have to respect that; but I do understand your predicament my dear, but, now I know that you're family, I'll help where I can. First of all let me reassure you that Pierre is not in any physical danger, well, there have been one or two occasions when he's tried to…To self harm; but he is very sick, in the mind." Martha tapped the side of her head and softened her voice as she spoke these last words.

An invisible cloud seemed to descend in the sun-filled kitchen and both women waited for the other to break the silence that followed. Eventually Lyn said, "Thank you Martha, I can understand now why Jennifer was reluctant to talk about Pierre. She did tell me that the nursing home is not far from here." In spite of the devastating news, Lyn's determination to see her father had increased, even though he might not care or remember the slightest thing about her, and Martha was her only chance of accomplishing this.

After a little hesitation Martha said. "The Resteasy Nursing Home is only a ten minute drive away; but I don't recommend you visit without the company of Mrs Beck." She stood and collected the empty cups and carried them over to the sink; signalling that she was unable to give any further information on the subject.

"Thank you again Martha, I think I'll take a stroll along the waterside. Oh, by the way, I tried earlier to follow the path that runs from the bottom of my terrace, but I couldn't find a way through, I'd appreciate a loan of that local map you mentioned."

Martha left the kitchen without saying a word and returned a few minutes later clutching what looked like a folded pamphlet. This was spread open on the cleared breakfast bar, revealing, in close detail, the layout of Twin Waters. A cross, in highlighting-green-ink, marked the position of the Beck's house. Lyn could see at a glance that she would need to walk a fair distance and circumnavigate several properties, just to arrive at the back of the house. "Why on earth would anyone block their access to a lovely walk along the waterside? It doesn't make sense!"

Martha released a heavily burdened sigh and said. "It hasn't always been that way, Lyn. After the tragedy, Mr Beck turned that corner into a sort of memorial to his son, adding sculpture and red-rose bushes that were obsessively tended by himself. But since the onset of his illness, Mrs Beck decided to lock the gate and allow nature to reclaim the space. She told me that it was time to allow the wounds to heal and move on. In the beginning, Pierre resisted her wishes, but gradually…Well he became too ill to argue.

The saddest thing, was that Jennifer wasn't able to give him another child, they tried, but after the second miscarriage they realised it wasn't meant to be.

"Oh how terrible Martha, I had no knowledge of their son's death" said Lyn, sitting down and pushing aside the map. "Would it be too much trouble if I had another cup of your delicious coffee, before I take my walk?

As both women lingered over the second cup of steaming coffee, Lyn was to learn, in detail, about the most harrowing episode of Jennifer and Pierre's life. Martha gave assurance to Lyn (and no doubt to herself) that the knowledge, she was about to impart, could be found in the media records of any library in Queensland. The tragedy had happened nearly forty years ago; but the newspapers resurrected the long-running, heart-rending saga whenever the hint of something vaguely similar appeared on Queensland's horizon. Martha cleared her throat in readiness as she stared into the steam of the coffee. Sensing that she had relayed this same story several times over the years, Lyn was determined to remain silent. To capture and visualise every scene and to be attuned to the nuances in Martha's voice.

"It was the day before Henri's second birthday, and the house was a hive of activity, preparing for the following day's celebrations. Sixty-five guests were expected, twenty-two of them children. Caterers, musicians, puppeteers and lighting engineers, all vied for the Beck's attention to make sure their preparations were perfectly in place. A large marquee had been erected at the back of the property and little Henri was playing contentedly under its shade with his dumper truck and a bucket of sand. Strings of bunting and fairy lights were being threaded from tree to tree along the Beck's section of the water's edge, where, during the evening, the adults were to be entertained by a classical trio.

Halfway through the morning as the temperatures climbed into the mid seventies, Jennifer, who had been supervising the two men working on the waterside lights, came indoors to prepare a tray of cold drinks. A phone call waylaid her in the preparation, but finally, after about fifteen minutes, she returned to the garden carrying a laden tray. Three things happened almost simultaneously: loud barking and furious snarls from Bess, their neighbour's German Shepherd, Pierre, ranting and raving at the electrical engineers for leaving the gate open to the waterside. After all, there was a large notice, on both sides of the gate, saying. **PLEASE KEEP CLOSED** And, the disturbing discovery that Henri was no longer in the marquee." Martha lifted her coffee at this point and allowed a small sip to moisten her drying voice. Lyn was spellbound and remained so.

Martha continued. "Panic set in as everyone frantically searched for the missing child. Pierre bounded towards the open gate and disappeared from view; but seconds later his anguished cries could be heard all over the neighbourhood. He had found his young son, face down in the water with blood surrounding the tiny form. As he lifted him from the water, the child's life-blood was still oozing from the gaping wound in his tiny throat. Within minutes the boy was dead!"

Martha reached into her apron pocket for a tissue and

blew her nose before continuing. Bess, the friendly dog from the neighbouring property, had given birth to four pups a few weeks earlier. Two of the pups had died in their first few days and Bess was particularly protective to the remaining two. And little Henri was seen as a threat! The inquest concluded that one of the pups had escaped from his enclosure and scampered down to the waters edge. The child, curious about a part of the garden he'd never been allowed to play in, was enticed through the open gate by the sight of the playful pup."

Another sip of coffee and Martha continued. "I wasn't there at the time. This happened over ten years before I came to be employed by Jennifer; but on that day, by the time the evening news was broadcast everyone in Queensland knew exactly what had happened. A journalist and camera crew, who were close friends of the family until that fated day, had been invited to record snippets of the lavish preparations. They seized the opportunity to capture, in graphic detail, what turned out to be, Scoop of the Year. The camera was rolling as Jennifer carried the loaded tray into the garden, and they kept on rolling even as little Henri gasped his final breath in the arms of his crying father!

A nasty court-case followed as the Beck's fought to have Bess put down; but after pressure from the animal rights lobby, the judge ruled that Bess, was only doing what came naturally to any mother; especially as she was on her own territory.

Deathly silence. Martha gripped her cup with both hands, staring into what was left of the coffee and lost in her own thoughts. Thoughts, which Lyn sensed weren't for sharing. She carried her own cup to the sink and emptied the cold, untouched contents and then rinsed it thoroughly. After folding the map and tucking it into the back pocket of her shorts, she placed both hands on Martha's shoulders and kissed the top of her head before whispering, "Thank you Martha; I'll see you later."

In her eagerness, to be away from the confining space where even the walls seemed to emanate an air of tragedy and sorrow, Lyn realised she had forgotten her hat. It was only 10am but the sun was already uncomfortably hot. Thank God, she thought, that the journey from the Beck's house to the nursing home was through a suburb of wealthy properties, all surrounded by gardens full of shade-producing trees. Attractions from all directions caught her eye, tempting her to stop a while, enjoy the feast of shape and colour, to use her camera and record for posterity the delightful scenes; but Lyn hurried on, intent on reaching the Resteasy Nursing Home as soon as possible. It wasn't actually marked on the map; but the first and only person that she'd seen—a woman clearing leaves from her lawn—showed her exactly where to head.

Within forty minutes Lyn was standing at the end of the drive of the nursing home, and it was here, it seemed, she was to remain. Security gates allowed no one to enter and no one to leave without the aid of an electronic pass. Tired from the exertion and the heat, Lyn perched on a nearby shaded bench to evaluate her options, regretting the fact that she'd also forgotten to bring water. Common sense told her there was no point in making a scene here, Jennifer Beck had already said in her brief note that she needed to talk, making it pretty obvious that Lyn had every right to see her father. After checking the map she decided to head down to one of the canals, canals which spread and opened into a large lake. And it was this body of water that lay to the back of the Beck's garden.

A refreshing breeze and a distinct smell of water hit Lyn after walking just a few minutes. A short distance, passed several large properties, and a sharp turn to the left brought her to the sandy slope of the lake's shore. To her astonishment and delight, a water fountain, spouting clean, fresh water at the press of a button, was the first thing she came upon as she headed toward a small wooded area, set aside for picnickers. After refreshing herself within the shade of this lovely oasis she headed in the direction she needed to go, allowing her mind to filter through all she had learned in the last few hours.

Jennifer had spent no more than half an hour in complete privacy with Pierre. During that time she'd held a one-sided conversation; relaying details of her trip to Sydney, including the early return with a guest who was anxious to purchase two pieces of her work. Pierre had appeared alert and focussed; but had remained silent throughout, his eyes never leaving hers. When the nurse had arrived to escort him to one of the therapy classes Jennifer had found herself feeling relieved, then guilty for feeling that relief.

On her arrival at the nursing home, the doctor had explained that Pierre's medication had been reassessed and altered. New drugs were being developed all the time for people suffering with dementia, and the latest, 'wonder-drug' seemed to be having a positive effect. Jennifer had grown used to such platitudes; but she had to admit, Pierre had seemed, more together, than she'd expected. She'd arranged to return at 2-00pm to take him home, Porter would by then be out of their lives; the last thing Pierre needed was to be confronted with a perfect stranger, calling him Daddy!

Feeling tense with determination, She drove into the garage and left the automatic rolling door in the open position. Martha was watering the potted herbs and greeted her with a smile; but the smile faded when she realised that Jennifer was alone.

"Is Mr Beck alright?" she asked, full of concern.

"He's very well Martha, I'll be collecting him after lunch, there are a couple of therapy classes the doctor would like him to attend; I suppose they feel that they need to justify their exorbitant fees. Thank you for coming over this morning, I do appreciate it. Off you go now, I'll finish the watering. Incidentally, is Lyn Porter about?"

"She arrived back from a walk just a few minutes ago. She's sitting on her terrace writing postcards. See you tomorrow then."

Jennifer stood at the threshold of the guest bedroom's open door, looking at the head and shoulders of her opponent through the mesh of the screens that led out to the terrace. This side of the house was in deep shade until the afternoon; but even in the diminished light, her likeness to Pierre was unmistakable. Relaxed and engrossed, with pen to paper, it could have been him (in female form) about thirty years ago. She closed the door with a loud 'clunk', and within seconds found eyes, unfamiliar to the bone structure of the face, looking at her.

Lyn Porter rose from the table and stepped into the bedroom, closing the screens behind her. Jennifer remained facing her, several feet away. "I hope you enjoyed your walk; now let's get this sordid business dealt with and you can be on your way. You're obviously here for money and I've no doubt you'll use the threat of exposure and publicity if you don't get it; but before I even consider any of your demands, I want proof of who you say you are." Jennifer watched closely as Porter's face blanched.

"Proof of who I am?"

"Your mother's full name—at the time she gave birth to you—and the dates when she…When she and Pierre supposedly had this fling."

Hatred rose like bile from the pit of her stomach as Lyn realised what Jennifer Beck was inferring. She marched forward, closing the gap between them and took hold of the older women's shoulders, turning her to face the wall of mirrored wardrobes behind. "You have her before you! A selfish mother who abandoned her baby, in order to live a charmed life in the sunshine!"

The shock and fear, at being suddenly man-handled showed on Jennifer's face; and was reflected back to both women. They stared at each other—two pairs of similar-coloured eyes radiating a hatred and contempt that was borne out of confusion and a deep sense of lòss. After what seemed like an eternity, and in a voice that was barely audible, Jennifer asked. "Who are you?"

Watching, through the reflecting mirror, Jennifer saw Lyn Porter move slowly to the bedside cabinet and remove her bag; she started to lift papers from the zipped side pocket and then hesitated—her head bent and her body forlorn and dwindled. A change of stance, and suddenly the papers were being tucked back inside and the zip closing. "I'm nobody you need worry about; can I use your phone to book a flight and then I'll be on my way".

Jennifer turned and faced the other woman taking a few steps closer as she spoke. "It's true, we did have a baby daughter; but she died of pneumonia when she was six months old."

Lyn turned on her, "And my parents died in a road accident when I was nine months old; but Hey Presto! Here we are, all alive and kicking! Kicking against the bloody truth! I was left behind with Gran, Edna Cartwright, your mother, while you sailed off to the land of sunshine and promise. You want proof of this, well here's the bloody proof!" She grabbed her bag, tore open the zip and removed the two letters and the Polaroid photograph, throwing them without care onto the pillow. She then took out the large brown envelope that was full of family snaps, and upending it onto the bed; spilling the captured moments of her life over the bed and onto the floor. "If you're the slightest bit interested, I have a daughter and a grandson and neither have an inkling that you or your husband exist. Maybe *you* prefer it to remain that way. I just felt that my father should have the right to decide for himself." She pushed passed her stunned mother and left the charged atmosphere of the room.

Lyn replaced the receiver with a sigh of relief. It had been a long rigmarole finding the right number and bringing forward her return flight to Sydney for later that day. It would have been much quicker and a lot less hassle if she'd returned to the bedroom and asked for help; but she couldn't face talking to her mother. Not yet.

She wandered through to the kitchen and helped herself to a glass of water. As she sipped the cool, refreshing liquid her mind was filled with thoughts of Sarah and her grandson. Was Lyn destined to be parted from her nearest and dearest family, just like Gran and Gran's daughter. As if summoned by the thought, Jennifer Beck walked into the kitchen and sat down on the opposite chair. Lyn's eyes remained fixed on the glass of water that was gripped in her hands. She heard the other woman start to speak, her words, hesitant at first, were soft and comforting; reminding her of story-time at school when all small children were encouraged to take an afternoon nap.

This story began many years ago when the Beatles were still relatively unknown and playing at the Cavern Club in Liverpool. A seventeen-year-old art student fell deeply in love with one of her tutors. He was eight years older than her and came from France. *His* feelings toward the student were just as powerful and each day their love grew stronger. One day the young student found that she was pregnant and made the mistake of confessing everything to her mother, emphasising their love and intention to marry. By the end of that month the tutor was sacked and hounded out of the country. Fortunately for the lovers, an opportunity arose where they could be together, and raise their family in a land full of hope and less discrimination.

Uncertain of the medical facilities while travelling to and on arrival at this new country; it was decided that the heavily pregnant art-student remain at home until after giving birth and the baby was deemed old enough to make the long six-week journey by boat. Reservations had to be made months in advance; and the days were patiently counted off until finally they were due to leave. At this time, Measles was rampant in the squalid, close-knit community of East London, where the art-student grew up, and the baby girl had contracted the disease, leaving the mother with a heart-rending dilemma. It was decided, that the journey was too much of a threat to the six-month-old-child, so the mother reluctantly left without her, promising her own mother, who was left in charge of the babe, that she'd return for her baby as soon as possible.

The six-week journey overseas was horrendous, storms and lashing rain were continual and the art student, although racked with guilt and misery about having left her daughter behind, knew she had made the right decision. The tutor met her off the boat and was deeply disappointed not to be able, at long last, to hold his baby daughter; but, they both worked like demons to raise the money to return for her. As soon as this was possible, they sent a letter to the art student's mother, thanking her for her support and saying that they would soon be arriving for their daughter. Before they had the chance to leave, a telegram arrived containing the few brief words that shattered their world.

Babe died of Pneumonia.
She was buried two weeks ago.

The art student, stricken with grief, now had to cope with the knowledge that her strong instinct to leave the child behind had been flawed. At least on the treacherous journey they would have been together. Even if she'd been destined to die on the rough seas, she would have had her mother's love to the very end. This realisation, created a void in the art-students heart which she knew would always be there.

The tutor's grief produced anger; anger towards everyone who had been party to the shattering of their dream. Most of his anger was aimed at the art-student's mother, whom he blamed for losing his job. He'd rant and rave continually, accusing her of all kinds of mischief.

The soft, soothing voice halted. Changes had taken place, just like in early school when you woke from story-time and found a warm blanket tucked around you. The cold glass of water was no longer gripped by Lyn; in its place were hands, reassuringly warm. Lyn raised her head and found her mother smiling but with tears rolling down over her pale cheeks. Her own eyes threatened the same but she squeezed them tight to prevent it and said in an accusing voice. "So, all this misery was Gran's fault, was it?"

"No. Not at all. Your grandmother loved you so much, she couldn't bear to give you up. You are aware from the letters you found that we tried to contact her. She uprooted from everything that was familiar to her, in order to prevent us finding you. She saved your life, gave you the opportunity to grow, develop and marry, eventually having a family of your own. Life and love are all that matter; if I'd taken you with me, you wouldn't have survived. Pierre grew less angry when I became pregnant with your brother. When Henri was born he became our light and our focus and everything was wonderful again. But…Oh God the cruelty of it! Before he'd even reached two years old…We were robbed again!"

Lyn felt the vibrations of her mother's grief pass through their joined hands as pressure increased. "I know all about my brother's death, there's no need for you to relive it. I'm so sorry, it would have been nice to have had a brother; but, I would like to see my father before I leave."

"I take it you're booked on the early evening flight, so that gives us a few hours to spend together." Jennifer held her daughters hands to her lips and kissed each one.

Lyn didn't resist, asking in a small voice. "Do you think my father will know who I am?"

"Probably not; but maybe on some level of his troubled mind, if you hold him close and whisper, Papa, it might bring him a little peace.

Chapter 30

Physically exhausted and mentally frustrated James climbed into bed with very little hope that sleep would come easily. He'd been with Peter Radcliffe the whole afternoon and evening; would still have been there had he not taken a firm stand. Peter, convinced that Victor Carlson may still show up, had clung to James's arm and begged him to stay each time he had made a move to leave. After speaking with Elena and hearing the background about Carlson's terminally-ill mother, everyone seemed to agree that Carl must have received bad news and he was on his way home. But Peter still hadn't been convinced. He'd suggested that James ought to make himself comfortable on the sofa and stay overnight. Exasperated, James had argued that he couldn't stay any longer, and was Peter aware of spiralling costs and expenses, incurred because of his so-called, marriage-of-convenience.

Peter had turned on him. "What do you mean costs and expenses?"

Having at last found a way to tap into the old man's

reasoning faculties, the solicitor had reeled off several things that could be construed as chargeable. "For starters, a two-man surveillance assignment plus equipment, runs into the hundreds of pounds."

The old man, sitting opposite and growing paler by the minute, as he'd taken on board what the solicitor was saying, was stunned into silence. James had continued. "Overnight hotel accommodation for Elena and her transportation costs to London the next day, and then of course, there are my own costs; and as you know Peter, a solicitor's hourly rate, out of necessity, is very high. I think two thousand pounds should just about cover it, if you pay cash. Or, if you prefer, I'll get my secretary to type up a fully-itemised invoice which will probably include several other things that don't readily spring to mind; plus of course, there's the V.A.T."

Without saying a word, Peter had shuffled out of his sitting room and returned a few minutes later with an envelope, only finding his voice as he unbolted his front door.

"Here's the two thousand." He'd said, shoving the envelope roughly towards James. "I don't expect to be charged for anything more or from anyone else: and, if Carl does show up, *you* can explain to him why his money is short."

With blessed relief, James had entered his own place, tossing the envelope of money into the top drawer of his desk. Two messages, demanding his attention were blinking on the answer phone. He'd wanted to ignore them and just climb the stairs to bed, but instead, he'd poured a glass of red wine and activated the first message. Lyn's voice, sounding forlorn, had filled his office. "James, I'm sorry I haven't been able to catch you again. I'm in Queensland and, well it would have been nice to talk. I'll try again later."

James had cursed Peter Radcliffe out loud as he'd moved to the second message. As expected, it had been Lyn, sounding brighter, but wary. "It's me again; I suppose you're paying me back for avoiding you. Sorry, I don't mean that; I know you're not as petty as me. But it would be nice to hear your voice. Hopefully we'll speak soon." Deathly silence had followed. How could he possibly speak to her; she hadn't left a number to reach her on and her mobile was constantly switched off.

Carl took the key from the tired-looking Polish attendant and walked over pitted tarmac to a row of shabby rooms. He'd been driving for hours without a break; desperate to reach the airport and then home. Heathrow was only a few miles away; and at this early hour could be reached in half an hour. There were still five hours before his flight was due to leave and a couple of hours sleep was all that he needed—two hours respite from the images that pressed against his aching head, hammering at the memory of a summer's night, when he was just a boy of fourteen. He'd pulled into the lorry park's service station for coffee and a few minutes rest after narrowly avoiding a collision with a coach. But, whilst sipping on the coarse brown liquid, he'd noticed the sign.

CHEAP ROOMS—BED, BOG & WASH

And decided that this opportunity, was too good to miss.

He turned the key and kicked open the metal-clad door. A stench of stale tobacco greeted him. The small space, which contained nothing but a single bed and wooden stool—positioned to be used as a bedside cabinet—had no window, the only ventilation coming through an air-brick set in the wall. One corner of the room had been partitioned off and a door, standing fully-open, revealed a stained lavatory and sink. Carl set the alarm on his watch for 3-30 and lay, fully clothed, on top of the single blanket before flicking off the overhead florescent light.

Elena lay wide awake in the plush hotel room. A pleasant mix of Candy's snoring and the crash of the waves rolling onto the hotel's beach soothed and relaxed her troubled mind. The strong sleeping tablets had left her body feeling disorientated and it was because of this, Candy had insisted that Elena spent the night making good use of the spare in her twin-bedded room. The constant questioning from her brother is what had troubled Elena more than anything. She was convinced that Carl was heading for home; having somehow received the news that his mother had died; but voicing this, hadn't stopped Stefan from interrogating her. He'd wanted to know how he could find the man who had held his sister captive and was prepared to marry her off for money. He'd wanted to exact his own type of revenge, without any thought to the consequences. Elena couldn't allow that, so she had kept quiet about most of the knowledge she'd gained from Carl and his private life. It had been hard to make him understand the reasons behind why she had agreed to marry Peter Radcliffe. Hopefully by morning he will have calmed down and he will agree to return to London with her and Candy. She needed to get back to work and put this mess behind her. If there was one thing she'd learnt, there was no easy way of acquiring a home here for her family But, thanks to Candy, she was in a position to work hard and save money.

Vinny's digital clock emanated a soft glow of blue-green light into the pitch-black of the bedroom. He'd been awake for ages, itching to get up but afraid of disturbing Stefan. It was only ten past four and normally he'd still be in the land of nod; but this was no normal day. With all the crap concerning Carl, Radcliffe and Elena out of the way, he could now concentrate on his expected trip abroad. He knew Jimmy had bought the flight, he'd seen him sneak the ticket into his briefcase; but what he didn't know, was when? Didn't matter; he'd pack anyway. He closed his eyes, allowing a thrill of excitement to run through him at the thought of Lyn Porter's surprised face.

Unable to wait a minute longer, he eased himself from the bed, crept towards the wardrobe and reached up to grab the handle of his suitcase, which rested on top. On pulling the case towards him, Vinny disturbed the baseball bat and hammer that had been shoved in front, (by him) only a few hours ago. After clouting the side of his head, the baseball bat landed on the floor with a loud clatter; followed by the almighty thud of the hammer. Vinny danced around the room on tiptoe holding his swelling head and cursing under his breath. Suddenly, the room was bathed in bright light and Stefan stood framed in the doorway.

"What is happening,?"

"Sorry mate, I didn't mean to wake you. Oh my fucking head is really hurting! Is there any of that steak left?"

Within a few minutes, both men were sitting at the kitchen table drinking coffee, one with a slice of raw steak draped across his left eye as he tried to explain to the other what he'd been up to at that ungodly hour.

Under different circumstances, Stefan would have found Vincent's accident very amusing and they would have both laughed it off. He'd sensed Vincent's relief that Carl had disappeared out of there lives, for now; but that didn't mean that the business was finished—not for him. Until the man was out of the way for good, he would always be a threat to his sister. Elena didn't agree; and because of her disagreement, she was keeping knowledge of Carl's whereabouts from him.

Whilst Vincent had been taking care of Elena in the Lyme Regis house, Stefan had been searching every inch of the place looking for clues on how he could track him down; but there was nothing. In Carl's bedroom they had found: two Armani suits, five expensive shirts, two pairs of leather shoes and several sets of underwear and socks. All were carefully folded and placed in a large black, plastic bag which Vincent carried away. Stefan was offered a share of the find; but all he wanted was information on Carl; but Vincent couldn't, or wouldn't help him.

The tempo of the watch's alarm rose to fever pitch, cutting into Carl's worst ever nightmare. Emerging from the trauma of it—thrashing and kicking his legs against the strong brutal arms that held him down—he fixed his mind on the clear and undeniable image of his mother. Sitting bolt upright, gazing without seeing into the cheerless room of the lorry park, he confirmed out loud what he had just seen. "She *was* there; *she* had known what had happened all this time!" Years of psychotherapy, hypnotherapy and countless other mind games, dissipated like mist as the light of truth cut through and tore aside the veil of deception. Everything that happened, on that hot, summer's evening, suddenly fell into place.

His father and four older brothers were on a three day fishing trip. The Vega Islands in the county of Nordland were particularly productive at this time of year. Young Victor was fourteen, old enough, according to Father, to work alongside his brothers on weekend trips. But Victor had no interest in fishing and the constant roll of the boat made him feel ill, so, as usual,he had remained home helping with the domestic chores.

An unpredicted heavy storm had erupted in the sultry heat of the summer evening, howling and blowing warm air through every crevice of the house, making it difficult to sleep. Mother became fearful and agitated, calling on Victor to help calm and sooth away her demons by singing to her. Victor obliged. He lay down alongside her stroking the tension from her arms and shoulders whilst singing their favourite lullabies. Soon, they were both asleep.

Rough, calloused hands, pulling and tugging at his exposed upper body, suddenly disturbed that sleep. Was it morning? Victor had thought, daylight was showing around the edge of the black-out-blind, but at this time of year, day light was almost perpetual. Bleary-eyed, he'd tried to make sense of why he was being part dragged and part carried toward the kitchen. He flailed his arms and kicked his legs; but the vice-like grip from behind, only tightened.

The nightmare shifted and became more sinister. Victor heard the waste-disposal-unit pulse into action and saw a hand reach for the scissor-like tool that Father used for trimming the fins from the fish he'd caught. Cold metal touched Victor's lower belly as he squirmed to break loose. He caught sight of Mother, framed in the kitchen doorway; eyes wide and stunned. He screamed in panic begging her to intervene; knowing that the nightmare would take its course. The sound of the Cut, followed by white-hot searing pain filled Victors head as warm liquid pooled in his groin. He was finally released, slumping in a heap on the cool tiles. Before passing into oblivion, Victor saw his captor grab the arms of his traumatised mother; spitting out the words "Remember, he's a sleepwalker who visits his mother's bed! Shame drove him to remove the cause of his problem!"

It was days later when Victor had awoke in hospital, heavily sedated from the second operation. He'd just been told that he would be incapable of enjoying a normal sex-life or fathering children. "But it's not all bad news, young man", the doctor had said, smiling over the tented sheet that had covered Victor's lower body. "Your second operation was very successful. You won't be needing that catheter for much longer."

In a stupor from pain-killing drugs, he'd barely

remembered his Mother's early visits and her explanation of his self-mutilation. How it had all been tied up with his fear of puberty and the emergence of urges he couldn't cope with. At the time, Victor had tried to argue that Father was the one who had ruined his life; but no one would listen. According to Mother, they were alone in the house and she knew nothing until his screams awoke her. And, according to his four older brothers, Father was with them, miles away, catching fish.

Holding back a reservoir of emotions, Carl slammed the door of the desolate little room and headed for his car. Clouds scudded against the dark sky as he halted; breathing deeply on the chilly, damp air. A sign ahead pointed left, guidance for joining the slip road that lead to Heathrow. He turned right and switched off his lights. Within minutes, an articulated lorry was heading toward him. Anticipating the lorry driver's instinct to swerve, he manoeuvred to counteract it. Flashing lights and the continual blare of the horn meant nothing. Carl's head was filled only with the image of his mother, wide-eyed and stunned. Impact!!! And Mother's image fragmented and disappeared.

8.00am
The ringing of James's doorbell sent him scurrying from the bathroom, wrapping the towelling robe around his damp body as he descended the stairs barefooted. It was Candy; fulfilling her promise to say goodbye before setting off for London. She apologised for arriving early and

explained that Elena wanted to have another go at persuading Stefan to return with them. James looked at the beautiful young woman who had been at the centre of all the trouble. The model, stood by Candy's Jaguar, smiling sheepishly.

"As you can see, Candy, I'm still dressing." James pulled the robe tighter across his body, embarrassed about his lack of courtesy at not inviting them in.

"I should finish shaving before you get dressed." Candy said, smiling as she pointed out a missed patch of whiskers to the right of his jaw. "We're going down to Vinny's flat, and after seeing Stefan, Elena would like to have a word with Peter Radcliffe, just to tidy things up, so I'll see you down there when you're ready. According to Stefan, Vinny's been up for hours."

James looked at his dishevelled appearance in the bathroom mirror as he slapped shaving foam on the side of his face. He would need to fit in a haircut sometime during the morning, he thought, grabbing hold of a handful of his tussled mane. So many other things were pressing for his attention; but he had made up his mind and nothing was going to be allowed to change it.

After tapping lightly on the lower flat's door it was opened immediately by Vincent who greeted James with a radiant smile. "Good morning, Jimmy, just got up I suppose."

"You seem very chirpy Vincent, considering the early hour." James stepped into Vincent's flat, just as Elena was leaving to pay Peter Radcliffe a visit. A suitcase, positioned in the hallway, caused him to step back and allow her to pass. A large colourful label was tied to the handle of the case showing clearly who it belonged to. With Elena out of the way, James reached into his pocket and withdrew two envelopes; handing one to Vincent, he said, "Here's a thousand pounds to cover your time and expenses. Are you off on a trip somewhere Vincent? You have been complaining a lot lately, saying that you needed a holiday."

"Come on Jimmy, stop keeping me in fucking suspenders, when's the flight booked for? I need to get organised."

Stefan appeared in the doorway and James handed him his envelope; which he tried to refuse, until James explained that the money was from Peter; gratitude for all their efforts.

Vincent interrupted, saying to Stefan. "If Radcliffe coughed up a grand each for us, he must have handed Jimmy here a good tidy sum, but I don't suppose we'll get to know about that." Turning to the solicitor he asked. "So, when is my flight to Australia? I know you have the ticket, and I do need to make my arrangements."

"*My* flight to Australia, leaves at 8 pm today, Vincent. I do appreciate your offer of help; but Lyn's my woman and therefore my responsibility."

Stefan held out his hand to James, holding on for several moments before saying in a low voice. "Can you give me any help in finding this man, Carl?"

James looked into Stefan's beseeching eyes. "I can only give a piece of advice. Stop looking my friend. Being caught up in the same way, may have cost me my future happiness."

Stefan nodded and turned to Vincent, lightly toeing his suitcase. "Shame to waste all this effort, my friend. Why you not join me for one week trip to Bulgaria? I return with Elena, for visiting my family. Then she coming back for working with Candy. I also will come back to find work. I no want to leave my sister here alone. Not yet. As my friend, I show you Bulgaria. My country knowing no bounds when it comes to criminals. You will learn much about this underworld. It will help you in your business, no?"

"I suppose the trip *would* be tax deductible," said Vincent, smiling as he scratched his chin. "Jimmy, before I place them on eBay, would you be interested in a couple of very nice Armani suits?"

Epilogue

Lyn sat propped against four pillows drinking her second cup of instant coffee. She was back in the Sydney hotel, wondering what to do with the remaining two weeks of her holiday. What she really wanted, was to return to England and pick up where she'd left off, but that choice had turned sour. On two occasions yesterday, she'd phoned James's office and been forced to listen to the same sickly-sweet voice of the unknown female. Each time, Lyn had cut the connection without saying a word. Desperation had driven her to phone his mobile; but that, seemed to be permanently switched off. With a heavy heart, she wondered again if the trip to discover her estranged mother had been worth the loss of the man she loved; even though there had been the added bonus of discovering that her father was still alive too.

Father and daughter had sat side by side in the back of her mother's car as they drove the short distance from the nursing home to the house in Twin-Waters. Pierre had been lost in a world of his own and Lyn had felt awkward,

308

stealing sideway glances every now and then, absorbing what she could from the distinguished-looking stranger. On entering the privacy of the Beck's home, a marked sense of relief and relaxation filled the air. Lyn was introduced to Pierre, as Fleur, their lost little flower who had come all the way from England to help mend their broken hearts. Pierre had said nothing, and gave no indication that he'd understood any of the softly-spoken words, delivered with genuine feeling. Lyn had reached out, and wrapping her arms around the father she'd never known, whispered, "Papa, I'm so happy to meet you." She'd held on tightly, trying to infuse the love of all the lost years. Eventually, she'd released her hold realising that he too had pressed his arms around her—arms that were strong and comforting. Suddenly the pressure slid away and he was smiling into her face as he said. "Thank you nurse; I've had a lovely holiday!"

The afternoon spent together hadn't been the outpouring of happiness that Lyn had expected; but it had been nice. No, it was better than nice; somewhere deep inside a, shift, had taken place, an adjustment, helping her to accept what can't be changed. Even the seeking out of the thief, Andy Fernley, who had made off with a bundle of her money, seemed pointless. In her heart she knew the chance of finding him was very slim, so why waste precious time and even more expense trying. Her mother had tried hard to persuade her to stay longer; but the flight to Sydney had already been arranged, and quite frankly, she had needed to be alone.

But now, with the empty day spread before her, she

wondered if she'd made the right decision. It wasn't until she'd arrived back at the hotel, physically tired and emotionally drained, that she'd found her mother's gift. Tucked out of sight in her case, was the cardboard tube, which Lyn, in a fit of anger had returned to the artist. Inside were four floral paintings and a letter.

Dearest Fleur,

You will always be our 'little flower', and how appropriate that you have chosen a career which embodies your given name. We have so much in common, my darling daughter. I hope that my fearful misunderstanding and my appalling attitude toward you might, in time, be forgiven and allow us to become friends; but please don't leave it too long. Believe me when I say, fame and fortune are nothing, compared to the love and companionship of family and friends. Please accept the four paintings enclosed, the two you chose and two chosen by me. The Gilly Flower, represents, Bonds of Affection, and The Celandine, represents, Joys to Come. As well as the gift of a daughter, we assumed to be long dead, thank you for the gift of your family (our family) photographs. You can be assured that they will sit alongside those of your brother, and we hope to be able to add many more over the years. Again, thank you my darling for seeking us out, we will remain, as we have always been, your loving parents,

Jennifer and Pierre Beck.

Again, Lyn read the letter as she periodically gazed at the lovely works of art—unrolled and positioned precariously along the foot of the king-sized bed.

The sudden ringing of the room's telephone shattered her reflective mood.

"Ms Porter, Mark at reception, I have a package for you, can I send it up?"

"I'm not dressed! I'll pick it up later, Mark."

"I'm sorry; but the courier is insisting on delivering it personally." Mark lowered his voice and said, "He probably needs a signature, and regulations state that we can't sign for guests. I am sorry."

Reining in a flare of irritation, Lyn grabbed her light-cotton robe and caste it around her body, hiding the T-shirt that once belonged to James. Footsteps approached and a burst of rapping followed. Lyn opened the door a couple of inches, eyes peeping through the narrow slit. A flat box, gift-wrapped, with a tiny box perched on top was partly visible. She widened the gap in the door; eyes fixed on the packages, asking, "What are they? Where are they…?" She looked up and saw the piercing green eyes and the warm smile of the man she'd fallen in love with over a year ago. A warm glow of happiness surged through her body. James kicked the door closed as he reached for her, demanding a kiss in place of a signature as receipt of the goods.

"What's inside?" she asked, knowing that once his hungry lips were pressed on hers, all else would become irrelevant and forgotten.

James tapped the larger package. "Well, there's a very sexy, French camisole and knickers in here. And in here," he held out the tiny box, is a diamond ring, which I hope with all my heart, you'll accept.

Against All Odds

Psychological Thriller—Forerunner to Blind Truth

Lyn Porter is a redundant florist who is on the verge of bankruptcy.

James Fairbank is an eminent, long-established conveyancing solicitor who owns properties in one of Torquay's most prestigious areas.

A chance meeting between the two, begins a catalogue of discoveries and plots which could, potentially find Lyn homeless, and James mercilessly swindled out of one of his properties.

Behind the scenes and pulling the strings, lies a rogue banker and his greedy accomplice. The former, delights in wrecking people's lives, while the latter, is stupid enough to think that he is improving his own…

To obtain a copy—ISBN 9780955971020—visit
www.margaretsherlock.net
or email shorelinespublishing@hotmail.co.uk